THE UNNAMED

L M WEST

Read more about the books at
www.lmwestwriter.co.uk

1. MARY

He sent a boy with the summons. He wouldn't come to me himself, not Thomas Johnson. Too good to be seen in the Lion now he is one of the godly men. No, his message was that *'Mistress Howldine was requested to attend upon Captain Johnson'* the next morning. Luckily the inn is never busy at that time, too many sleeping off the night before, so it was not an inconvenience.

I knew what he wanted me for – Widow Wade. Some still think she is poor and confused, but for years many have been at the end of her sharp tongue and malicious comments. And now that old, foul-tempered widow has been accused of witchcraft. It is said she cursed a neighbour and I can well believe it. For we all know that the Devil has entered this land; that his evil spews from the mouths of those whom he has brought into his fold. Women, who have ever been weak and wilful, are now willing to be seduced and enticed into wrong-doing, instead of choosing a godly path, and have taken up with Satan himself. This is what is preached from the pulpit, talked about in hushed tones in the market square. And now Joan Wade is to be seized for a witch. Captain Johnson will need a good woman to accompany him when they go to arrest her, one who is God-fearing, who will speak up and speak truthfully, and he has chosen me, for he knows I can be relied upon. He knows that I will be able to persuade others. He believes I will be his creature in this thing and he is right, for witchcraft is a blot on this land, an evil which must be rooted out and destroyed, and, if I can play my part, I am content to do so.

But I am also thinking that people will want to know all about the Aldeburgh Witch. That they will flock to my inn to hear me talk of her. That money is to be made here.

Captain Johnson leads the way towards Slaughden. I am glad he is not on his horse, for I would be hard pressed to keep up. As it is, I stumble over the rutted road, once turning my ankle and crying out, only to be silenced by the intake of impatient breath from the Captain. He has brought two guards with him for the purpose, and the Reverend John Swaine, our new minister, whose hard unsmiling face makes me grateful I am not the one accused. But I am pleased to be included, proud to be thought of as a good and godly woman, and I know this evil that has come amongst us must be weeded out before it has a chance to take hold.

The house, when we see it, is barely the height of a man, a rough place hidden by bushes. It looks old, but has the feeling of being cared for, although the small garden is tall with weeds and there are no chickens. A thin wisp of grey smoke comes from a low chimney and the door is closed firm. Captain Johnson strides up to it and bangs hard. He hammers again, then, not waiting for a reply, pushes the door open with the end of his stick, a look of disgust on his fine face, and waves his hand for the Reverend and I to enter.

I follow them in hesitantly. The smell of earth and unwashed clothing is overwhelming. It is the smell of poverty, and I remember it, from long ago. Remember how hard it was to be poor, how I swore I would never be so again. So I worked hard and become respected, I married well and did my duty, and the times changed, and my life was better. But the witch's house brings back that old fear and I push it away before it takes hold of me, turning my thoughts back to the reason we are here.

The house feels damp, even in the late-August sunshine, light limping through the one grimy window. There is a wooden trencher on the table, with a portion of bread upon it, a pitcher of milk, a mug. Small things, everyday things.

'Mistress Wade?' The Captain's voice is harsh. He is used to being obeyed. 'Mistress Wade, show yourself.' Reverend Swaine moves to an alcove at the side of the room and sweeps aside a single, thin curtain. A shower of dust and dead insects float slowly through the air in a sudden shaft of sunlight. The old lumpy mattress has the indentation of a body, and a red coverlet, quite clean, has been thrown aside as if the occupant has only recently left. There is a wooden cupboard, its door ajar, pushed against the corner of the room, a worn chair and a three-legged stool.

The two men move around the room, sweeping everything aside in their search. I have to do something, so I open the cupboard and look hard at the dusty shelves. There are bundles of dried herbs – I recognise lavender, sage, thyme – and the memory comes of my mother, my childhood, picking herbs together from the garden, tying them into bunches. When we were happy. Before. I push this memory away with the other and apply myself to my task. There are jars of waxy fat, wooden implements and cloths and, as I scrabble through the cupboard, my hands pulling aside the witch's few clothes and possessions, I occasionally touch crisp seed-heads which throw up the scent of summers long past. There is a clean shift, a coif with strands of grey hair clinging to it, a winter cloak, and a clean skirt. Of Widow Wade there is no sign.

We search every corner of the room, and find nothing. But you can feel when a place is empty, and this is not. I turn to the hearth and hold my hand over it – still warm, the fire has only recently been put out, dead furze from the common is still smouldering. She cannot be far. I look around. Above the hearth, on the shelf, is a small carved wooden spoon. I take it down and smooth the wood with my thumb. This is something to be treasured, something I would not have left – unless I had no choice. Unless I was still here. The men have moved outside now, searching for her in the heath around the cottage, thrashing with staves in increasing anger. I stand, stock still, and then I hear it. A small jolt of breath, stifled, but there. I turn back to the bed and lift the edge of the red coverlet. Something glints as I pull it to one side, and I see a tiny figure, eyes fixed on me. She is huddled down in the small space between the end of the bed and the wall, and reminds me of a baby blackbird I once found long ago, fallen from its nest. Her eyes are rounded in terror, dark and sparkling, wordlessly pleading, and I wonder, if I were to leave now, if she would go unnoticed, for the men have already searched in here – only I am left. And I think I could replace the coverlet, let her be, for I feel her power, her eyes on me, and I think to walk away, but then the sounds of the men outside break her hold over me and, when she sees this, those eyes narrow in hatred, she purses her lips and spits at me. Any sympathy that was forming dissolves into dust and I picture instead dead crows, black and glassy-eyed, hung from a post by the farmer to frighten the other crows away.

Staring her straight in the face, I open my mouth and call for the Captain.

2. JOAN

Joan knew they would come for her, that it was only a matter of time. She knows that many in the Town despise and fear her, she has watched as people cross the street to avoid her. Children throw stones and call her names and she shouts at them and threatens them, because that's all she can do. She has no power any more. She is an old woman, angry and spiteful, no longer an object of pity but one of contempt. And, ever since this talk of witchcraft and evil stalking the land began, she knew they would come for her.

Now they are here and she huddles as tight and small as she can in the space at the end of the bed, the only place she can think of, but an intake of breath, stifled too slowly, is the undoing of her. As the edge of the coverlet is lifted she expects to see a man but it is not. It is a woman, of middling years, plump and self-important, her mouth pursed in judgement. She looks straight at Joan who gazes back numbly, willing her to pass by, not to to give her away. Then, through the open door, come the voices of the men outside, and the woman straightens. Joan thought she had her, that she would soften and not betray her, but now she knows there will be no escape. And she doesn't know why she does it, for it makes matters worse, but a sudden anger rises in her, a hatred of the woman's smug, sanctimonious look, standing there in her spotless white coif, her soft woollen cloak, her look of righteous contempt, so she sucks at her mouth and spits. The globule splatters wet onto the woman's clean white apron and she looks down at it in disgust, then back at Joan, and calls for the men.

Joan's legs fail her as she is dragged from her hiding place, terror overwhelms her. She is pulled upright in front of a man she has only ever seen at a distance, but knows of. He is one of Parliament's men, a military hero and the Town stands in awe of him. He is known for getting things done, for being godly and pure, a true Puritan, and she shrivels inside to find that it is he who has been sent for her.

'Mistress Wade, you have been accused of witchcraft.' The Captain's voice is harsh, loud in the small room. 'You are accused of bewitching a cow and cursing its owner to cause him harm. What say you?' But she is struck dumb by fear and can only gaze at him, trembling. They bring cord and bind her wrists behind her. It drags at her shoulders, the pain burning and growing as they pull her between them towards Aldeburgh, like an animal taken to market. When she stumbles they pull the ropes to keep her upright, and the hemp gnaws deep at her skin. She is not used to walking this fast and they are going at a pace. Her hips pain her and she mumbles a prayer, then catches herself doing it and stops, in case they think her possessed. The men and that woman do not talk amongst themselves but look straight ahead, walking briskly until they reach the edge of the Town. Joan has not been here for many months, for it is not a place for an old woman with a short temper and a long memory. Recently she has relied on neighbours to bring her food, for she still has some coins hidden. Had. Her heart sinks as she realises that the men may go back to her cottage now they have seized her, they may find the loose brick behind the hearth. She should have moved the stiff leather purse hidden there, buried it. Too late now. All her money. The thought ignites her anger and overtakes her fear of the men.

She begins to struggle, swearing and cursing them all the way.

3. MARY

As we walk back with our prisoner, the old woman stumbling along in front of me, a wind rises, bringing with it the smell of the Town; salt and fish and tar and hemp. At the centre, the grey flint of the town hall gleams before us, chiselled and knapped, but sharp as blades, imposing in the lowering light. Stone steps on one side lead up to the red brick, half-timbered courtroom which shines with damp, the dark door to the gaol below. Rumours that a witch has been taken have swooped through the Town like the swallows on a hot summer day, and townsfolk are assembling, standing silent, watching closely as we pass, the only sound the brawl and clatter of the pebbles as they are pounded by the sea a few streets beyond.

The gaoler spies us and strides forward importantly, unlocking the heavy studded oak door, and the men push the witch inside. She has cursed us most of the way here, but when she sees the cell she stops swearing and pulls back, trying to free herself. I see the guards fingers sink deep into her scrawny arms as they tower above her. She is too small, too frail, and I watch as the fight leaves her. Captain Johnson waves for me to enter and, as I lower my head to step through the low stone arch of the gaol, the musty smell of the close-packed earth floor fills my nostrils and damp wraps me like a shroud. The walls inside are powdery plaster, the stone crumbling in places, and I can see signs and marks that have been scratched by desperate hands. The cramped room is divided by iron bars which shimmer with wet, but I can tell it has been recently cleaned. There is straw, a blanket, a pail, and it strikes me that the cell is little different to her hovel. But it is still a prison, and for such evil as she is accused of, if it is true, she deserves to be punished. There are two small barred windows which light the room, one facing east to the sea, the other west to the Town. I think that although today the air is still warm, the coming winter will bring the snow-winds and warmth will be hard to find, but I harden my heart. After all, she has been accused of witchcraft and such evil must be rooted out, its followers brought to justice. And surely she will not be imprisoned for that long.

The men stare at the old woman, their presence and authority filling the small space. She has crumpled into a black heap to the floor and is hugging herself in fear.

And then I hear it.

The witch starts keening, a low soft crying that pierces our souls, and we step back as if she is summoning the very Devil himself. I try to silence her racket by pushing the thin blanket towards her with my foot, but she just looks down and continues.

I turn to Captain Johnson.

'Will that be all, Sir?' I know my place – deference and humility, that is the way with men such as he.

The Captain looks away from the snivelling mound at our feet and nods to the gaoler who shows us out into the crisp, fresh air. We all take a deep breath to rid ourselves of the smell of damp and despair.

'Mistress Howldine, the prisoner will need to be fed. Nothing much though, the Town is not made of money and, after all, she is likely to hang. Bread and ale each day, at dusk and dawn, should suffice. Are you willing to provide this until she is tried?'

'Of course, Sir. I will set up an account and will enter all I supply into it, and then it can be settled each month . . .'

'It will be settled when this business is over, Mistress, and not before.'

I curtsey and lower my head at the sharp tone of his voice. Knowing when to give in, that's the key.

'Of course, Sir, that will be most acceptable.' The Captain turns on his heel, the Reverend Swaine following like a trained dog, back to his high house with his servants and wife.

Behind me, in the gaol, the witch falls silent.

THE INN IS BUSTLING WHEN I RETURN, THE POT-BOY RED-FACED AND rushing, but all heads turn towards me as I reach the serving hatch. I smooth my apron and straighten my coif in readiness.

'Yes, gentlemen, what can I get you?' They look at each other, not wanting to be the first to ask, for they think nosiness is the prerogative of women. They think they are being subtle, but I can see desire for gossip shining in their wide eyes and wet mouths.

'Well, is there a witch? Have they seized her? Come on, woman, speak.' The fish merchant cannot contain his glee, his stinking breeches and stained apron quivering with anticipation, and I give him my most withering look.

'I demand manners of my customers, Sir, courtesy. This is a respectable inn.'

Another voice breaks in.

'Mistress Howldine, do you have any news of the witch, if you please.'

I know the farmer's boy is mocking me but I turn to him and fix a smile.

'Yes, there is news.' The room rustles with tension. 'An old woman, Mistress Wade, from Slaughden way . . .'

'Ah, her, such a wicked mouth she has.'

'Vicious old hag, no more than she deserves.' The voices rise, each full of their own accusations.

I raise my voice above the hubbub.

'Gentlemen, if you will, pray silence.' You can hear a coin drop. 'She has been taken up by Captain Johnson and the Reverend Swaine . . .' The men exchange glances. '. . . and is now secure in the Town gaol.'

'And how is she accused?'

I face the men, their faces flushed with drink and excitement, drawing myself up, standing straight. Although not tall, I have learned to carry a room.

'I hear that Master Lamb has claimed she used spells and enchantments to bewitch his cow, so that its milk dried up. It is stricken now and like to die . . .'

'What, that old beast that he has left on the common land? I'm surprised it's still able to bear milk, the lack of care he gives it.' A fisherman shrugs his shoulders. 'But if she cursed him, now that was wrong.'

'He says that she asked for a cup of milk and he refused her. He says she then cursed him with foul language, pointed her finger at his animal. He claims he knows she bewitched him too, says that since that day he has felt ill and weak.'

The men nod and shuffle in their seats and reach for their ale. This is proof enough for them, and they talk amongst themselves as the room settles. After the storm and God's curse on the Town, we are all cautious, keen to do good and redeem ourselves in His eyes. The seizing of this witch seems a fair price to pay for our redemption.

NOW THAT WE HAVE ONE WITCH IT SEEMS THERE MAY BE OTHERS. Townsfolk have become emboldened by the imprisonment of Widow Wade and begin to remember their old grievances and feuds. They listen and repeat the stories which fly around this corner of East Anglia until the Town is a-buzz with tales and rumour. So the Captain and Burgesses of Aldeburgh make a decision. They send word to a man in Essex, one whose name is mentioned in whispers, behind hands. And Captain Johnson pays me another visit that evening.

The inn is noisy and full, but, as he enters, all fall silent. Caps are doffed, heads are lowered – he inspires deference, does the Captain. He has petitioned Parliament on many occasions for arms and defences against the Dutch and for help for the fishing trade, and his crusade to make Aldeburgh a godly place is much supported. He is to be respected.

I straighten my coif and drop a curtsey.

'Captain Johnson, to what do I owe this honour?' I keep my eyes lowered as I show him into the back room, for there will be no privacy in the front, ears are already stretched out. I close the door behind us and the noise muffles. He refuses my invitation to sit but removes his hat.

'Mistress, you may have heard tell of the request to attend our Town that has been extended to a Master Matthew Hopkins?' I look up, fixing surprise to my face, as if he is telling me something I do not know, but, in truth, the inn has been rife with this tale for days. Aldeburgh can no more contain news than a net contain seawater. 'He has accepted our invitation – at some cost to the Town I might say – but he does the Lord's work and I have no doubt we will fare the better for it. He comes tomorrow.'

'And this Master Hopkins – will he be staying with you, Sir?'

The Captain's brow furrows.

'No, no, he will not – that would not be appropriate. That is the reason for my visit. The Town wonders if you could provide him with a bed here at the Lion?' I hide a smile – I have the very room. 'And one will be required for his assistant, a Mistress Phillips I believe.'

I look up sharply. This is the first I have heard of an assistant, and a woman too.

'Sir, mine is a respectable establishment.'

He holds up his hand and I pinch my mouth closed.

'You misunderstand, Mistress. Goodwife Phillips will require her own room, she is Master Hopkin's searcher.' I wonder at the term. But whatever she is, she will be welcome in my inn. I am already calculating the provisions I will need to order, the servants I will need to hire.

I can already hear the clink of silver.

4. JOAN

The dark door of the gaol yawns before Joan as they shove her inside. She pushes against them, resisting to the last, but they are stronger, and it is pointless, so she stops struggling and lets them cut the ropes from her wrists, rubbing the soreness away as she looks around. The gaol smells of damp and it's warm, surprisingly warm. It looks as if some effort has been made to clean it, and the breeze blows through the windows and keeps the air sweetened. Joan's cottage was like this once, when she could be bothered to keep it swept and tidy, and she thinks there may be worse places to be. She's slept in some. When her husband died so suddenly she had nowhere to go and had a spell of sleeping in the open, finding trees or a thick copse for shelter, nestling down into the leaves and bracken. It was hard, and she was full of fear, but she was free. She could look at the clouds and predict the weather, and the birds were her watchmen, for they rose and chattered at anything approaching. People were kind in those days and she could beg a crust, a dish of milk, in return for work. So she made her own way, had no need of a man, no need of anyone, but she was still young then, still had hope. Seven short months she'd been married, not long enough for the joy and pleasure to wear off, and it was hard when he'd gone. She'd always wanted children, a babe of her own, but they'd had too little time. Instead she made a life for herself, tending animals, being a servant, nursing the infirm, any work she could find, and it was a comfort. But she is old now, bad-tempered, intolerant, and the world seems noisier, more difficult.

Her legs wobble and she sinks to the straw. That at least is clean. The walk to the gaol has exhausted her, and she finds she is mumbling to herself again. The men stand there watching as if she was an insect and a shaking overtakes her, so she clasps her arms to herself and starts to cry. The woman that betrayed her pushes a blanket towards her with the toe of her boot, as if she cannot bear to touch anything that will touch her. The blanket is a comfort, although her betrayer would be horrified to think so.

Joan keens to herself quietly. She knows who she is, who she was. She knows the life she led, how it has has brought her to this place. She knows what will happen to her now she has been touched by this madness. For madness it is – she may be the first, but she will not be the last.

5. MARY

W hy accuse such women, you ask, why now? For all know that there have been cunning folk, white witches, for centuries, accepted and appreciated. Well, the fighting in other parts of the country did not help, our food and horses being taken for the soldiers use, our men leaving for war. War means people live in fear, especially when father turns against son, neighbour against friend, and that fear grows and thickens, and every event takes on meaning, becomes portentous. And Aldeburgh was touched by this. We had our own sign, that day of the great storm three years ago, a true sign from God that evil had come and that the Town had moved away from the righteous path and slid into sin.

It changed Captain Johnson. It changed all of us.

IT HAD BEEN LATE AFTERNOON WHEN CAPTAIN JOHNSON CAME INTO the Lion and I was very surprised to see him for, as a godly man, he eschews all strong drink, and, anyway, the fishermen, farmers and sailors who sit here are not normally for the likes of him. But that afternoon had been strange.

The storm had blown up suddenly. Not unusual for a hot

August afternoon I know, but the ferocity of this one was unnatural, its noise deafening, a banging and crashing such as we had never seen in this lifetime, and we all feared the end of the world. The tide rose high on Aldeburgh beach and the shingle shattered sharp against the boats and clamoured against the cottages as it was thrown up by the sea. It seemed to go on for hours, but then stopped as suddenly as it had started and, as the town began to put itself together again, people emerged from their houses and men crowded into the inn to exchange stories.

Then the door opened and Captain Johnson came in, white-faced and shaking, asking for brandy. He had William Thompson with him and I was pushed to say who was in a worse state. I poured two glasses of my best brandy and looked hard at the Captain as he downed his in one gulp. He gestured for a refill then, seeing my face, reached in to his coat and put a heap of coins on the table. There was enough there for the whole bottle so I set it down before them. The two men did not look at each other, just stared into space at first, each in their own thoughts. But then the door creaked and the carpenter came in, him a long time crony of the Captain.

'Thomas, William! I had not thought to see you here.' Then he spied their faces. 'What has happened? You look pale as ghosts.'

The Captain turned to him.

'Thompson and I. That storm. We saw . . .'

'You were not caught in it? The wind was fierce . . .'

I wished the carpenter would stop interrupting.

'We'd been to Woodbridge to look at launching my new ship.' The Captain wiped his mouth with the back of his hand and I saw the brandy start to soften his shoulders. A crowd was beginning to gather round them, faces blurred with drink and anticipation, but there was a muttering from the men, as there is ill-feeling about the Captain having his ship built at Woodbridge when there are capable men in Slaughden. 'We were on the heath, nearly home, when the horses went skittish. There was a change in the air, they could sense it. You could smell it.'

Thompson nodded agreement.

'Sulphurous it was, and the sky blackening all the time 'til it was like night.'

'Then . . .' The Captain seemed to be seeking the words 'We thought there was an army invading. The sounds – they were like cannon-fire, like shot discharged, and we feared that the war had reached here, and us not knowing. We spurred the horses, but they would not obey in their terror, so we dismounted, thinking to lead them on. There was no cover and they were like to run off, so all we could do was stand and wait.'

William Thompson spoke up.

'I have never seen the horses like that. Their eyes were white, their ears back, they had the look of the very Devil, and ready to run at any moment. And the noise didn't stop. For nearly one hour . . .'

'Nearer one and a half.'

'. . . it carried on, it deafened us, so we made ready to mount up and make haste back here to prepare, in case there truly was an invasion. The noise – it was as if we were in the very heart of a pitched battle. It was not as any thunder I had ever heard, it followed us and we were in fear for our very lives. But . . .' He looked around as if seeking an audience but then I saw he, too, was terrified. 'Then it ceased. It just stopped, but as it did, this *thing* hurtled out of the sky and crashed into the heath before us some six or seven yards. Thomas's dog howled and hunched low, but he brought us to it.'

The Captain reached under the table to pat the head of his hound, who crouched there, shivering still, then looked down at his empty glass. I topped it up, my breath held, as William Thompson continued. 'The thing was buried in the grass and earth, and the dog was standing over it, whining and shaking with fear. We got down and pulled him back and bent towards it and . . .'

His hand shook as he took another nip of brandy, his teeth rattling the glass, and the Captain took over.

'It was hot. I thought it was shot – from a cannon – but . . .' he reached into his coat, '. . . it was this.'

The whole inn leaned forward in thrall as he put a lump of rock on the table in front of him. It looked nothing much, just like any flint that is pushed up on the beach here. It was about eight inches long and five inches broad and two inches in thickness, brown and grey in colour, but from it came a dark smell as if from the grave. That was the strangest thing about it.

One of the old fisherman leaned forward to touch it with the tip of a grubby finger.

'It is a flint.'

'No, Sir, it is not. You can see deep into a flint. This is solid, like brick. It fell from the sky itself. We saw it.'

We all pulled closer, gazing at the item in wonder, though some start to pull back from the stench.

'What is it?' Several whispered the same question.

Captain Johnson looked around the room. It was dark in the corners but the table was lit by a ray of late afternoon sunshine, illuminating his face.

'This rock is sent to us as a warning from God. Our Town is full of sin and, by sending it, He has shown us His displeasure. We must win back His favour. This is a sign from Heaven. We must repent and ask God's forgiveness. We must flush out the evil in our midst and cleanse ourselves. Our Town must be made pure again.' He slammed his hand loud on the table for emphasis, his voice rising.

And in his eyes I saw the dazzling light of the zealot.

THAT ROCK BROUGHT US NOTORIETY. THE CAPTAIN BROUGHT OUR Members of Parliament to see it, he published a pamphlet about it in London. He put the rock by the stocks in the market square and everyone wondered at it. And all came to believe that Aldeburgh was a sinful place, in need of cleansing, and that the Captain was the one appointed by God to lead it. And the following year, when Parliament sent Dowsing to break our church, Captain Johnson, together with the Reverend Swaine, then the very terror of the poor folk of nearby Westleton, did not wait for Parliament's men to break up our church. No, they took the staves and bars from the men and broke up the church themselves. Paintings and statutes and glass, all gone. Other towns and villages had stood by and watched while this destruction took place, but not ours. Here, Captain Johnson and Reverend Swaine took charge, glorifying themselves in the eyes of God, Parliament and Dowsing, showing themselves to be true believers, as they battered and destroyed our images and carvings. Not for them a reluctance to wipe out decades of beauty and tradition. No. They hammered and smashed as if crushing Satan himself. And, as the church was destroyed, their names rose. The windows were replaced with plain glass, the walls limed, and only the ghosts of the saints remained as faint outlines, trying to push their way out of the shrouds of paint, their hands raised in sorrow and supplication.

AND WE THOUGHT THAT WOULD BE ENOUGH. THEN OUR MINISTER, Topcliffe, was removed, but the eyes of the godly continued to look around, seeking out sin and devilish things. Everyone said it was the day the great storm came upon us that was the cause of all that followed, but I don't think it was – in fact I am sure it wasn't. The sign of God's anger that fell from heaven that afternoon certainly changed us, made us afraid, and that fear set men higher than they should have been set. But it wasn't the storm that began it. For, as the great and the good of Aldeburgh spoke out against Reverend Topcliffe and ousted him from his ministry, the accusations against his curate also flew. Like seabirds over a dead fish they clustered and grew, screaming through the Town. No, it was not the storm. It all started with that scurrilous curate Maptid Violet.

Maptid Violet. He was young, tall – and very beautiful, some might say too beautiful for a young man. One such as he should never have entered into the Church; he was not suited to it. For, above all, even above the Lord, Maptid Violet loved women. He charmed them with those dark eyes, always half-closed in humour or suggestion. Reverend Topcliffe was at least a God-fearing man of faith, although his dislike of sermons and his costly decoration of our church infuriated Aldeburgh so much that they sought his removal. But his curate was different, he should never have been ordained. But ordained he was, and our Town had the misfortune to get him. And it wasn't just the women, I think he would have been able to control his base urges with time and age growing upon him. But there was the other thing. Maptid Violet liked to drink. And with drink upon him he became a very Devil.

AT THE START, THE YOUNG CURATE WAS THE DARLING OF THE TOWN. His presence next to the Reverend in the church on Sundays was enough to attract a larger congregation than of late, the women of the Town watching his every movement with kerchiefs held against their mouths as if stopping up their very thoughts. He had a smile for them all, a kind word. He assisted at the services and the bible-black of his surplice only added to his good looks. The women of his congregation hung on his sleeve, his every word, and he could not resist them. He meant well, I am sure, but he could not fight his nature, and his nature was to be a pursuer of women, and the drinking made this all the worse. He tried to seduce a respectable widow. He drank for days in Orford, and in Saxmundham he was accused of pursuing a maid into her chamber. And worst of all, it was said that he had thrown another maid over a chair and used her most foully. He denied all of this of course, claimed his accusers were saying this out of malice and spite, demanding that evidence was only to be given by men of quality. I might have believed him. I liked him at first. But he came to my inn one night with a group of rowdy young men, the type he would have done better never to associate with, and the ale flowed freely. I kept serving him, for trade is trade after all, and a curate's coin is as good as any other, but then they became loud and unruly, knocking over the jugs of ale, and Violet started shouting about how much he could drink, and that he *'had a very Devil in his belly that would never get out.'* The inn went quiet, shocked at this speech from a man of the cloth; they were waiting for me to throw him out, wondering how I would deal with curate in his cups. I had already looked around for the pot-boy, just in case. But he quietened and I thought all was well, until he started up again. Then he climbed upon the table, mug in hand . . . I can scarce bear to think of it even now . . . and bellowed *'Give me a woman's belly, and come let us sin, for the more we sin the better we shall be accepted.'* Well, that was too much for me, even for the men. Some were rising to their feet and I feared a fight, so the draper, George Nun, and I grabbed him and put him out into the street, throwing his friends out after him. I cannot afford to get a reputation for running a low establishment. There was already talk of regulating the inns in the Town and I did not want the Lion closed and I lose my trade, so when Violet's case came before the Suffolk committee and I was asked to bear witness to his behaviour I did so, without hesitation. Violet had the effrontery to deny it all, said we witnesses were of *'small or no reputation'*, that he would never do such a thing. But I know what was said – I was there. I bore witness to his shame and disgrace.

And this act has emboldened the people of the Town to speak out. We have caused a minister of the church to be removed, and his curate, and this has given us confidence, made us feel as if we are all coming together to cast out sin and bring our Town to right-eousness, in line with the new teaching.

It has given us power. And this was when we first heard talk of witchcraft.

6. JOAN

Joan is leant against the bars of the gaol window watching the sunrise, just able to glimpse the sea beyond the houses. Her eyes follow the pale orange light which transforms the skies, as the sea changes from pewter to silver. There is a low mist and she cannot see where sky ends and sea begins. These last days of August are a dusty stretching time, and she has long loved to watch the sun come up. Her first night in this place has been short, but she already misses her home, her own things around her. She drops her gaze to the side of the window and sees, in the plaster by the stonework, lines, shapes that have been scratched by others held in that place. She runs her fingertips over them, feeling their presence, then has a sudden urge to leave her mark, so she crouches, scrabbling on the earth floor until she finds a small flint. It is so tiny she can barely grasp it, but she moves back to the wall and pushes the sharp point to the plaster. She has never learned her letters, never been able to read, and has only been asked to make her mark once before, when she married all those years ago. Now, carefully and slowly, she scratches the shape of a 'J', her own mark, into the damp surface.

.   .   .

A CLATTER OF FOOTSTEPS, AND SHE PULLS HURRIEDLY AWAY, DROPPING the flint, and sinks back down to the straw. There is a clash of keys, a creak of oak, and the woman who betrayed her strides in, her face tight with importance. Joan stares hard at her.

'Here – food.'

She is torn between her hatred of the woman and her hunger. Hunger wins, and she pulls the plate towards her, saying nothing, watching as a jug of ale is set on the floor.

She grabs at a nub of stale bread then glances up.

'Who are you anyway?' The bread is churning wet in her mouth as she continues to push food in. She feels as if she has not eaten for weeks, although it has only been one day.

'I am Mary Howldine, keeper of the Lion Inn across the square. I am charged with looking to your care while . . .'

'Paid, you mean. You are their paid lackey' She spits the words out and the innkeeper starts back. Joan smiles inwardly. They imagined her to be old, of unsound mind, but her words are quick and sharp and they bite.

The innkeeper recovers herself but her eyes narrow in hatred.

'I am paid to provide for your comfort. Bring you bread and ale. That is all. The Town may have hired me to do this, but I am my own woman.' She glances around and turns on her well-shod heels. The door clangs behind her, the lock turned and the Joan is left alone, chewing thoughtfully, to watch the sun come up.

7. MARY

The rooms are aired, the beds changed, floors swept and all is ready for the coming of Master Hopkins and his searcher. I have taken on another boy to run errands and am keeping a careful note of my expenses in a new ledger, bought from the town scribe for this very purpose.

It is late in the afternoon when they come. I am looking around to make sure everything is in order, moving to the window as I hear the jangling of harness and the clop of hooves which signals their arrival in the yard below. I straighten my clothes – I have bought a new apron and collar for this occasion, adding the expense to my ledger under 'victuals' – and go downstairs. The pot-boy opens the door for me and I stand in the sunlit courtyard to greet them.

I am not sure what I expected from a witchfinder who has been ordained by Parliament, but it was not this. I thought he would be tall, old, distinguished, a man of experience and solidity. I have read the pamphlets, seen his image; tall hat and big boots, stern expression, but the man who slides from his horse and turns to face me is so young. He is slender and short with curling brown hair. I lower my gaze and curtsey, noting his shoes have heels. A man who feels a need to make himself taller.

'Mistress . . . ?'

'Howldine, Sir, welcome to the Lion Inn.' He glances behind him at the woman moving stiffly from her horse, the yard-boy's hand reaching for her elbow as she staggers. She brushes him off and hands him the reigns, turning to us, straightening her dress which is grey, like the strand of hair that escapes from the scarf tied under her wide-brimmed black hat.

'This is Goodwife Phillips, who assists me in the searching of witches. She is most experienced in dealing with such persons and has for many years known how to search out the Devil's marks.' The woman nods and I curtsey in return. She is sturdy and hard-faced, strong – I would not like to wrong-side her. My visions of comfortable evenings in the back parlour making small talk with another woman crumble into dust and are lost on the breeze.

I gather myself again and hold out my hand.

'This way, Sir, Madam – I will show you to your rooms. My boy will bring your packs.' I nod to the yard-boy, who shoulders the leather bags he has unfastened from the saddles, and follows us upstairs. I have given Master Hopkins the best room at the front, with a high bed, a table and chair and a view to the sea in the distance. 'The day has been warm so the fire is not lit, but it can be, Sir, if you wish?'

The Witchfinder looks carefully at me. His eyes are the colour of river-silt.

'That will not be necessary. I do not require much. I am not here for comfort.' His voice is high, his words perfectly formed. He turns to his pack and I curtsey again and attend to Goody Phillips.

'Mistress Phillips, your room is through here.' I have chosen a room at the back, overlooking the yard. It is smaller but with a soft bed and a table and chair. The smell of the horses can barely be noticed if the window is closed. She looks around her, unsmiling, but nods her approval then takes her bags from the boy. He stands there for a moment, hoping for a coin, but catches her look and bows himself out.

'Will there be anything else?'

'No thank you, I can make myself comfortable here.'

'Dinner will be in one hour if it suits?'

She has already turned away and is unpacking, but she gives me a cursory nod, and I turn and leave, shutting the door behind me. Across the corridor Master Hopkin's door is already closed.

I lean back against the wattled walls and breathe in slowly. Deep inside I feel a sensation quiver and I wonder at it. Then I realise – it is a prickle of fear.

EARLY EVENING. I LEAVE THE POT-BOY IN CHARGE WHILE MASTER Hopkins and Goodwife Phillips settle in, and rush across the square to take food and a jug of ale to the witch. She has clearly not eaten well in days and, again, stuffs the food into her as if it's her last meal. She chews with mouth open, noisy and wet, and chunks fall out onto her grimy skirts. But her eyes are still sharp and I realise she is not demented as I had first thought. She glares at me with hatred.

Master Hopkins is taking the air in the yard when I return, looking up at the sky as if for divine guidance. He looks even younger without his hat and the evening light on his face.

He smiles at me and it softens his face.

'Is the witch being kept in good condition?'

'Yes, Sir. I have taken her food and ale as instructed.' I search for the words. 'It will not be easy. She is evil-tempered, that is sure, old and full of spite.'

Master Hopkins' words are almost tender.

'I know this can seem difficult for godly women such as yourself, but you must keep the Lord before your eyes always, and he will protect you. It is only too easy for a woman to be seduced by Satan, Madam, weak and full of sin as they are. This one is just the first. Who knows how many other witches we will find in this Town?'

I can feel the blood drain from my face.

'But you are here only to try Widow Wade? I am sure there are no more ...'

'There will be more, Mistress Howldine, be sure of that. They are found in nests in a Town like this, they live like rats, breeding and spreading their foul contagion, and I am the dog who will chase after them. I will sniff them out, nip at their heels until they are constrained and brought to justice. This Town will have a cleansing such as it has never seen. I am here to bring it back into the light, into the favour of the Lord. For more witches there are, Madam, and they will be found, they will be tried and punished and God's will shall be carried out.' His face is no longer soft, his voice harsher.

And in that moment I see a black maw open up in front of me, jaws wide, tongue swollen, breath foul, and I can only stand and wait for it to swallow me.

8. JOAN

The sky is darkening into night when the innkeeper finally appears with more food and Joan grabs at it, chewing carefully, feeling her teeth rocking in the back of her mouth at the hard bread, watching morsels dropping to the floor, as hunger makes her slovenly.

'Ah, my gaoler. Mistress Howldine. Have you come to provide for my comfort?' She splutters in amusement.

The innkeepers face hardens.

'I merely carry out my duties as required.'

'You may think that, Mistress, but you are as bad as they, worse maybe, for you know what you do.' She raises a gnarled finger and points. 'Mark my words, you will regret this.' The innkeeper recoils and raises her hand before her, placing her thumb between her two fingers in the old sign against witchcraft. The hand is trembling and Joan sees her fear. She laughs in delight and feels part-chewed bread falling from her opened mouth. 'You think that will protect you? Seventy years and more have I lived, and I have yet to see a witch, though many suppose their existence. They accuse me of cursing a dumb animal when I merely cursed its master for his meanness. I am old, I do not care what people think. If they cross me I curse them, and feel the better for it. If that is witchcraft then we are all witches.' The innkeeper looks hard at her, face pinched and tight, bursting to speak. 'Well?'

'He is here to examine you.'

'Who is?'

'They sent for him. The Town.'

Joan's irritation rises and the word snaps out.

'Who?'

'Him. Matthew Hopkins. The Witchfinder. He is summoned here to search out more witches.'

Joan freezes, she can feel the blood drain away from her face. His very name strikes terror deep into her.

'Hopkins? He has come here?' All the fight leaves her and she slumps back into the corner, the crust falling from her fingers. 'Then I am not long for this world.' She, closes her eyes and pulls her shawl over her face. Her whole body trembles.

9. MARY

Master Hopkins is as good as his word, it is clear why the Town has invited him. For, over the next two days, visitors are invited to his room. Townsfolk, hats in hand, heads bowed in deference, march up my stairs with heavy tread, to pour out tales of loss and illness, death and curses. It seems that the whole world has been damaged and seeks to blame others for it. When I take him a jug of ale I find he has pulled the table to the window and is sitting behind it, his head bowed, scribbling furiously in a black notebook, pausing only to pay attention to the person before him. I have noticed how he looks at people. He sits still as a statue while they speak, looking full at their faces. His eyes are full of sympathy and understanding and he nods in encouragement, his head tilted to one side. Goody Phillips sits to the left of him, her hands clasped in her lap, listening, and occasionally, as he writes a name, he glances at her.

So many come that, on Saturday, proceedings are moved to the courtroom above the gaol. The Town has prepared it well. A long table at the far end for Master Hopkins, a chair for Goody Phillips, seats for others who will attend to watch the proceedings. The accused will be kept standing.

·   ·   ·

THE INN IS BUSTLING THAT AFTERNOON, THE RUMOUR OF THE SEIZING of more witches bringing in the customers, but the atmosphere is subdued, they are all poised as if for flight. George Nun is in his usual place by the counter and he tips his hat to me as I return to the bar.

'Mary.' We are old friends, I allow him the informality.

He nods towards the door.

'This is a sad business and no mistake.'

'Do you know who has been taken now, George?'

'I hear it is Mistress Butts, the fisherman's wife, from South Town, and her daughter. That girl isn't right in the head, hasn't been for a long time, always preaching and praying.'

'She was such sweet child. I remember her playing on the beach.'

The memory smashes into me, like a tall wave, cold and hard. A tiny girl, blonde curls flying about her chubby face in the breeze, her cries of laughter joined with the screech of seabirds as she toddled across the pebbles in pursuit, waving her little arms at them. Unexpected grief takes me by the throat. For I so wanted a daughter, but no child came. Any babe would have been a blessing, but I yearned for a daughter. I did have one once, that's the thing, but she was not meant for this world; she only lived a few days, and the midwife had so much trouble birthing her that I was unable to have more. And for months afterwards, once I was strong again, I would go to the beach to watch the children and wonder what my own girl would have been like, how she would have looked . . . And that was the end of my marriage too. We were unhappy anyway, before then, thought the child would save us, but it was the finish. I couldn't rid myself of the ill-moods that swept through me and he couldn't contain his anger and disappointment, so when the inn at Orford came up and he wanted to take it I let him go – alone. I stayed at the Lion and we are still married, our vows remain unbroken, and that is the whole of it. But sometimes I still ponder how my own child would have been.

I swallow the memories down and move to fill up George's mug.

'So why isn't the Butts girl right? What happened to her?'

George taps his finger to his nose.

'No one knows for sure. That Martin Butts, he's a rum 'un. Got religion bad, for all his bluster and harsh words. That wife of his, she never stood up to him, a mouse of a thing. Some say he is still handy with his fists when a temper comes on him.' He drains his mug and stands. 'Daresay we'll find out soon enough what's what. Sad business though, when even decent folk can't be trusted. Witches.' He spits thoroughly onto the floor then sees my face and scrubs at the wet gobbet with his boot. He drops his coins onto the counter and lurches to the door. As he throws it open I see a crowd has gathered outside the town hall. Their faces shine with fervour.

IT IS NOT UNTIL EARLY EVENING THAT I CAN GET AWAY TO FEED THE prisoners. There are scraps from the tables to be used up and I enter the amounts carefully in my ledger. Three prisoners now, all to be fed and watered – my quill scratches away.

I expect all to be quiet in the gaol but I can hear sounds as I approach. The gaoler is standing outside.

'Evening, Mistress. More now for you to feed.'

'I have heard.'

'Can't stand the noise in there. I hoped to have them settled before you came over, but the young 'un won't keep quiet.' He unlocks the door for me and stands aside. The room is dim, the outside light fading, and I can make out three figures. Widow Wade's face is expectant as I enter, and she snatches at a piece of bread from the tray I lay on the floor and shoves it into her mouth. The new ones are in the far corner, the mother's arms around the girl to calm her, but the daughter is nothing like calm. She looks like a small child, and her head is uplifted, her face shining.

' . . . and I open my heart to the Lord God, for he will be merciful, he will forgive my sins. For I am a sinful and wicked girl and I must be punished ... '

'Hush, hush.' The mother turns and I see her face is streaked with tears, which glisten on her cheeks, wending their way over a dark bruise on her face.

'Mistress Butts? I am Mistress Howldine, keeper of ...'

The woman scowls.

'I know who you are. My husband used to frequent your inn – before he found the Lord.' I wrack my brains to think of him but I cannot remember. There are so many people that come through my doors, I am hard-pressed to recall them all.

'I have brought you food and ale. My advice is to eat quickly before she ...' I point at Widow Wade. '... takes it all, for she will.'

'Mistress, we have been wrongly accused. Isbel here is a God-fearing ...'

'I do not know how you come to be accused, nor the rights and wrongs of it, I am merely employed to ensure your comfort.' Widow Wade hisses at my words and I glare her into silence. 'I am sure that your husband will speak for you, that your case will be heard fairly, as the law requires.' Mistress Butts turns to her daughter, quietened now with a crust in her mouth, and smoothes her hair. The child's golden curls are gone, her hair colourless and greasy, and her face is blank. She looks nothing like the carefree toddler I remember.

Her mother looks at me dully.

'That will not happen.'

I look at her askance. The witch in the corner sits up, listening.

'But your daughter. She is clearly devout and has the Lord in her heart.'

Catherines Butt's voice cracks in a strangled laugh.

'They say she has been seduced by the Devil and that I allowed it. My husband beat us, Mistress, he tried to drive Satan from us, says only by suffering will we be cleansed and come to the Lord. But he was too late, too late!' She reaches for her daughter and pulls her close, then runs her hand over the front of Isbel's dress and I see a small swelling.

I draw back in horror, clasping my hand to my mouth. At that moment Isbel turns to me. Her face is white, her eyes rolling in her head. She moves her hands down to where her mother's have just been, then lower. Widow Wade gasps in the shadows as the girl speaks through cracked lips.

'Evil girl, bad girl, the Devil has taken you. Evil girl, bad girl . . .' Her voice is harsh and old, the litany recited over and over, as I call for the gaoler and lurch towards the door and out into the fresh sea air.

Overhead, seabirds scream in a darkening sky as I swallow the vomit rising hot and bitter in my throat.

It is later that evening when the Witchfinder comes to my back parlour, knocking gently on the open door.

'Mistress Howldine?'

I rise from my ledger entries and curtsey.

'Master Hopkins. How may I help you?'

His smile is warm but it does not reach his eyes.

'I am sorry to disturb you but I am wondering if you would be able to assist me in the morning?'

'Of course, Sir, if I can.' I return his smile warily.

'I will be examining further the young girl brought in today, and I wish to have women present to make sure all is as it should be. There must be no suggestion of irregularity with such a sensitive inquiry such as this. I know you to be truly God-fearing, willing to speak out against evil and wrongdoing, and I would have your presence in the courtroom while I question her.'

He has heard about my standing against Maptid Violet then – how fast gossip travels in this Town, even to the ears of strangers. And then I remember it is his job to root things out about people, to listen to all that is said.

'I am not sure if I am able, Sir, the inn is busy . . .'

'Mistress – you would be doing God's work, you would be helping me in this task I am set. It would just be a case of hearing what she says. Goodwife Phillips will attend, Captain Johnson and the Reverend Swaine as well. I need witnesses to every word the girl speaks. And the court will sit in the early morning, so your trade would not be badly affected, I am sure.' He sees my hesitation. 'Of course, there will be payment for any additional duties.'

He has the measure of me, as I have of him.

'Very well, Sir.'

'Thank you, Mistress Howldine, you are a true servant of the Lord.' He turns to leave and I make my decision.

'Sir, Master Hopkins?'

'Yes, Mistress?'

'This girl – Isbel – who is to be brought before you tomorrow. I fear she may be with child.'

His face closes in on itself, sludge eyes narrowing, breath hissing between his teeth and when he speaks his voice has an edge that was not there before.

'Then we will treat her kindly until we find out if that is true and who has done such a thing. After all, it is the truth we seek, over all things.' He nods at me and goes, leaving behind him the small smell of sulphur.

10. JOAN

J oan is dozing when she hear footsteps, her head bowed on her chest, a string of dribble hanging cold from her mouth. She rubs it away with her hand and straightens up as the gaoler enters. She sees the Captain behind him, stern and unflinching, and two more women are pushed into the room. Joan glares at the men as they turn to leave, the door slamming behind them, as keys clank in the lock.

She stares at the women. One is of middling age, small, thin, bowed down, and she has her arm around a slender girl who cannot be more than ten years. The child is startling. Pale silver hair like the birch trees on the common, light blue eyes. She could be pretty, should be, but her eyes are blank hollow pools. Her lips move constantly, and Joan can see immediately that her soul has gone. Her mother, for she is clearly so, tries to sit her daughter down on the straw but the girl will not bend, moving instead to stand by the barred window, muttering, her hands plucking at her skirts, gazing out towards the sea. Her mother drops to the floor in despair and rubs her eyes.

'They have brought you too?' It is all Joan can think of to say.

There is a large dark bruise shadowing the left side of the woman's face and, as if by habit, she lifts her hand to cover the damage, but then drops it again resignedly. The hardness of her life is etched in her face.

'Myself and my daughter both . . . but we have done nothing.' Tears start in her eyes and Joan softens.

'What is her name?' She nods towards the girl at the window who is singing to herself now, softly swaying from side to side.

'Isbel.'

'And yours?'

'Mistress Butts – Catherine.' She looks at the old woman. 'I know who you are. The mad woman from down Slaughden way – Joan Wade. People say you are possessed.'

'People should mind their business.' Joan snaps the words out and Catherine recoils.

'They say you are a witch, have done for years.'

'I know what they say. Let them. It keeps people away, leaves me on my own, in peace. I am content with that.' As Joan says this she realises the truth of it. She managed well enough, people avoided her, but they still came for remedies and potions when they needed her help. Oh yes, not too proud then, were they, not afraid of the witch, and they paid – coins sometimes, but mostly food, milk, ale. Gifts left outside by strangers who would have kept their distance, except they wanted something from her.

'But Isbel and I are not like you. I do not understand why we are accused. We are not witches. My girl is only fifteen years old.' Joan blinks at this for she looks far younger. 'She is a good girl, all know that, her father has kept her in line, kept her away from ordinary folk. She is a saintly girl, she has God before her eyes . . .' Catherine's voice trails off and it comes to Joan that the mother knows why they are here, why they have been accused. And the daughter is the cause, Joan is sure.

By the window, Isbel clasps her hands together and starts to sing a psalm, as if that will help her.

11. MARY

Monday sees us in dark procession in the lightening dawn as we walk across to the town hall. Master Hopkins, tall in his shining boots and black hat, Goodwife Phillips behind him, me taking up the rear. We are climbing the stone steps to the courtroom just as Captain Johnson and the Reverend Swaine approach.

We nod in greeting, but no one speaks as we settle ourselves around the room. Master Hopkins seats himself behind the long table and pulls piles of paper from his bag, a bottle of ink, two quills, and a black book, and, lining them up precisely on the table before him, sits and waits, still as a statue, eyes closed, lips moving in prayer. The only sound is the wind outside, buffeting the flint, whistling through the mullioned windows. I have never sat quiet in this room before. It is light and airy, it's beamed ceiling arched high – it is beautiful.

The first one to be brought in is the daughter, her arms clasped in the firm grip of the guards, whose gleaming faces betray their excitement. The girl looks all around her, her lips in constant move-ment. Although the guards make a big to-do, as men are prone to, I can see she does not resist – she looks numbed, unseeing. Master Hopkins moves and brings a chair which he sets down before the table, facing her. His voice is kindly, but he is like an adder. Poised. Poisonous.

'Isobel, be seated here before me.' Isbel looks at him, then at the chair, and sits, modestly, her hands in her lap, head bowed.

'Isobel, I have brought you here to ...'

The girl looks up, her face stilled.

'Isbel.' The Witchfinder pauses, looks at her enquiringly. 'My name is Isbel.'

His eyes narrow briefly but the mask of kindness snaps back onto his face.

'Indeed, my apologies. Isbel, I have brought you here to answer some questions.'

'I am an evil and sinful creature, Sir, the Devil is within me.'

'And that is why you are here.' His voice is sharper now but still quiet, still deadly. 'You and your mother have been accused of consorting with the Devil, for having imps and demons to do your bidding. It is said that you both contrived to bring about the death of your grandmother – your father's mother – by spells and curses. Do you understand?' Isbel looks at him blankly. 'Your grandmother, girl, she died.'

Isbel's eyes light.

'Evil old hag she was. Cruel to Ma, cruel to me. Nasty tongue on her. Had us all at her beck and call. Good riddance. Better off without her.'

Hopkins face is a studied mask of horror.

'So you bewitched her, causing her death? You and your mother?' I hold my breath. Surely she could not confess to this. All know that Widow Butts was a foul mouthed old harridan, that she had been ill for some time with the wasting sickness. Surely her death was of natural means? I will Isbel not to speak, but she looks up at the ceiling, her hands clasped before her as if in prayer, her eyelids flickering.

'My Ma, Sir, she got a poppet.'

'A poppet. And where did she get such thing?' His words are

calm, precise. Isbel clamps her mouth shut. 'Tell me about this poppet, girl . . . who made it? Was it your mother?'

Isbel's eyes are blank again and her voice, when it comes, is faint.

'Wax it was. A little doll, cloth and cord wrapped round it and a thorn to prick it with. She made it for me.'

'Who? Who made the poppet for you?' He has stopped wheedling now, his voice is rising, sharp as a knife. 'Tell me, girl. Was the poppet made to harm your grandmother?'

Isbel's eyes clear and I see she is back in her wits.

'No, no, Sir, not Grandmother. She just died. No, the poppet was for me, the Widow made it to protect me.'

Hopkins hisses like a snake and darts in to strike. I can almost see his tongue forking.

'Widow? What was her name? Protect you from whom?' He leans in now for the kill. Isbel gazes at him.

'Gardner, Sir, Widow Gardner, over Hazelwood way. She helped me. She helps people. She knew about my trouble, you see. She knew what he did, so she made it to help me stop him. But I did not use it, Sir.'

The air thrums with tension, the name hot in our mouths. Widow Gardner. She who lives by the creek, who has made a living looking after children while their mothers work, who, all thought, wouldn't harm a fly. Who sells herbs, elixirs that she makes for common ailments and those less ordinary. A cunning woman, a helper. Nigh on forty years she has been widowed and in all that time she has made her own way, not begging, never a drain on the parish. She has kept herself quiet and unnoticed. But poppets. The church has warned us about such ungodly, evil enchantments – I cannot believe that any Christian woman would make such a thing.

Matthew Hopkins clears his throat, leans forward in his chair and looks straight at Isbel.

'So, to be clear. You say that this Widow Gardner made a poppet for you to to stop . . . whom?' Isbel's head drops.

'I cannot say, Sir, for the man told me not to speak of him. He promised me that I would only be safe if I did not tell. He promised me he would save me, bring me to the Lord, if I would only let him come to me at night, but he made me swear not to tell.' She is crying now, her pale hair falling in limp strings around her face.

We sit, horror etched on our faces, as Hopkins picks at the truth like a needle in cloth.

'Satan visited you? In what guise did he appear to you? You must tell me now, confess, and all will be well. Were you lured by the Devil into sin?'

Isbel's thin body shudders and I see in that moment she is resolved to tell all. Her voice drops even lower as she starts to speak and all crane forward to hear her.

'He came to my bed at night, Sir, always in the dark. He was all darkness.'

'Who was it? Speak, girl!' Reverend Swaine's voice cuts in sharp and loud and Master Hopkins snaps his head round to glower at him, raising his finger.

'Master Swaine, if you would allow me.' The contempt in his voice sears the room. 'Now, Isbel, who was it that came to you? What took place?' I flinch at the question. Surely anyone can see what had happened here, but no, he wants details. 'Mistress Phillips, as this is a delicate matter, perhaps you . . .?' The search-woman leans forward in her seat, unsmiling.

'Well, child?'

'He used me, Mistress, most cruelly, not just once but other times too.'

I gasp and hold my hand to my mouth. Goody Phillips does not flinch.

'And what was he like, child? When he lay with you. What sort of man was he?'

Isbel hesitates and her voice comes out in a whisper.

'He was cold, Mistress, his . . . his yard was icy cold. It hurt me, inside. I burned but I could feel his seed was cold too.'

She is mumbling now, barely heard, but Goody Phillips persists. 'And he came to your bed, what, once, twice?'

'Maybe more times, Mistress, I did not count. I just did his bidding.' Her voice tails away as if the realisation of what she has said has just struck. The search-woman sits back, satisfied.

'And why did you do his bidding, girl? What did he promise you?' The Witchfinder's voice is losing its softness. He can sense the kill.

Isbel lifts her head.

'He promised to save me from eternal damnation. I was so frightened, Sir, of the torments of Purgatory, the fires of Hell, and he told me I would be blessed, that he could take the evil from me. He promised me. And he seemed kind, although when he . . . when he used me he was not so kind. But he said the pain was cleansing, that it would make me pure, and so I suffered it.' She raises her voice and speaks firmly, confident now. 'He promised. He promised me.'

THE ROOM SEEMS TO SHIMMER, BRIGHT AUTUMN SUNLIGHT NOW pouring in, making diamonds on the oak floor. The breeze is getting up outside and I can hear the shouts of the fishermen on the beach. No one moves, no one speaks. Master Hopkins clasps his hands before him, eyes lowered as if deep in prayer. He seems to compose himself and looks again at Isbel, who is smiling now, her confession made.

'So you had a poppet made to stop this man?'

'Oh, no, Sir, I did not. Twas my Ma who did so. She went to Widow Gardner after the Devil had visited me again, to get a potion, for she feared I may be with child, but the Widow would not give one, for she said that to stop a child was against the teachings of Christ, that all children are a blessing in the eyes of God. But she gave my Ma a wax man. We used a little piece from Pa's shirt to dress it, wrapped some hemp from the nets round it. I was going to prick it, Sir, for she gave me a thorn for the purpose, but I did not. When the man appeared again I showed him the poppet, and it stopped him, for he never came to me after that. And I am here now. And we are safe.'

She sits back in her chair as if a huge weight has been lifted from her and looks around the room. Master Hopkins scratches away with his quill, the chink of the ink-pot as he dips it rings like a bell in the silence.

He looks up.

'And now you are with child?'

Isbel looks at him in horror.

'No, Sir, how can I be? I only lay with him a few times and he promised I would be saved, that I would be freed of all sin, made pure.'

'And what of your mother?'

'She only went to Widow Gardner because of me, she was trying to protect me. And the poppet worked, Sir, for the dark man never visited me again. I do not know why I am here. I do not understand who has accused me, for I have done nothing.'

Master Hopkins looks at his notes.

'It is your father who has made the accusations against you.'

Isbel flinches as if hit, her face blanching, her mouth falling open.

'No, that cannot be. My Pa loves us. He is sometimes ready with his fists, that is true, but it is for our own good, for we are full of sin and must be cleansed.' She looks from side to side as if for help, her eyes are rolling, and I fear her wits are leaving her again. She is trembling with shock, her world has turned, all that she thought true is not. She drops her head. 'It cannot be.'

'You have been seized because your father has laid an accusation of witchcraft against you and your mother. He says that you lay with the Devil, that you carry Satan's child, and that he is afraid for his immortal soul. What do you say to this?'

But Isbel is gone into herself now, rocking on her chair and, very faint, I hear her muttering. 'Evil girl, bad girl, the Devil has taken you. Evil girl, evil girl . . .'

MASTER HOPKINS NODS TO THE GUARDS WHO PLUCK ISBEL INSENSIBLE from her seat and half-carry her to the doorway. Her head is drooping and her legs barely moving as they push her down the outer stairs. She makes no noise.

Captain Johnson sits back on his chair.

'I would never have countenanced such thing happening here, in this Town. I am shocked, horrified.' He puts a kerchief to his nose as if to ward off a noxious smell. 'I understand that Master Butts is a godly and righteous man, frightened of the evil spirits surrounding him, and this foul work going on in his very house without his knowledge . . . he must be tormented indeed to accuse his own wife and child.'

The Witchfinder gathers his papers and looks at the Captain, his head tilted.

'The girl has freely confessed to using witchcraft and she has accused her mother. We all heard her. No duress was used. It will be the case that her mother made her a witch, for these things are kept in families, passed along from old to young, I have seen it only too often on my mission. My suspicion is that the grandmother may have died through witchcraft, but it is of no matter. The girl has confessed, has named her mother and this Widow Gardner. The mother must be examined for marks by your good self, Mistress Phillips. Widow Gardner must be seized and brought in before she can carry out any more evil deeds.' He is all briskness and efficiency now he has the bit between his teeth. His eyes sparkle with zeal as he stands and faces Captain Johnson and the Reverend Swaine. 'Sirs, this is only the beginning. This Town will be cleansed of witches and I will be the one to do it. You must make space in your gaol. There will be more.'

· · ·

THE MEN HUDDLE TOGETHER AS THE COURTROOM IS CLEARED, INTENT tight on their faces. Hopkins looks at them.

'Widow Gardner – does anyone know where this witch can be found?' The men do not stir so I pipe up, eager to be seen to do my bit.

'She lives at Hazelwood, Sir, has long been known as a healer.'

'Has she now – I wonder how many people she has 'helped'?'

'Sir, people have long relied on such folk, for potions and herbs. She is known as a cunning woman, not a witch.'

Hopkin's eyes fasten mine.

'So how do you explain the poppet?'

I cannot. I lower my eyes and crawl back into myself, reprimanded. Hopkins face softens. 'Mistress Howldine, I know you to be a God-fearing woman, a pillar of this community. But you are, after all, merely a woman, and as such will not always be able to see when evil is before you. That is why men preach, why they rule. For women are the weaker sex, prone to hysteria and imaginings, and must be guided by their betters in all matters.' His words are said kindly but I bristle. I would like to see him run the Lion, separate men fighting in drink, try to halt the swearing and blaspheming that an inn, especially one frequented by sailors and fishermen, fills with when the ale is flowing. But I know my place and do not want to lose it so I drop a curtsey and Hopkins is satisfied.

He turns to the Captain and the Reverend, his face flushed with enthusiasm.

'Gentlemen, we must call the guards, form a search party. This witch must be seized before she can do more harm, we have no time to lose.' He strides across the courtroom, the oak boards creaking under his boots, and flings open the door. I move to follow him but he stops me with a look. 'Mistress Howldine, you will not be needed, this is work for men. But be prepared, for there will be another in the gaol by the end of the day for you to feed, you have my word.'

As the men go to leave I catch at the Captain's sleeve.

'Captain, do you think the Town should employ someone to see if the girl truly is with child?' He turns on his heel and looks questioningly at me.

'Goody Phillips may . . .'

'I was thinking of a midwife, Sir, one trained in such things. She may be more suitable than Mistress Phillips.'

He ponders for a moment.

'You are right, Mistress Howldine, please arrange it, but make sure she is a godly person of good character, for we want no further taint of witchcraft clouding these matters.'

I drop a deep curtsey.

12. JOAN

The girl Isbel seems barely in her wits when the guards bring her back. Her mother cries out and rushes to her side as they drop her onto the straw, then turns to the men.

'What have they done to her? Surely they have not pricked her, ducked her . . .' She is wailing and tearing her hair now as the girl lies still as a corpse.

The guards laugh loudly.

'Look at her, woman, she has not been ducked. She is dry as a bone. And anyway, ducking is forbidden.' Catherine looks across at Joan – they both know that forbidden does not mean not done.

One of the guards steps forward, full of importance.

'She has not been touched. There was no need. Confessed all she did, to sinning with the Devil. Said you were to blame an' all.' Catherine looks up.

'Me? But I . . .'

'Said you enticed the Devil to her bed, let him lie with her. Your own daughter, a slip of a girl. Hanging's too good for you I say – burning, that's what should be done to the likes of you, and with green wood too. See how you'll scream innocence then, when the fire is biting your legs, catching your scrawny arse.'

'That's enough, for pity's sake.' Joan raises herself up slowly, her knees creaking, and stands to face him. She has to tilt her head far up for, now she is standing, she sees he is even taller and wider than she thought. He glares down at her.

'Shut your mouth, you old crone. You witches will stick together now, even more than before. Master Hopkins will search out each and every one of you. We want you out of this Town, done away with once and for all. You are to blame for all this, you and your creatures.' He wipes spittle from his mouth, his eyes wide and sparkling. Joan backs away from him, not daring to anger him further, and gazes down at Isbel who now clings to her mother. Anyone can see the girl is not in her wits, how can they believe her stories? But deep down she knows they will snatch at anything to prove the existence of witchcraft in this Town, even the ramblings of a half-witted child. And even deeper down a voice tells her 'but look at her, look at her stomach.' For someone put the seed in her. Someone's child is in her belly.

And then even she begins to wonder if the Devil really is come to this place and a cold finger of fear pricks at the back of her neck.

13. MARY

I am collecting pots, sweeping the floor, tidying away after the midday drinking when a tall woman knocks at the door of the Lion

'Mistress Howldine? You wished to speak to me?'

'You are the midwife?' She nods. I have not seen her before – in the end I had to send to Saxmundham for her, as the woman who has always assisted with such things in Aldeburgh seems to have melted away and cannot be found. 'I have a need of your services.' I see her sweep me with a professional eye. 'No, not for me. There is a woman in the Town gaol who needs your attention. Captain Thomas Johnson . . .' I can say his name with authority, for I have his ear now. '. . . has told me to arrange for her care. The Town will pay your fee.'

Her eyes narrow.

'Mistress, I am a midwife and this woman . . . I hear she is old, infirm.'

'Yes, but there is now a girl. Three have now been taken up.'

'Three? I had heard there was but one?'

I ignore her and continue. I am on Town business, I expect deference.

'But you have skills, do you not? Healing powers? I too hear things and I have heard that you are clever with herbs and salves? The Captain has told me to point out to you that it is our duty as God-fearing citizens to root out such evil and that he expects you to …'

'Mistress, in these present times, such skills that a woman may have can be seen as unnatural, un-godly. I am merely a midwife. I aid babes into the world, tend their mothers. I do not dabble with spells and potions. I follow the Lord's teachings in all things.'

'As do we all.' I try to soothe her agitation, for I need her help. 'But there is a girl who may be with child, who has confessed to witchcraft. Aldeburgh must be seen to be a caring Town, for the Witchfinder …'

'He is here? Hopkins?' The midwife's face whitens and her words hiss from pursed lips. 'Then I will have nothing to do with this. I have heard tell of his methods, his persecution of such women. He has them searched, watched. I will not do it, you must find another.'

'You will not be required to search the women – he has brought his assistant, Goody Phillips.'

The midwife looks at me scornfully.

'Goody? Goodwife? I hear of her methods too and I do not think she could ever be referred to as good.'

I smile inwardly. This midwife has courage.

'But, nevertheless, the Bailiffs and Burgesses have deemed it necessary to invite him and it is not our place to question it. The witches will be tried and God will decide their guilt or innocence. This is holy work we do, Midwife, and you would do well to remember that. I am merely carrying out an order, and that is to find someone to attend the accused girl. It will not be onerous work, for the Town will only pay for the minimum of care. After all, if she is found guilty and hanged, any money will be wasted.'

'I cannot. I have sworn to do no harm.'

'But this would not be harming her, it would be helping her in her hour of need.'

'I will not work for such as the Witchfinder.'

'Then work for me. Help me to carry out my instructions. After all, it would take only one word from, say, a disgruntled father, a bereaved mother, and the eyes of the Witchfinder could light on you. I can protect you, but only if you help me.' I can see she is wavering. 'You would be making what may be her last days bearable. The girl has confessed to lying with the Devil and needs attention. You would be doing good, not ill and, more importantly, you would be seen to be doing good.'

'It seems I have little choice.'

'No, you have a choice. But be careful, very careful, what it is you choose.'

The midwife lowers her gaze but I can see she is not happy. I hope there will not be trouble.

I ESCORT THE MIDWIFE ACROSS THE SQUARE, HER RED CLOAK billowing in the chill air, her bag slung over her shoulder.

'If we are to work together I should know your name.'

The midwife pauses and looks at me. Her gaze unnerves me. It is as if she can see something behind me. She blinks, and the look is lost, but my feeling remains and I am suddenly uncertain.

'My name is Rose.'

'Rose what?'

'Just Rose.' The midwife's smile does not reach her eyes.

I look at her curiously now. I had not noticed before, but she is ghostlike. Her skin is white, and her eyes pale, almost invisible. I can see little of her hair, tucked as it is under her coif, but a strand that is caught in the breeze is silver. I cannot tell her age.

'You may call me Mary.'

The midwife nods and we stand aside as the gaoler unlocks the door and bids us enter. The sky is grey and forbidding this day, and the gaoler passes us a lantern, for it is dark in the cell. Rose takes it from him and lifts it high, looking around her and I see the horror on her face, quickly masked.

'Which one amongst you may be with child? Speak, I am a midwife, I have been sent to tend to you.' The figures hunched on the floor begin to rustle and move, encouraged by the tone of her voice, which is low and calm.

Then Catherine speaks.

'It is my daughter, Isbel, but she is not quite right.' She stands and pulls her daughter towards her, fumbling at the fastening of her bodice, undoing it and letting it drop to the straw while the girl stands motionless. Isbel's body is thin, the slight bulge of her stomach just visible through her shift. Her eyes are glazed but fortunately she is quiet, sucking on a finger that is hooked into her mouth. She looks like a small child.

'Come closer to the lantern, Isbel. What a pretty name. Come, I will not harm you.' She holds out a hand and Isbel moves forward into the circle of light, finger still in mouth. I can see a string of wet trailing onto her chin and I have a sudden urge to wipe it away for her, for this could have been my own child standing before us. The midwife reaches out and presses her hands onto Isbel's stomach, feeling over and around the swelling there, searching with her fingertips.

'How did this happen, Isbel? Do you know how long ago?' The girl looks at her feet and I realise it is with shame.

'I am an evil child. The Devil is within me, he must be put out.' Isbel's voice drops to a murmur and I stand in silence while Rose looks at Catherine.

'I cannot tell if she is with child as she is very small. It is not normally possible to tell until a child quickens in the womb. Do you know what has happened to her?' Catherine shakes her head and keeps her eyes down as Rose sighs. 'I do not believe this to be the work of the Devil.'

Catherine's head shoots up.

'Yes, Mistress, it is, Isbel told us so. My husband got the truth out of her. He beat us, Mistress, until she confessed. And he was full of horror that this had happened under his roof, and him such a god-fearing man. So he could do no more than come forward and denounce us to Master Hopkins, as any good man should.'

Then, from a dark corner, Widow Wade's voice crackles and barks.

'Devil be damned.'

Rose spins to look at the old woman and I see Catherine's hands move to her mouth, her eyes screwed tight. 'Look closer to home, Midwife. It is clear what has happened. I daresay the man who forced her was no Devil, not in that sense of the word. It is the father you should look to. Ask him how a babe might have got there.' She coughs into her sleeve, then fixes her black beady eyes on me and I wilt under her gaze. 'Devil's child indeed. I have lived long enough to know that devils are normally much closer to home. The gospel says *"He that is without sin can cast the first stone"* – aye, Mistress, I know my Bible too. The child's wits have gone along with her innocence. It is her Pa that should be in here, not her, not us. Evil is all around, aye, but not always where men choose to look.' Her cough takes all her breath now and she reddens with the force of it, unable to speak more. And I back away to rest against the wall and all is horror.

Rose's face is a mask, unreadable.

'Very well, I expect the matter will be looked into when she stands trial. And if she is with child she could plead her belly.'

Catherine looks at her.

'I do not understand.'

Rose crouches before her and takes her hand.

'If she is found to be with child, and it is not certain yet that she is, they will not hang her . . .' Catherine stifles a cry. '. . . for it is a sin to take the life of an unborn child.'

'So she may go free?' The Wade woman speaks from the shadows.

'No, if she is found guilty of witchcraft, she will not go free. She may be imprisoned or she may hang. But they will not take her to the rope until the babe is born.'

'So there is a chance?' Catherine pleads with her eyes, but she knows the truth of it as well as I.

Rose sighs and looks down at her hands.

'Mistress, your daughter would first have to wait here in gaol until it was certain she was with child and this will involve . . .' she pauses, looks again at Catherine, '. . . certain examinations. I understand Goody Phillips is experienced in these things, having once been a midwife herself. But think what they will do if they consider this to be a child of Satan? How they will treat Isbel? How they will treat a babe? They will keep her locked in here until the birth, but I suspect that then they will not hesitate to hang her.'

The midwife swallows hard and squeezes Catherine's hand. 'I think it is just that her courses are late, caused by her treatment here – and elsewhere. There are herbs to bring them on.' I stiffen at her words for this sounds like witchcraft, and Rose looks across at me as if she reads my thoughts. 'Mistress Howldine, such herbs have been used for centuries and their use is well recorded. If Isbel merely dreamed she was visited by Satan, as she says, then she cannot be with child. Such a potion would resolve this.' She turns to Isbel. 'Child, what would you have me do?' Isbel's face wobbles as tears start, and she looks younger than ever as she scrubs at them with curled fists. Rose puts a hand on her shoulder. 'Look at me, Isbel.' She tips up her chin with a long finger and looks deep into her eyes. 'You are old enough to decide – no, do not look to your Mother, look at me. What ever you wish to do, you must tell me, for I am trying to help you.'

Isbel blinks.

'I do not believe I am with child. He told me I would be safe . . .' Her voice tails off.

'Then I will prepare a draught for you.' The midwife turns back to me. 'It will contain garden tansie, master-wort and some other common herbs in a little wine, Mistress. There are many reasons a woman's courses may stop and start and this is a well-used remedy.'

I look at her and I look at Isbel's small stricken face and I nod my agreement.

14. JOAN

After the innkeeper and midwife leave and the cell door is locked, Joan shuffles across to Isbel and takes her hand. The girl's skin is soft, smooth and white against her own dry, wrinkled fingers and she remembers that she, once, was this young, this soft, before time and life had drained her to a husk. Isbel looks at her, but she doesn't pull away.

'Girl, did you say that you lay with the Devil? Is that what you told the Witchfinder?' Isbel's eyes widen, then it is as if a veil is drawn over them and she snatches her hand back and starts to rock from side to side. She closes her eyes and begins to mumble her prayers, but Joan shakes her back. 'Did a man come to you at night, Isbel?' She nods. Joan glances across at her mother and sees her face, and in that moment she realises that Catherine knows. She knows what has happened to her daughter and has done nothing. Her anger rises and she turns to the girl again. 'What was he like, this man?'

Isbel opens her eyes and for a moment her mind is clear again.

'A dark man, clothed in black. His feet were hard like hooves on my legs.' She frowns at the memory. 'His hands were rough and his body was cold, 'twas how I knew him to be the Devil, his sharp feet and his coldness. ' She looks at Joan beseechingly. 'I did not want to do it, Mistress, I knew it to be wrong, but he promised me I would be saved and he told me I am an evil girl . . .'

Joan shakes her again before she goes off into her muttering.

'And his breath, child, was it foul, as the Devil's is said to be? Did his body give off an unnatural stench?' Isbel looks up, big eyed and puzzled. 'Was there a foul stench about the man who came to you in the night, and used you so?'

Her face clears in understanding.

'Oh, no, Mistress. He smelled just like Pa.'

EVENING HAS COME WHEN THE MIDWIFE RETURNS WITH A SMALL CUP. The gaoler looks on as she puts it to Isbel's lips and the girl drinks thirstily. She brings clouts, tucks them beside Isbel and looks around at the women.

'We know what has to be done.' Catherine speaks softly into the gloom and the midwife nods abruptly, gathers her cloak around her, and strides through the door without a backward look.

It is as the night thickens that Isbel's pains begin and Catherine and Joan tend to her as best they can, rubbing her hands and stomach, soothing her with their voices. They pull up her skirts and push clouts between her legs, changing them as the blood seeps through, keeping her clean. And as the dawn breaks and the sun slides upwards over the sea Isbel gives a great groan and is still. They bind her, working together as one, until at last she sleeps.

15. MARY

The witches are still asleep when I bring their food in the morning, the girl pale but breathing gently. I rattle the tray on the floor to rouse them.

'I have brought you some bread and ale – it is all that can be spared at the moment.' Widow Wade blinks at me with those beady eyes and reaches for the bread. 'And what of . . .' I point towards Isbel Butts.

'The child's courses began in the night, Mistress. There was no child.' The old woman nods towards a bundle tied up in an old apron, set beside the pail. 'The clouts need to be got rid of.'

I signal to the gaoler and he pulls his scarf over his mouth and picks up the bundle and the pail.

'The pail must be emptied and those cloths must be burned.' I can see the distaste in his eyes over his mask but stare him down – he is paid well enough. I turn to the girl's mother. 'The Town will be reluctant to pay for any more visits by the midwife.'

Catherine nods dumbly.

'They will not be needed. The child has her courses, that is all. Just bring fresh clouts.' Widow Wade glares at me but we understand each other. The matter has been resolved, no one has been harmed. But underneath my skin, a prickle of unease has lodged.

For it is only God who should change the course of things, not man, and certainly not woman.

THERE IS A HUM OF EXCITEMENT IN THE TOWN AS I STEP OUT OF THE gaol, I can feel it. The market is bustling, but I can tell that few have their minds on their tasks, for word has spread that the Bailiffs have gone to seize Widow Gardner. Heads snap up at every hoofbeat and people talk behind their hands, whispering and muttering. There are new faces here too, for rumours have spread to the outlying hamlets and people are gathering. It has the feeling of a festival, before such things were banned, and I wonder at people's thirst for malice. But it is another thirst I am here to quench and I hurry back to the inn. The Lion is already filling with all the usual regulars and I find that today I am reassured by the familiarity, that it helps to calm the clenching of my heart. For this matter is affecting me now, and I did not think it would. I thought that it would be an easy thing to help seize witches, to watch them imprisoned, to throw them scraps, to keep them alive until such time that they may face justice. I had not considered the other thing. That they are a little like me.

IT IS PAST MIDDAY WHEN THE MEN RETURN. THEY CANNOT HAVE needed to search hard, for a woman is tied across the back of the last horse like a sack of grain, coif-less head low, grey hair dancing in the dirt. I cannot see her face. They untie her and she falls to the ground, senseless, then the guards pick her up as the gaoler opens the door to the gaol and they throw her in. I do not see what they do then for I can only stand frozen in the doorway of the inn. The crowds are jeering and jostling, trying to get a glimpse of the witch as the guards push them back. There are cat-calls, some swear, some spit at her, but I notice that, behind the crowd, in places, a few women stand apart, stock still, their faces drawn and fearful, exchanging glances with each other behind the backs of the menfolk.

People begin to disperse as Captain Johnson crosses the square towards me, leading his horse, the reigns twisted through his hands, a satisfied smile on his face, acknowledging the doffed caps with a haughty air.

'Another one for you, Mistress. She put up a struggle, this one, but the men soon saw to her. Please include her in your ministrations. The Town will pay.' He hauls himself back on to his mount and spurs it into movement. The gaol door clangs shut and the square clears of the last of the onlookers.

It is a quiet Monday afternoon, the seabirds circle above, the sea hisses and thrums on the pebbles. The Town is as it has always been, but now all is changed.

16. JOAN

The women are sitting listless in the heat of the afternoon when the door crashes open to a bustle of men and sweat, leather and fresh air. They carry someone between them, slumped and silent, and they lift her to the far corner where they throw her to the floor. She does not stir.

'Another one of you.' One of the guards spits in contempt and kicks the prone figure in the ribs. 'Won't be any trouble, this one, we let her know who was in charge. At least she knows when to give in. Mind you, we made sure of her silence first.' He grins. 'Sleep well, for it may be your last.' He turns to leave, ushering the others before him, all laughing, heading for the inn no doubt, their work done.

The woman in the corner begins to stir, then pushes herself up, wincing, to look at their retreating backs. Her face is bruised and bloodied, grey hair falling around her shoulders. Her clothes are caked with filth and she has lost a shoe but still she manages to raise herself. And she fixes the men with such a look that Joan's heart surges. For it is a look full of dignity and pride, but also of hatred and anger. The new woman does not curse, does not speak, but the power that emanates from her fills the small stinking cell and gives Joan courage. For she recognises it and knows she is no longer alone.

17. MARY

E arly on Tuesday morning the Captain sends another message. He wishes me to accompany the men to Hazel-wood to search the house of this new witch. I expected the summons, although hoped it would not come. But I must be seen to be helping and we will be back by the afternoon, when the inn fills up, for I cannot afford to lose my livelihood; this extra income will not last forever.

Outside the witch's cottage are signs of a struggle. The ground has been churned by the feet of several men and a coif lays in the dust, blood spotting one side, a boot mark clear. This house is larger than the last one, better built, with a brick fireplace. There are clean reeds strewn on the floor and the air is sweet and fresh. It is tidy and neat with dried herbs bundled on shelves, pots and bottles and a small bench with a sharp knife and a grindstone. The place does not look like that of a witch. It looks like that of a woman who is used to caring for herself, who is organised and particular. Now it fills with men, all sweat and stale breath, and immediately it is made smaller. Captain Johnson's voice booms, he is used to ordering, used to people doing as he says.

'I want this place searched from top to bottom. There will be signs of witchcraft; wax images, foul potions. This one is clever, she will have hidden the tools of her dark trade well.' He looks at me. 'Mistress Howldine, please be good enough to search the coffer over there. There may be such items hidden amongst her most personal things.' I nod and look at the large wooden chest under the window. It is carved with a flowing design of deer and vines, pretty, and I wonder where a woman such as she got such a valuable possession. It is cared for, polished; and free of dust. I wonder what will happen to it, whether I could . . . As I haul open the lid I smell beeswax and lavender, cinnamon and thyme and I am reminded of my grand-mother, for she used such herbs to repel moths and keep clothes fresh. With a pang of horror I realise that maybe she too, in these times, would be seized as a witch. The thought makes me shudder.

The chest is full of clothing, old but serviceable, darned and mended in places. I pull out three skirts, a plain bodice and a patterned one, and four aprons. There are coifs in here too, and all is clean and sweet-smelling. As I dig deeper I find shifts, creaming with age, but spotless. There is a shawl and, towards the bottom, a bundle wrapped in a linen cloth. I peel away the cloth and cannot help an intake of breath.

The Captain turns.

'Have you found something, Mistress? What is that?' He comes across and stands over me as I fold the edges of the linen cloth back. It is a bodice and it is beautiful. Pale blue silk is embroidered with tiny green shoots and pink buds which entwine themselves across the front. It is old-fashioned, the style worn by the Old Queen, but as fresh as the day it was made and I realise that this woman has kept her wedding gown.

The Captain turns away, disappointed, but I cannot stop touching the garment. I have never seen anything so beautiful, never worn such a lovely thing, even on my own wedding day. I run my fingers over its surface, feeling each flower and leaf, admiring the delicate stitching. It is a thing of great beauty and I tuck it back into its wrap carefully.

I turn back to the chest which is nearly empty now. I am surprised such an old woman has so many clothes. She has lived a long life so maybe she was just careful. But then I spy something else, deep down, hidden in the dust and dark and I reach for it. I lift it out. It is a poppet made of cloth with stitched eyes and mouth, grubby, a toy for a child, not like the wax image she has been accused of forming. It has been carefully placed in here, it was precious. But now she is seized as a witch and this may be the evidence I am told to look for, so I put it to one side for Captain Johnson, then turn back to the coffer. Right at the bottom are pieces of folded linen, bleached and soft with use, and I pause. I remember such things, although I have not had any need of them for many years now. They are clouts. It seems odd, as courses stopping are one of the few advantages of old age, and most women are happy to fling any reminders on the fire or use them for rag. The witch is old, like me, she cannot need them, so why has she kept them? I turn away but then pause as a thought hits me. The many clothes, the clouts. The witch did not live alone. There is a younger one.

THE HOUSE IS TURNED OVER. THE MEN HAVE SLICED INTO THE mattress and straw spills out, whisked around the room on the wind blowing through the open door. Shelves have been cleared, bottles and jars lying broken on the floor, their contents soaking into the reeds. The guards have bundled up the food that was there, for she will not be needing it now, and I wonder again about the embroidered bodice, but I am not a thief. Her possessions will be sold, whether she is hanged or freed, to pay for the costs of keeping her in the gaol, so I may well be able to buy it. The men are outside now, digging up the small vegetable patch, flinging earth and plants into the air, saving anything that looks useable. I stand in the doorway and watch, as the Captain moves to my side. I hand him the cloth doll. He nods and we stand and watch the men sweating and cursing.

'What are they searching for?'

'We know she must have the tools of her dark trade somewhere. She will have buried them. It is clear she knew we were coming.'

'I wonder that she did not flee.'

The Captain turns to me with a wry smile.

'Where would she go, Mistress? Aldeburgh is a small place, this Hazelwood even smaller. Beyond are only marshes and water, dangerous and wild. She has nowhere to hide, no one to hide her.'

I think again of the clothes, the clouts.

'Do you think she lived alone?' I am reluctant to voice my thoughts now.

'She is old, useless, I understand there is no family. Who would live here? No god-fearing man or woman would have anything to do with one such as she.'

I think of the woman, living here, unprotected and alone, how it would feel to be taken up . . . I shake myself to my senses. She is named as a witch. Isbel Butts has accused her of making a poppet and these things are wrong, such evil must be rubbed out. The Captain and Master Hopkins are right in their teaching, right to do this. Our Town needs scourging to bring it back to the true path and what is one woman's soul when compared to that of the whole Town? They are right to take her and God will judge her in a court of law. I settle my thoughts and fold my hands over my stomach as I watch the men dig. Deep inside, though, a thought takes hold. Her wedding bodice. A child's toy. Once she was loved.

18. JOAN

The women in the gaol are trying to sleep but the small space is cramped, rank with the smell of unwashed bodies. Isbel is mainly silent, which is a blessing, and the one they have just brought says nothing, but Joan knows she is taking it all in. Catherine cannot look at her and keeps her head bowed, her arms round her daughter.

'You must not blame yourself, Mistress Butts.' The new woman's voice is low and husky. 'It was not Isbel's fault.'

Joan looks square at her.

'You know each other?'

'We met but once, recently. I have not seen Isbel before now.'

'So, who are you?' It dawns on Joan that Catherine has not spoken a word since the new one was brought in last night, in fact has barely spoken since Isbel was returned from the courtroom, now she comes to think of it. The woman turns to her.

'I am Alice Gardner of Hazelwood.' Her head is held high, her bruised face proud.

'Joan Wade, widow, from Slaughden. I have heard tell of you.' She remembers this woman now, and remembers why. Alice Gardner is known as the cunning woman, one who you go to for love potions, herbs to settle a stomach, roots to heal wounds. And now such people are taken up as witches.

'I am also a widow, Joan, married but seven years. And you?' Her voice is soft and rhythmic and Joan can imagine how you would come to tell her your secrets, for she makes you feel safe. And it is a long time since someone just said her name. It lures her to familiarity.

'Not one full year of marriage for me. Henry his name was, a farmhand.' It is many years since Joan has spoken of him but he still comes into her thoughts, especially now in this place, where she has little else to think of. What might have been, the life she could have had, children . . . Joan is drifting when Alice's voice comes back, low and gentle.

'You must have been on your own for many years?'

'I have seen seventy winters now, I think, I was seventeen when we married, so yes – a long time.' Alice makes Joan feel calm, and for a moment she loses the constant anger that she has carried for many a year. 'I got by, always found work although often it did not pay well. But I managed. I have rarely had to beg, unlike some.'

'We cannot judge those who are worse off than ourselves, for there, but for the grace of God, go we.'

Joan accepts the rebuke.

'It was begging that brought me here. I made the mistake of asking a neighbour for a cup of milk.' Joan's bitterness has returned at this thought. 'And you, Alice Gardner? No children, family, to care for you?'

'We were not blessed but I have made a living caring for the children of others and that has been a comfort to me.' She smiles at Joan and it seems strange in this place. Her face is ageless, lined, but Joan can see she would have been beautiful once. 'And now we are here.'

Joan looks around. The air is cooling, the walls dampening. Autumn is coming in fast. And she wonders, with a rising fear, if they will see winter.

19. MARY

Master Hopkins must have risen early. He is collecting his papers together when I take his breakfast to his room.

'Mistress Howldine, a busy day.'

'Sir?' I set the tray down on the table.

'The witches are to be searched today. The Butts woman, who was accused by her daughter, and the other two.'

'Not the girl?'

'She has confessed, so there is no need. And, of course, she is very young.' He grimaces as if the thought pains him. 'Mistress Phillips will take charge. She will be using the courtroom and will require some food and ale at midday, for hers is thirsty work.'

'Very well, Sir, I will arrange it.' I drop a curtsey. But as I move to leave, he reaches a hand and touches my sleeve. I turn, startled by this familiarity, but his face is set and I see he means nothing by it.

'Mistress . . .' He pauses, finding the right words. '. . . please ensure that it is you who takes the midday tray, not your pot-boy.' I look at him curiously. 'There may be . . . sights . . . that would not be suitable for one so young.' I feel the hairs on my neck rise and a deep sinking in the pit of my stomach. It has begun.

. . .

I WATCH FROM THE DOORWAY OF THE INN AS, ACROSS THE SQUARE, the first one is taken from the gaol and pushed roughly up the steps to the courtroom. Her head is down and I cannot see clearly which it is but I think it is the mother, Catherine, for the figure seems younger, thinner, than the other two. People are beginning to gather again, they have heard the news, for such stories whistle round the Town faster than an autumn gale. The weekly market is becoming swollen by strangers who travel here to try and see the witches for themselves. The inn is thriving and I hear the stories multiply and enlarge as the days grow dark and the ale flows. I am kept busy this morning and at midday I am tempted to send the pot-boy with the food anyway, but I have given my word so I wipe my hands on my apron, put a cloth over the tray of meat and ale, and walk through the crowds across and up the stone steps.

A guard stands outside the dark oak door. He stiffens at my approach.

'I bring food for Mistress Phillips.' His eyes narrow at the name and he turns to knock on the door. I am not used to being kept waiting and click my tongue, but he waits for a muffled reply before pushing door open for me.

At first my eyes cannot take in the scene. The room is dimmed by dark clouds scudding over a September sky outside, but, as they clear, I gasp in horror. The long table where Master Hopkins sat has been pulled to the centre of the room and Catherine Butts lies upon it. Her clothes have been removed and her shift is pulled up over her face so I cannot see it. I can only hear her low moans. I look away from her nakedness but not before I have seen her body is pitted and speckled with blood. Goody Phillips stands beside a smaller table, her leather bag open. I cannot see what is in it but as I move to put the tray down beside it I have to stifle a cry, for on the table lies a stained cloth and a tool with a wooden handle and a metal spike. There are several others of different sizes carefully lined up in a stained leather wrap. I look at Goody Phillips.

'This is searching?' I never thought it would be like this, never imagined the horror. I look back at the tools. 'What are these?'

She smiles grimly.

'Prickers. To test for the Devils marks.'

'Marks?'

'Teats, spots – anywhere the witch can suckle her familiars. The Devil sends his imps to such women, to feed on their blood, this is his pact with witches. And the Devil's teats do not bleed and that is how you tell a witch.' She folds her arms across her stomach in satisfaction and nods towards Catherine's prone form. 'That one had a number of marks and I have found them all. Master Hopkins will be pleased. Her child had already accused her so there was no real need to search her, but best to be certain, we agreed, and he wants to do a good job here. There must be no suggestion of failure.'

I put my hand to my mouth. I had seen the pamphlets, heard the talk, but this . . . Catherine lies silent now, only her chest heaving, her breath coming hard, and I suspect she is praying that it has stopped, but expecting it to begin again. I turn back to Goody Phillips.

'And has she confessed?'

'Oh, yes, my dear, they all confess in the end.'

I turn to the door, resisting the urge to run, but I find myself pausing as I reach the bottom of the steps. Behind me I hear Goody Phillips speak to the gaoler.

'You can take her back, she is finished. Bring the next one. I will be able to get them all done today.'

THEY HAVE THE NEW WITCH READY TO BE TAKEN UP. As I PASS THE gaol I see Alice Gardner, her head held high, shake off the hands of the gaoler and walk steadily up the steps. I wonder at her calm – perhaps, after all, she is innocent of the charges. But they are serious. To make a poppet to cause harm, that is a hanging offence.

I am not there when she is returned to the cell. I do not see how she is changed. But those present who tip into the inn to wash away the bitter taste of hypocrisy tell me.

'She was sent back in just her shift, Mistress, all bloodied – they had taken her clothes. But they say she did not confess and there was no witches marks found on her. People say that means she must be innocent.'

'Nothing innocent about that one. She's been making potions and spells for years, all knew of her and what she did. Looked after children I was told, years ago. Wonder how many she sent to their deaths?'

'I knew a neighbour whose wife got a spell from her to get with child and the next summer, there he was. A boy-child, as bonny as you like, and they dote on that child still, even though he's full grown. They won't hear a word said against her.'

'They were lucky then, for if you can use spells to make a child, you can use spells to get rid of one an' I bet there's many a young lass who's been helped in that regard.' The men nod sagely and pull at their ale and talk moves on to the coming winter and how it will be. The hedges are already full of berries and the blackbirds are feasting and all know this means a hard winter to come. But I continue to think of Mistress Gardner, for this has reminded me of something I had forced myself to forget, something I had pushed to the back of my memory for shame. A time when I yearned for a daughter of my own so badly I would do anything. How I crept out one evening, when my husband was at the inn, to seek out the cunning woman. How the herbs had been sharp and bitter on my tongue, burning my throat, searing my belly. I think of my joy when they nourished a little knot, nurtured it into being . . . but how, even then, I could not bring it to life.

And how I have always cursed the person who had given me hope, only to have it snatched away so cruelly. The cunning woman. Alice Gardner.

20. JOAN

Joan cannot bear to look at Catherine when she is brought back. They take Alice in her place and Joan's heart is full of a black dread, for she knows she will be next, and she does not wish to see what they do.

There is a little water in a pail for washing, so she tears off a piece of her underskirt and soaks it. She passes it to Isbel, nodding towards the jug of water, so she can tend her mother's wounds, but the girl is pulled in on herself and just sits, eyes closed, prayers winnowing her lips, so in the end Joan does it herself. Catherine is pricked all over but the small punctures will heal in time. She makes her as comfortable as she can, laying her on her side so the hurt does not touch her so much. She seems to be sleeping but then her eyes flicker and she looks up.

'Thank you, Mistress.' Joan pats her hand as Catherine's eyes close again. Fear claws at her guts and her entire body shakes.

Thoughts are still spinning like whirlpools as the gaol door rattles and opens, and Alice Gardner is thrust back inside. Her proud look is still there but her body seems reduced. She is dressed only in her shift. a fresh bruise colours one side of her face and, like Catherine, there is blood everywhere.

She sits down heavily on the straw as if her legs can no longer support her.

'Joan, just tell them. There is no escaping this, no way to save yourself. Tell them what they want to hear. Save yourself the pain.'

Joan considers her words. She is old. Her time is coming to an end and she has little fight left in her. If she does not hang she will be forever reviled, she will be the witch that escaped justice. Her life will be a misery. Maybe it would be best to end it now, quickly.

'Is that what you did?' Her voice wavers and she sounds as old as she feels.

Alice turns and opens one eye, her face glowing with the bruise, scratches scouring her neck and shoulders, and laughs, and Joan wonders where she finds the strength.

'No, not me. I gave them nothing.' Alice reaches out to her and puts a warm hand to cup the side of Joan's face, and strength flows through it and into her like a smooth white tide.

Then they come for her, pull her to her feet and half-drag, half-carry her out of the door and up the steps.

21. MARY

When Goody Phillips returns to the Lion later that afternoon there is an expression of satisfaction on her face. She knocks on Master Hopkin's door and he opens it so fast I know he was standing behind it, waiting for the sound of her step. I follow her in, for to be alone with a man in his room would not be seemly, and anyway I want to find out what has happened.

'Mistress Phillips. And Mistress Howldine, come in, come in. Such a sad business.' Master Hopkins looks anything but sad; his thin fox-face glows. The search-woman drops her bag to the floor and I shudder as I think what her implements have done this day. 'What news? Do you have their confessions?' He indicates the bench and we both sit. We could be friends visiting, waiting for wine and cakes, looking forward to a neighbourly gossip.

Goody Phillips puts her beefy hands on her knees and leans forward.

'The first one, Butts, confessed to asking Gardner to make her a poppet. She said it was a doll, a plaything for her daughter, but I knew the truth of the matter. I had to test her sorely to get at the truth but the truth came. My pricker finds out faster than anything.'

Hopkins smiles grimly.

'That is good. And the others?'

'More troublesome, Sir. The Gardner witch said nothing. I pricked her thoroughly but she made not a sound. She is inhuman, for no good Christian woman could withstand such a thing.'

'But were there witch marks? Did you find teats that did not bleed?'

'Sir, I could find nothing. She bled as anyone would each time the bodkin entered her and she did not make a sound. She has conjured this, to put us off the scent, but I know her type. She is as guilty as sin, as true a witch as I have ever come across.'

'But there were no signs on her body?' He looks sideways at her now, his eyes narrowed and dark.

'Not in the normal way, no.'

'So she will have to be watched?'

'Yes, Sir.'

I have heard of this watching, I did not think it too hard a thing, but having seen what has already happened I am uneasy.

'And the last one, the old witch that was brought in before I arrived. The one who was the start of this?'

Goody Phillips furrows her brow.

'Widow Wade. Well, that's the strange thing, I thought she would be the easiest, given her age and temper. I thought that a few strikes of the pricker and she would babble like Beelzebub himself. But she told me nothing, despite her thin skin. Just cursed and swore at me like a sailor, such foul words she used.'

Hopkins tuts and shakes his head sadly.

'So we must watch her too?'

'That would be my advice, yes, for she is old and full of spite and we need a confession. We do not want to be accused of persecuting them. I have heard some begin to say that this mission . . .'

Hopkins holds up his hand to stop her.

'I too have heard the rumours, Mistress, but we both know that our undertaking is sent from the Lord. I only have a few more days here, so watched they will be. Tomorrow. I will make sure the room is prepared, employ men to sit. We will get those confessions from them before I go, you have my word on it. These women are witches, I know it in my heart. '*Thou shalt not suffer a witch to live*', that's what the Holy Gospel says, and that is what will happen. I thank you for your efforts, Mistress Phillips, I know how this business tears at your soul.' I look between them – if I did not know better I would say that Goody Phillips simpered. We both stand, drop a low curtsey and leave, her to her room and I to the kitchen. For I have meals to prepare, customers to serve. The horror I swallow down.

THE WITCHES ARE IN A SORRY STATE WHEN I TAKE THEIR BREAD IN THE morning. The girl Isbel has her head turned to the wall, and does not move when I am let in, but the others stir and hands reach shakily for the food. There is a jug of ale too and they pass this between them as if it was their last. The Gardner woman is clothed only in her shift.

'Where are your clothes?' I ask.

The bruise on her face is purple, yellowing a little, but it is covered now with scratches and pinpricks of blood. She is still defiant.

'Taken from me yesterday, by that foul woman upstairs. I need them back.'

I agree with her, it is most unseemly that she should be dressed so indecently, especially with the gaoler outside.

'I will see what has happened . . .'

She looks at me, her face curious.

'Have we met, Mistress? You seem . . .'

'Why would we have met? No, you are mistaken.' My heart thumps beneath my bodice – if she were to recognise me, to name me. Then she nods and looks at the others and I think myself safe again, though my chest still pounds.

'And water, we need more water and cloths, to cleanse ourselves of this filth.'

I hesitate, for this is not something I have been paid to provide, but it is not right that she should be left like this and I cannot afford to wrong-side her, for she may still remember. And it will cost little, and may enhance my standing in the eyes of the Witchfinder.

'I will see what I can do.'

'You do that, Mistress, and soon. You would not wish for gaol fever in this place I am sure?'

When I get back to the inn I go straight up to Goody Phillips' room and knock on the door. She bids me enter and I find her sitting majestically in the chair, her sewing on her lap, looking like a stately matron, happy with her lot.

I come straight to the point.

'The clothes from the Gardner woman.' Her face narrows. They were good and clean – saleable – and all at once I know she has taken them.

'I have them here, Mistress Howldine – for safekeeping.' She lies and we both know it, but we let it pass.

'It is not seemly that a woman should be kept in her shift, even a witch. We have standards in this Town and I ask that they be returned to her.' I see her hesitate, so hold out my hand.

Bending to her bag with a sigh, Mistress Phillips pulls out a roll of cloth and passes it to me.

'You will ensure they are returned to her?'

I know what she is suggesting and I bristle at the idea that I am one such as she.

'Of course, for they do not belong to me.' We stare each other down. We are pacing round each other like a pair of curs, our teeth beginning to bare. We are getting the measure of each other. I pluck the bundle from her hands and tuck it under my arm. From it wafts the faint, sweet smell of lavender and summer. Of a better time. A safer time.

'BACK AGAIN, MISTRESS?' THE GAOLER LETS ME IN AND I PASS THE bundle of clothes to the Gardner woman who catches it deftly. She unrolls it to check everything is there and then stands.

'Cloths? Water?'

I glare at her for indeed I have forgotten, but I do not want to lose face by admitting such.

'They are being prepared.' She looks wryly at me – we both know the truth of it. 'I will be but a moment.'

The inn is filling and I have work to do, but I bustle across to the gaol for a third time, a jug of water sloshing in my hands, old rags tucked under my arm. This is taking too much of my day and I wish I was not so involved. But involved I am, and if I want the payment they have promised me I will need to carry out my duties diligently, even those not asked of me directly. I turn and nod at the gaoler who lets me in then stares at the woman standing tall before us. I follow his eyes and see that Alice Gardner's shape is pressed against her soiled shift and that, bloodied and damaged as she is, she has the body of a younger woman. Then, to my horror, as she spies the water and cloths, she reaches down, pulls the shift over her head and stands before us naked as a babe. It is unnatural, ungodly, a filthy thing. Beside me the gaoler breathes heavier.

'Look elsewhere, Gaoler, for fear you commit the sin of lust!' He has the grace to look sheepish at my catching him out and shuffles away, closing the door behind him. I turn back to Alice Gardner. 'Be quick, Mistress, I do not have all day.'

The witch seemingly has no shame as she reaches for the cloths. She dampens them with water from the jug and, one by one, passes them to the others, then begins to clean herself. I do not know where to look. Catching my eye, her face softens a little and she has the grace to turn her back, as she finishes washing and begins to dress. She puts the soiled shift back on, pulls up her skirt and laces her bodice. She combs wet fingers through her hair. It is wild and tangled and she has little success, but it is an improvement. The others are busy with their cloths, grey shadows, wraiths, moving slowly as the room rustles and shimmers before me and suddenly it seems as though the women are moving as one, dark and sinuous, power crackling from them. It is like looking into the very maws of Hell and I can only close my eyes and wait.

22. JOAN

J oan told them nothing.

She thought that if Alice Gardner could be silent then so could she. But the pain. The fingers, pinching and prodding at her bones, the sharp sting and throb of the point going in, pulsing. She could not bear it and she had come so close to telling them what they wanted to hear to make it stop. But then she had pulled into herself and breathed deep, and thought of the sea and the marshland. In her mind she walked through the reeds, the birds warbling and fluttering deep in the leaves, and thought of all the things she has loved. The smell of lavender in the garden, the hum of bees. The feel of fresh well-water on her face, summer rains, autumn winds. The crunch of snow under her boots, the fresh stinging of winter air. All these things had flooded to her aid and she rose with them, away from the broken body on the table, blood-spattered and bruised, away from that moment and into another. And she knew that it was Alice Gardner who had given her this, who had blessed her with the power of flight from her own body.

But then Joan came back into the room and she was a mass of pain. She had looked down at her hands, her legs, smeared with blood as they trembled before her, and she had felt her whole body shaking.

But she told them nothing.

23. MARY

M aster Hopkins is once more at his desk when I take bread and ale to him the next morning. He tears at a piece of the loaf and places it carefully in his mouth, dabbing the corners with a napkin, then takes a draught of ale, and springs to his feet, leaving the rest of his meal on the plate. I look down at it. It will do for later, it will not be wasted.

'We will be watching the accused today, Mistress Howldine. Captain Johnson has arranged men to sit with them, so you will not be required to take food to the gaol.' I see the profits in my ledger shrink.

'All of them, Sir? I thought the Butts woman had confessed after her daughter . . .' He turns and smiles at me but his eyes are cold.

'No, not all of them, Mistress. We will watch the Gardner and Wade women who have yet to admit their sins, but it will do the other two no harm to be without food. It is only the cost that prevents them also being watched – indeed, there is no need, for I am satisfied of their guilt and they have confessed all. No, the two widows will endure it until they speak out, or their imps come to them and God sends us the proof we need.'

I have heard tell of imps, imagined small black bitter sharp shapes dancing around with forked prongs and spiked tails and I shudder, but underneath rises curiosity.

'Will such creatures appear here, Sir, in this Town? For they are servants of the Devil, are they not, to be contained and feared?'

'Imps come in all forms, Mistress, but you need not be afraid, for they do not attend godly women. Sometimes they are as big as cats or dogs, but most often small creatures – mice, bees, flies, beetles. Why, only a few weeks ago in Rushmere two sisters admitted sending lice-carrying imps to a neighbour. Imps were used in Halesworth, one even being sent to help Prince Rupert with the King's Army.' He looks horrified at this event, and I see that he believes his righteousness in this matter. He truly believes he is on a mission from God, with the sanction of Parliament. He is deadly dangerous, for he knows himself to be right.

THE DAY SEEMS LONGER WHEN I DO NOT HAVE THE WITCHES TO FEED. No trips across the square, just the customers, more and more, coming into the inn, asking questions. And the only subject on their lips is the Witchfinder.

'What is he like, Mistress?' A crabbed hand, one of the sailors, grabs mine as I serve him his ale.

I shake it off with scorn.

'He is very polite, keeps himself to himself. A good guest in every way.' But they want more.

'Does he have you all praying for redemption?'

'Is he going to search out more witches?'

'Does he have a book?' This last question makes me stop, for I have heard talk of this book. It is said that Master Hopkins has the Devil's own list of all his servants.

I turn to the man, see the excitement in his eyes.

'I have seen no such book, Sir, but it may be that he keeps it hidden in his room, away from prying eyes.'

'Let's hope he's hidden it well then, lads.' A young sailor is pointing at me, making goggle-eyes, but at least he has the grace to look shamefaced when I turn and glare at him. I wonder whether to throw him out, but the ale is flowing so I leave him. Men will speak unwisely when in their cups and I do not want to lose valuable custom. George Nun is propped in his usual place at the bar when I return. I top up his mug, unasked.

'This is a bad do, Mary, a bad do . . .' He fastens his lips to his mug and takes a deep pull.

'The Town has invited the Witchfinder here, George, and it was right to do so, for the place is going to the dogs. Time was when you could go about your business undisturbed, without fear of curses and spells.'

He looks thoughtfully at me.

'But there have always been arguments, neighbour cursing neighbour, jealousy, spite. What I want to know is why now, why are people accusing each other of such things now?' He looks at me, his eyes damp, and I realise that he is getting old, muddled.

'You should not speak so, George, not so publicly. You don't know who is listening. You can trust me, but there are some that could repeat your words, relay your doubts, and then where would we be? Men have been taken up as witches too you know. This Town; the Bailiffs, Captain Johnson, the Reverend – they are our masters, they know what must be done for the best and they have deemed that an invitation to Master Hopkins is the way to cleanse our Town of sin and evil.'

George looks at me as if I am possessed.

'Sin and evil . . .' He spits forcibly and doesn't trouble himself to rub it out with his foot, even when he sees my face. 'What sin and evil? No more than usual, no more than other places. It's people, that's all, the way people are. They have always fought, always argued, and they always will.'

'But that curate, Maptid Violet, you cannot tell me he wasn't evil. The way he acted, the women he touched. He was a drunkard and a fornicator, and no one will tell me otherwise.'

He looks at me with rheumy eyes, one clouded. He is not the man he was.

'Violet behaved badly, that is true, and the Town was right to get rid of him, but have you thought that he was just a young man, unused to freedom, to strong drink . . . unsuited to the priesthood?'

I flap my hand at him in frustration.

'George, we were both here that night, we saw what he did, heard what he said, and someone had to stand up and speak, and, as for the women he molested – one was a mere servant girl. We all know what men are like, but a curate? He should have known better, have been above such thoughts and actions. No, you and I were right to speak out, and I stand by it.' I soften my tone at George's startled expression. 'And what of the omen, the rock that appeared before the Captain and Master Thompson? Do you not believe that it was truly a sign from God, a comment on our wickedness? It is right that Aldeburgh does what it is doing, to beg forgiveness for our sins, right to cleanse this place of evil. And now, with these four women seized, and the cleansing continuing, well, it is a godly thing, I am sure of it. I do not question my masters on this, and you would do well to do the same.'

His head drops and he waves a thin hand at me.

'You are right of course, Mary, I should not give voice to such things.'

I pat his bony shoulder to show he is forgiven.

'Best to go home now, George, will you find your way?'

'Aye, Mary, g'night.' I open the inn door for him and watch him stumble into the darkness, whistling tunelessly. I glance across to the courthouse. All is dark in the square below but above, behind the patterned glass of the upper room, where the watchers sit, candles gleam as if it were morning and a shaft of uncertainty edges itself into my mind.

·   ·   ·

FOR SOME REASON SLEEP ESCAPES ME THIS NIGHT AND I CANNOT STOP thinking of the two women in the courtroom. I am told that witches are made to sit, sometimes tied, and they are watched for hours on end, to see if their familiars visit them to suckle, but it surely cannot be that bad? Then I try to lie still in my bed and it is not long before I feel the mattress tickle, my nose itch, my joints start to ache. I must not dwell on it. I shake the thoughts away and, throwing the covers back, slide out of bed and move to the window. Beyond the houses the moon shines on a calm sea, clouds scud across the darkened sky in a stiffening breeze, and all is peaceful. But the sight of the candle-lit courtroom has disturbed my thoughts. For there will be no peace in there. The women are witches, almost certainly, and Master Hopkins knows what he is doing, he would not have seized them without cause, but what will happen after they are tried? If they are guilty they will be imprisoned or, worse still, hanged. If they are not guilty they will have to go back to their lives and live in shadow and fear. I shudder and reach for a shawl, pulling it tight around me, then sit on the window-seat and wait for morning.

24. JOAN

The watching has destroyed her.

She did not think of how it would be. She thought it would be bad enough to have all eyes on her when she is only used to her own company, to be made to sit still, but that it would be bearable, for it was only sitting after all. And for the first hour it was. But she is old, her joints stiffen quickly and she could not sit still, so they tied her legs to the chair and bound her arms. They hoisted her skirts up so that any familiar that came to her would not be hidden, and all she could think of was their eyes on her ankles. She could not see Alice Gardner, they were bound back to back, but she could feel her. The warmth from her body, the regular movement of her breathing, it soothed Joan to know that she was there, that she was not alone in this. But soon the pain was blinding and she lost all sense of where she was, what was happening.

When darkness fell she thought they would let them go, but then candles were lit so there was no night. Men sat around the room, their eyes gleaming, and others would come and take their place as the hours dragged by. When she closed her eyes, the men would shake her and shout, then pull her up and walk her around so she could not sleep. She could feel Alice behind her, moving quietly, trying to ease the agony, as she was doing, and every now and again they walked her too. Then a mist grew over her and time stood still and she drifted, as if floating on the sea like a corpse, alone and cold. She remembered her husband, Henry, drowned after only seven sweet months of marriage, dreamt she heard him calling to her, and she thought she would be better off dead with him. She thought her life was ending at that moment and she was glad of it. But then a shuffling, a murmuring and her eyes sprang open.

The pain. Such pain flooded through her, she was panting and crying with it all now, and then she glimpsed it. A poor brown tangled thing, its nose quivering in the unexpected candlelight – a mouse. The men saw it and the room came alive.

'An imp – look, it comes to them . . .' The men hissed in whispers, the susurration whirling like devils around the room, like the dust storms of high summer on the fields where the hogs root and wallow.

'One of them has summoned her familiar, it comes to her aid.'

Their voices were taught with excitement, tinged with fear.

'Which one will it go to?'

'Perhaps they share, perhaps they are both in league.'

Joan could no longer see the creature as it ran under her chair and she felt Alice tense.

'Look, it goes to the younger one – there, by her foot – it is running around her.'

The men leaned forward, expectant and she felt the other woman trembling, her whole body moving, and in her mind's eye she could imagine the creature touching Alice's foot, damning her, condemning her, so she did the only thing she could think of to save her, to take their minds from it.

'I confess.'

The men spun round and looked at her. Joan tried to swallow, to wet her mouth, and as she forced the words out again, she felt her dry bottom lip split and begin to bleed. The blood tasted sharp and salty on her tongue and it revived her, so that the words just seems to pour out. The men jumped to their feet, all thought of imps forgotten.

'I am guilty. It was as they said. I cursed Master Lamb, swore at him and I bewitched his cow . . .'

'She confesses – fetch Master Hopkins.'

Even through her pain she smiled inwardly at the thought of him being raised from his sleep, having to dress in the dark, summoned to hear her. Such little things give faint pleasure, even now, even here. She felt Alice slump in her chair and the horror of what she had spoke began to creep through her.

She is done for. Now she will hang.

It has destroyed her.

25. MARY

I am woken by the sounds of footsteps outside the inn, a hammering, the outer door unlocked. I hear men coming up the stairs, pausing on the landing, then muffled voices, the creak of floorboards, a shift in the air. Something has happened. I glance outside. Candles still burn in the courthouse but the sun rises over the sea, fast and bright. Morning has come.

I rise stiff and aching from the window-seat and pour water from a jug into my wash-bowl. I splash my face and scrub with my palms, trying to remove the grittiness of a poor night's sleep. I am weak with exhaustion. I lean heavily on the table top and bend down over the water, and, as it stills, I see my reflection. But the face that is looking back at me is old, lined, and my heart thumps, for it is the face of that witch in the gaol, Joan Wade. Then the image dims and I see myself, black smudges around my eyes, my hair unkept. A woman of middling years, her looks fading, age creeping up. I blink to clear my mind of the strangeness and stand up straight, rubbing at my back with my knuckles, gradually regaining my composure as I dress. I am only tired, that is all, the extra work is taking its toll, I need to rest. But I cannot clear my head of the witches.

. . .

As I enter the downstairs room Master Hopkins comes hurrying in from outside, bringing a cloud of salt air with him.

I curtsey.

'Master Hopkins, is all well?'

'The old witch has confessed, Mistress, and the other one's familiar came to her this night. It is a good outcome.'

'So what happens now, Sir? Are they to be taken for trial?' All of a sudden I want him gone from my inn, money or no. The women will go to the gaol at Ipswich or Colchester, with all the others he has found, and this Town will be done with it. I must not begin to think what will happen to them, I must let matters be.

'I move on tomorrow, Mistress, I have business in Ipswich that I must attend to. But Aldeburgh, it seems, is pleased with my work here, and I have been invited to return. The Captain and Reverend have kindly asked me to continue my searches, for there are more witches to be found, I know it.'

This is news indeed.

'But what will happen to those already seized?'

'They will remain in the gaol here until I return. The Captain has been pleased with your co-operation and diligence and so have I, Mistress, you have proved to be a true member of God's anointed. Captain Johnson will speak to you with the intention of asking you to continue to provide for the prisoners. They need little now, as they have confessed, but they must be kept in reasonable condition for the trial. We must be seen to be fair, we are not barbarians.'

'And when will you return, Sir?' The extra payments will be useful but I need to know what to expect. I can hold the rooms for a few days but others may wish to stay, especially when news gets out of more witches to be found.

'My business takes me further into the county. The Town will settle my account tomorrow and then I will return in December.'

'December? They will stay in the gaol until Christ-tide?' His eyes narrow at my presumption and I lower my gaze. 'I am sorry to speak sharply, Master Hopkins, but I am surprised. I thought the matter to be done well before then.'

'It is not something that must be rushed, Mistress. Each complaint must be examined for falsehood, each case must be considered carefully. And many are asking for my services now, and those of Mistress Phillips. So December it must be.'

I AM LATE IN TAKING THE BREAD AND ALE TO THE WITCHES, SO I bustle over, my mind spinning with the web of opportunity this news has brought. A further search would give me the chance to be rid of the fear of poverty that has haunted me since childhood, it will bring me certainty and security. But at what cost? Thoughts jangle and foment in my head and I am so caught up with them that I do not remember the watching until the gaoler swings the door open and I step into the dark cell.

No one speaks. None move. They are huddled apart around the cell and have their heads down as if asleep. All but the old one, Joan Wade, who is lying on the straw, bent and twisted. She stirs a little at my entry, but no gnarled hand grabs at the plate as I set it down, no sharp face looks up at me in contempt as she has been wont to do.

'What is wrong with her?'

I address them all but it is Alice Gardner, of course, who answers and her words are spat out.

'What do you think, Mistress Howldine? What in God's name do you think we have gone through? Have you even considered how the watching would be with one as aged as her?' I say nothing, for, I confess, I have tried not to think about it. 'Well, let me tell you. She was bound hand and foot to a chair, as we both were, for a whole day and part of a night. We were given no food, no drink. We had to soil ourselves as they would not allow us to move. We were leered at by men we did not know, who spat and looked at us as if we were already dead. Your joints seize up, Mistress, you are unable to straighten them or ease yourself and it becomes agony. You burn with thirst but you forget hunger for the pain takes that away, it is all there is. And she withstood this, Mistress Howldine . . .' She speaks my name as if it is a bitter thing. '. . . she held out, until a mouse came and ran over my foot.'

Alice's voice breaks. She crawls stiffly to take Joan Wade's hand, holding it gently, and looks up at me, tears in her eyes.

'And she thought it would be the undoing of me so she confessed, Mistress, to save me, to save us both more pain.' She looks back down at the old woman on the straw, who stirs and groans as she tries to move her legs. Catherine Butts pushes the tray of food towards them and I watch as Alice Gardner breaks a soft piece of bread, dips it in the ale, and puts it to Widow Wade's mouth. She is able to take a little and chews slowly, her eyes closed. Her lips are cracked and bleeding and I think I will bring her some fat to grease them, for I suddenly pity her. All her spirit has gone. That spiteful, vicious-tongued harridan is no more. There is only the husk of a woman left, all her courage spent.

Four pairs of eyes glitter at me as I back away and push at the door. For once in my life I have no words.

26. JOAN

Joan feels more than sees the innkeeper's presence, for her eyes are dimmed, although she finds her hearing seems clearer. She hears the tap of the tray on the floor and the shuffling of the others. She hears Mistress Howldine's voice but she cannot make out what is being said. Then someone puts some bread to her lips and she opens them and takes it in. The bread is fresh, soaked in ale, and it is bliss. She opens her mouth and someone gives her more, and slowly her senses begin to return. She forces her mind to focus on eating, to keep away the pain which is rising and spreading through her body, until she thinks she must cry out. She focuses on the bread, wrapping her mouth around the softened texture, sucking the moisture from it as she hears the door of the gaol clang, smells the waft of fresh air as the innkeeper leaves.

Then Catherine puts a hand behind her head and lifts it, putting a mug to Joan's lips, and she realises that she is desperate to drink. She can hear the noises she makes, slurping and spitting, but it tastes so good as it floods through her body she cannot stop.

'A little at a time, do not rush it. You have been without too long. Stop now, and I will give you some more in a little while.'

The mug is taken away and her head laid back gently on the

straw. It is many years since she has been tended like this. She opens her eyes, sticky and crusted as they are, and her vision swims into focus. Alice Gardner is next to her, Catherine alongside. Isbel hovers above them like a ghost, a look of concern clouding her thin face. Then the horror hits her, she feels again the ropes binding her, the chair hard beneath her. A mouse . . . she cries out in fear.

'Be still, Joan, it is over now, you are back with us.' Alice's voice is strained but tender, and she remembers. Alice was there, she suffered too.

27. MARY

I send another jug of ale to the gaol. It has not been requested but the sight of those women has quite undone me. I thought I had seen life, knew all there was to know about the ways of men, for inns are places where all humanity passes through, good and bad, young and old. I thought I had seen it all. But those women; to be treated with such – inhumanity – I had not thought it possible in a God-fearing town like ours, that such things could happen. I thought us different. We have all heard of cruelties elsewhere, but they have never affected us here, in the depths of the countryside. Even the war hasn't reached us in the east. Men speak about the fighting, boys and money are taken, but the King's stand-off with Parliament is only talked about here, it hasn't affected us directly. People in these parts take the view that things will always be as they will, that nothing much will alter. But this searching-out of witches has brought change. It has crept in like a thing of the night, unnoticed, its tentacles reaching out slowly out of the dark to touch us all.

MASTER HOPKINS MUST HAVE NOTICED THE CHANGE IN ME, FOR HE asks me if all is well when I take his evening meal to his room.

Unusually, Mistress Phillips is there, although the door is open. I place the plates and dishes onto the table, now cleared of the papers which have been carefully arranged over it for the whole of the week.

I hesitate before answering.

'I have been a little concerned, Sir, about the witches.' I know I need to speak with great care and wish he had not asked. I think of lying, but I have seen his face as he looks at the townsfolk who come before him and I know that he sees all. 'I had not imagined that the watching could be so . . .' I bite my lip as I search for the right word, '. . . painful.'

Goody Phillips looks at me shrewdly.

'Fear and pain are the only things such people understand,' she says. 'They are all in league with the Devil, they entertain his familiars, do his bidding. Why, I could tell you –'

The Witchfinder raises his hand and she stops dead.

'Mistress Howldine, you are a good woman and your sympathy does you credit. It is as I would expect. But Mistress Phillips is right in all that she says, the evil must be expunged from them, this Town made clean and if we can do that, then the suffering of a few poor godless souls is the price that must be paid.' His voice is smooth but has an edge of hardness to it.

I bow my head.

'My apologies, Sir, I was shaken by seeing the results of their treatment, that is all. Now you have explained it to me I understand better, and I thank you for your reminder.'

He nods and smiles thinly.

'I am here to do God's bidding, Mistress, and to spread his goodness and forgiveness in a place that has lost its way. But we are making progress.' He glances at Goody Phillips who nods modestly. 'We will be leaving here at first light, Mistress Howldine, so I ask that you continue to provide for the prisoners as you have been doing until we meet again.'

I pull myself together – at least this is over for the time being – and drop a deep curtsey.

'You have been an ideal guest, Sir, you too, Mistress, and I hope you have been happy with your stay, that all here has been in order?'

'It has, thank you, and I shall look forward to enjoying your hospitality again, although I wish it were under less sombre circumstances. Now, I expect Captain Johnson shortly as he is coming to settle my fees. Please be good enough to show him up as soon he arrives.'

'Of course. Master Hopkins, Mistress Phillips.' I curtsey again and move to the door, leaving it open as propriety demands. The knowledge that fees are finally being paid heartens me and helps me to push the vision of the witches slumped on the straw away.

IT IS NEAR ON AN HOUR LATER THAT CAPTAIN JOHNSON ARRIVES. HE leaves his horse in the yard and comes in, flustered and sweating, through the bar, his cloak swirling around him.

'Mistress Howldine, where is Master Hopkins?'

I curtsey.

'Good evening, Captain, you are expected.'

'I'm sure I am, Mistress.' He seems angered, unlike his normal habit, and I realise that he is a man used to being in charge and, at this moment, he is not. He does not like being beholden to another.

'This way, Sir.' I show him towards the stairs and follow him up. His tall boots are muddied and scratched, the heels worn down. Master Hopkins has his boots polished to a shine each day, he is fastidious in that. He has only been here a week and already I know his ways. Experience, that's what it is, experience of watching and listening to people, to men in particular. For they think you cannot read them, but they give themselves away in these little ways.

The Captain knocks firmly on the Witchfinder's door, even

though it is open. He bows to Goody Phillips and then to the Witchfinder.

'Master Hopkins.'

'Captain Johnson, please sit.' Master Hopkins indicates a chair and the Captain folds himself into it with a frown. No, he is not used to this at all. 'You have come to settle my fees on behalf of the Town, I trust?' He says it with a smile but his eyes are sharp. I stand by the door, pushing myself into the shadows, hoping I will not be noticed. This I must see.

'The Town has received your costs, Master Hopkins, but we were surprised to find the extent of them.'

'Surprised, Sir? I know not why, as all was made clear when you invited me. God's business is not cheap. It cannot be done other than thoroughly and properly, in accordance with the laws of this land, and I am sure you must be satisfied with the results.' He is still smiling but his look is that of a fox stalking its prey on a moonlit night.

Captain Johnson clears his throat and Master Hopkins stiffens in readiness.

'We are delighted with the work you have carried out here this week with such diligence and efficiency but the Town . . .' He shuffles in his seat. He already knows he is bested and I think he would have done better to bring someone with him for support. 'The Town feels that two pounds for one week – my labourers do not earn this much in a whole year, Sir. And not only that, there is the additional costs of your searcher.' He turns to Goody Phillips. 'Begging your pardon, Mistress – and those of the men who watched.' He splutters to a halt, and sweat sheens his brow. No one has asked him to remove his coat and it comes to me that this is the Witchfinder's way. This is how he coerces and controls, how he is able to make people respect him. Not by shouting orders or by using his stature, for he has none, but by deliberate quietness. In this he is like a spider, unmoving, relentless, and the Captain and the Town are like flies in his web. He watches their struggles and waits for them to exhaust themselves. Then he strikes.

The Witchfinder's face is a mask of control as he leans towards the Captain.

'Captain Johnson, I am sorry that you and the Town feel that way, but my payment was agreed at the outset. Two pounds for myself, one pound for Widow Phillips and any additional payment for the watching which, in this case I believe, was thirteen shillings and ten pence. As I have said, it is a costly exercise doing God's work. I have expenses to meet and, after all, you did invite me here, and I have carried out my duties as I promised. And the Town has asked me to return in December.'

'That was before we realised that the cost was . . .'

Master Hopkins continues smoothly, as if the Captain had not spoken.

'As I said, my fee was agreed at the outset, and has already been agreed for my return. Captain, I am sorry you feel like this, but if the Town feels I have given bad service . . . ?' He has him now and all know it.

The Captain sighs.

'No, Sir, we have all been impressed by your work. It is a right-eous and godly thing that you do.'

Master Hopkins smiles.

'Then we are agreed, and can put this – question – behind us?'

The Captain reaches into his cloak and brings out a leather purse. It is heavy with coin, I can almost feel the weight of it.

'It is all here, Sir, payment in full as requested.' Master Hopkins reaches for the purse and sets it on the table before him.

'Thank you, Captain, and I look forward to returning in a few weeks time.'

The men stand and shake hands.

'Where do you go to next?' The Captain is all civility now the moment has passed and his dignity is restored.

'Mistress Phillips will return home to Manningtree for the time being, until she is needed again, whilst I have to be in Yarmouth tomorrow, more witches have been found there.'

The Captain raises an eyebrow in enquiry.

'I wonder that you are not attending the execution of the woman in Ipswich, for it has been the talk of that place?'

The Witchfinder lowers his head and I prick up my ears.

'No, Captain, I do not need to attend her end, I know it will be carried out in accordance with the Law. I questioned this Mother Lakeland myself. Indeed, she was proved to be a Royalist and a witch. It was also said that she was a minister of religion, although all know that women are not capable nor even allowed to preach God's Holy word. She was accused of murdering many people, and, most shockingly, of the bewitching and murder of her own husband. She broke down eventually, they all do, and confessed to her monstrous sins, and tomorrow she pays for them. A terrible case.'

The Captain nods in agreement.

'Hanging is too good for such as her.'

'Indeed it is, Captain, and that is why she will not hang.' I want to stop up my ears, I do not want to hear, but I stand still as a rock. 'No, for a woman to kill her husband is high treason, so she will burn. They are to put her in a barrel of tar and burn her at the stake, and all will see how such foul evil is rubbed out in this county.' His face is raised, his expression radiant, and Mistress Phillips stands beside him, her eyes lowered as if in modesty. The Captain stands open-mouthed, staring, and I slide out of the door unnoticed, rushing outside into a fresh sea breeze as the bile rises and burns my throat.

28. JOAN

The Howdine woman appears the next morning with some odd assortments of leftovers and a jug of stale ale. Isbel has started her crooning again and the women are tense and uneasy. Joan thinks the innkeeper seems changed somehow, diminished, as if her spark of confidence has been snuffed out. She puts the tray down before them and Joan is helped to sit by Alice, who puts an arm around her, handing her a crust of bread which she gnaws on gratefully. The others take their share and the only noise is chomping and chewing. The innkeeper stands there, twisting her apron between her fingers, waiting, and the women exchange looks.

Alice, as always, takes charge.

'What news, Mistress Howldine? There must be something, else you would have high-tailed it from here by now. Is it not enough that we are persecuted for nothing, that you have to stand and stare at us. Or is your master, the Witchfinder, summoning us again?'

Joan shivers at the thought of him – her body will not take any more, and anyway, she has confessed. What more could he want?

'He is gone.' Mistress Howldine raises her eyes and looks at them in turn and Joan's heart thumps in her chest.

Beside her, Catherine speaks.

'Gone. Are we to hang then?'

Isbel starts moaning.

Joan's nerves are set on edge, so her voice comes out sharper than she thought.

'Well, speak woman! What is to do?' They all sit back in surprise as her returning strength empowers her.

The innkeeper looks down at her.

'He has gone to Yarmouth. But in Ipswich – a witch is to die there in the morning. She is to burn.' They look at each other in horror. They have all had thoughts of hanging but burning is a terrible death. As one, they think they are to be told that they will meet the same end, and horror flattens their faces.

'And what of us, Mistress?'

'You are not to burn. Your trial is not to be held yet, for Master Hopkins will not return until December. The Town have invited him back then to search for more witches.' Joan turns her head to one side, shuddering, and spits forcibly. His very name strikes fear into her.

'But what is to become of us? What is to happen to Isbel?' Catherines voice wobbles and pitches as she reaches for her daughter and holds her close.

'You are to remain here. I am to bring you food, keep you in good condition for the trial that will come.'

Joan sits back, her heart thudding faster. Winter will soon come, and all who live here know how harsh it can be on this most easterly coast. There is no glass in the windows in this cell, no fire. The walls already run with damp on days when the air is chill, and cold seeps up through the floor. They have been here little over one week, three women and a girl, in a small dark room, and they are already degraded. How can they survive what is to come?

29. MARY

I have done my best. No one can say that I have not. For the last three months I have fed the witches, provided ale, and water to wash in once a week. I have taken them some old clothes since the weather closed in, and the gaoler has stuffed a piece of cloth into the window-space for warmth. There were four old cloaks as well and that was done out of the kindness of my heart, for they cannot die in my charge, I would not want that on my conscience, it is heavy enough as it is.

But word has come that the Witchfinder will return in one week's time, that we are to expect him on the thirteenth day of December, and now the Town is in a panic as to the condition of the witches. For none have seen them save me and the pot-boy, and that brief enough, for I have only been putting the food inside the door and pushing it at them with my foot, the stench in there is that bad. The gaoler empties the pail once a day, well, he says he does, but the place stinks to high heaven and even passers-by have been complaining.

It is the Reverend Swaine who is sent to see about them, and he comes to me first.

'Mistress Howldine, I have been tasked with assessing the condition of the witches imprisoned in the Town Gaol.' He is very fond of his own voice, the Reverend, and his Sunday sermons get longer and longer, though I have managed to keep awake so far, unlike some. 'How do they fare? I have also been tasked with providing for their spiritual health, as they are soon to stand trial.'

I think he would have been better tasked providing more food, as I was only asked to provide the very basics.

'I do not know, Sir, I merely take their meals to them each day as requested. I have not seen or spoken to them for some weeks.' He tuts loudly, but it is not my job to care for them, and I cannot afford to become too involved. I consider pointing out that they are his flock too, but think the better of it.

'Very well, we will go this afternoon and see. Please tell the gaoler to have them ready.' I am not sure the gaoler will be too pleased, given the state of them, but I nod in agreement.

I SEND A MESSAGE ACROSS TO THE GAOL – SPOKEN, NOT WRITTEN, AS I am not sure that gaoler can read, he is the poorest sort of person – telling him to expect the Reverend Swaine and I. It will be black out there, it gets dark so early now, so I am not sure what the Reverend hopes to see, but I search out lanterns and my warmest cloak and wait for my summons.

The wind is blasting east from the sea as we cross the square, the sound of the surf loud on the pebbles. It is bitter, the coldest I can remember and I think how the September hedgerows were weighed down with berries this year, the birds feasting, and realise the hard winter that foretold has now arrived. I wrap my cloak tight around me and walk behind the Reverend for shelter. The gaoler is waiting, lantern in hand, a scarf wrapped around his mouth as he swings the door open. I think he is just muffled against the cold until the stench hits me and I gasp. The Reverend has blanched, I can see his face paling even in this dim light as we hold our lanterns out into the cell.

It is like a scene from Hell. The women's bodies are melded into one brown mass which stirs little at our entrance. I look around in horror. In the corner the pail has overflowed and a hardened mass of turds is piled next to it. I determine to have words with the gaoler about this, I told him to make sure they were kept clean, and now the Reverend has seen the lapse. I glance at him, but his eyes are staring at the scene before him as he puts a kerchief to his mouth.

'Dear God in heaven, what is this? Why are these women not rising in obedience as they should?' He addresses the dark figures 'I am your minister, a man of God, where is your respect?' But they do not move.

Then, slowly a crabbed hand appears and pulls a cloth away from a face lined and stained with dirt. I cannot tell who it is until she speaks.

'Reverend Swaine, our apologies, Sir. Had we known you were coming we would have been better prepared.' She cackles mirthlessly and I recognise her by her spirit. It is Alice Gardner. We hold the lanterns closer and I see her eyes glittering and blinking in the unaccustomed light.

'Why do you sit like this? Well, speak woman? How do you not keep yourselves in better order? Where is your self-respect?'

'Gone, Sir, blown away with the wind, starved and frozen out of us. We huddle together for warmth, for there is none here. We have forgotten what respect is in this place.' Her voice cracks. 'But we are all alive, no thanks to you.'

The Reverend can take no more. He rushes past me, coughing and gagging into the December afternoon and I follow hard on his heels.

'Mistress Howldine, I am horrified. How did you allow this to happen? This matter must be given your immediate attention and I am authorising you to have the women taken out tomorrow. They must be given clean clothes and washed thoroughly, and the cell cleaned. Gaoler, you must find someone to carry this out or you must do it yourself. For the Witchfinder cannot see them like this.

Our reputation as a God-fearing town must be maintained, d'you hear me? What is the Captain going to say?'

It is on the tip of my tongue to point out that no one has said anything and that is why this has happened. No one checked, no one was responsible, and I am not going to be held to account for this. I have done everything asked of me and now they seek to blame me. They will pay for this. They will pay.

DAWN BREAKS OVER A FROSTED TOWN, AND FOR ONCE THE GAOLER HAS done as he was instructed. He has the night-soil man standing ready with his cart in the pale morning light. The Town is still quiet, the witches forgotten about for now. I feared it would be left to me to oversee this, but then I hear the thump of boots and turn to see Captain Johnson striding towards me. He is wrapped in a warm wool cloak and holds a nosegay in his gloved hand. Behind him come two men armed with tall pikes.

'Mistress Howldine, the Reverend Swaine has advised me of the situation and I am here to make sure that all is done correctly. The witches must not be allowed to use this opportunity to conjure their devilish familiars or try and flee justice.' I am glad he is here, for I did not want this to be my responsibility alone. He turns to the gaoler who is bowing and scraping before him.

'Master Gaoler, you are to fasten the women with these irons and bring them forth.' The Captain's man steps forward and passes over a sack, heavy with clanking metal. 'They will be chained together until the gaol is cleaned. Has fresh straw been brought?'

The gaoler pulls at his cap.

'Yes, Sir, the night-soil man has brought some, clean from the farm.' He nods towards a dark figure who is already forking fresh straw from his cart into a pile on the damp earth.

The Captain sighs.

'Very well, all is ready. Men, be alert. Gaoler, bring the prisoners out.'

30. JOAN

The women hear the noise outside and begin to stir. The cloaks and rags are muddled together so they each try to pull something around themselves as they slowly straighten their aching limbs and attempt to stand. Joan cannot manage it so Catherine puts a surprisingly firm hand under her elbow and pushes. Bone on bone. These months have made them skeletal. The door creaks open and the gaoler comes in, cloth wrapped around his face, carrying a sack. He drops it to the floor with a loud clank and they realise what is within, what is to be done.

'Arms.' The gaolers voice is gruff, muffled by the cloth, but, above it, his wet eyes betray his excitement. Catherine and Isbel hold out their wrists and he fastens rusting irons around them. Isbel's arms are like white sticks, the chains loose, and Joan thinks that she will be able to free herself, but the girl stands still and unblinking as he turns to the others. 'You too – arms.' He fastens the metal bands around Joan's wrists. They immediately chafe her skin and the weight of them causes her to bend forward. They are made for men, they could easily be pushed off but what then? She cannot run, where would she go?

He runs a long chain through the rings on the irons and tugs it, pulling the women together, then takes up the end, winding it round his wrist securely, grunting in satisfaction, then glares hard at them.

'Right, don't try anything, d'you understand? There are armed guards out there so don't even think of summoning the Devil, your master.' He hauls on the chain and they shuffle to the door. It opens and they step out into blindness.

31. MARY

The women stumble out in a cloud of fetid air. The Captain hurriedly puts his nosegay to his face and I pull up the scarf I have worn under my cloak.

The first thing I realise is that they cannot see. They have been kept in the dark so long that even the weak December half-light has blinded them. They shuffle forward, brown wraiths, one holding on to another, chains clanking, wheezing and coughing in the sharp air. It is bitter cold and the breeze takes the stench away from us as they stand, huddled together, shaking with cold, hunger and terror.

It is far worse than I thought. Their hair is matted and stringy, thick with grease, crawling. Their clothes are soiled and stinking, and my mind goes to the pail and its overflowing mass. The two older women are still in the skirts that they wore to the watching, dark stains at the back, and I remember that they were not allowed to relieve themselves, but were left to sit in their own mess, and they have had no change of clothes since then. And thin – they are so thin, skeletal hands grasping the poor rags to them, trying to find some little warmth. Twelve weeks and they no longer look like women. They look like witches.

.   .   .

CAPTAIN JOHNSON GESTURES TO THE NIGHT-SOIL MAN, WHO ENTERS the gaol with a large pitchfork and bucket, and begins to remove the stinking straw, loading it onto his cart, brown and shimmering, no less foul than the midden heaps he normally clears. The Captain turns to me, his face full of blame, as I knew it would be, but I am ready for him.

'Sir, I was not asked to care for their bodies, merely to provide enough food and ale. The Town did not request any more than that from me, and I have carried out my duties religiously, ever since the prisoners were first contained.' He nods resignedly and I breathe a small sigh of relief, for I had feared he would berate me, threaten to take this commission elsewhere. I feared he would not pay me.

'Mistress Howldine, you have done your best but we must remedy this now, for the Witchfinder and some of our gentler townsfolk will take us to task if this is seen. Gaoler, have you brought water?' The gaoler nods and points to several buckets standing by in the lee of the wall. There are torn cloths and a large pile of old clothes next to the buckets and I wonder where these have come from, but then recall how the witches houses were searched, their contents seized.

'Gaoler, remove the chains but leave their shackles on. Guards, be ready. You prisoners, you are to wash. Remove your clothes.' Four heads come up as one, four grimy pale faces blink and contort. 'You heard me, remove your clothes and wash yourselves.' I lower my head – surely he cannot mean for them to stand naked in the street, before the already leering guards, but he does. And I do not know whether it is the desperation, the degradation, the humanity that has been stripped from them by three months of imprisonment, but slowly crabbed white fingers begin to pull at clothes, garments begin to drop to the floor and then they stand there, covering themselves with their hands as best they can, heads bowed, in silence, but for a faint mewling from the girl. Bitter cold air blows hard around them and I watch as their skin goes blue and mottled under the dirt and grime, but one then another reaches for a cloth, push it into the bucket, others follow, and they slowly begin to scrub the filth from their shivering bodies. They dip and rub, all modesty gone, washing under arms, between legs, then bend oily heads into the buckets, pulling through wet hair with bony fingers.

'Captain, they must be allowed to dry themselves, to dress. They will freeze to death.'

He gestures again to the gaoler. The women are huddled tight together now, naked and frozen, trying to find some warmth, their hair straggled and dripping over their faces, so close I cannot make out who is who. The gaoler moves swiftly forward and picks up the first bucket, and, before he can be stopped, throws the soiled water over the women. They scream as he goes to the next pail, and the next, until all is despatched and the women are left crying and shaking, icy with cold but at last clean. I move hurriedly towards the pile of old clothes. There are some old worn shifts, patched and darned, and I pass these to the women to cover up their nakedness. They snatch them from my grasp, pulling them hurriedly over their heads. The clothes follow, skirts tied around thinned waists, ribbons and tapes fastened, bodices laced with fumbling fingers until they are half decent again. There are some threadbare cloaks too, and I pass these around and the women seem to sink into the unaccustomed warmth. The last one goes to the child, Isbel. She is dressed in a shift and skirt, both too big for her, a bodice too loose, but she smiles at me, a pale imitation of a girl, then opens cracked lips and I expect her thanks, but it does not come. Instead she starts her chanting and it sounds like prayer; but it cannot be for she is a witch.

'The Lord is my Shepherd, I shall not want . . .' I look at her then, properly, deep into her eyes. They are black and blank and hollow. She is gone quite mad.

THE CELL HAS BEEN SCOURED OUT WITH SEAWATER AND SAND, THE pail replaced and fresh straw laid. I bring a jug of ale and some warm gruel as the women are led back in and their shackles removed. They are standing, rubbing grazed wrists, but they snatch the bowls from me as soon as I enter, sinking to their knees, swallowing greedily. There is bread, too, dried and hard from leftover meals, but it does not have weevils, so I hope it will do; they dip this into the gruel to soften it, bolt it down then pass the jug of ale round, guzzling and dribbling.

'There will be more food, the Town has ordered it, and cloths for washing.' They look at each other, none speaking.

'Did you hear me? There . . .'

'We heard you, Mistress, we just wondered why, when we have gone so long . . .?

I feel a twinge of shame.

'Master Hopkins is returning to search out the remaining witches from our midst.'

'Ah, that explains it. We are to be displayed as examples of your good and godly treatment.' Alice Gardner laughs hollowly and exchanges looks with the others, and as she does so I realise that the women are in conspiracy. They have been so long together that they have bonded, become one. I glance at them all in turn. Widow Gardner has some of her confidence back, even the Butts woman seems stronger, but Widow Wade seems to have shrunk, looking even more like the small black bird I first saw all those weeks ago, when this thing started. I think she must be ill, diminished by her treatment, but then her head turns, she fixes me with glittering eyes, and, just as she did before, she leans forward and spits on my shoe.

32. JOAN

Joan can feel the panic around her and knows they fear that they will never see again as they step outside into the freezing air, but she is used to the dark and she knows their eyes will clear. It became too cold, that was the trouble. The two cell windows let in just about enough light, and sometimes the gaoler left the door open to clear the stink while he stood guard outside. But when the weather had closed in and the autumn mists that always cloak the marshland hereabouts wound their way into the cell, they had asked for something to be done about the cold, and the answer was to block the window that faces east to the sea with cloth. It helped a little, for those easterly winds are vicious, but it forced them to live in the dark like moles.

And now they are outside for the first time in months, their vision is clearing too slowly and all around are shouts, orders, and it confuses them. A man's voice commands them to remove their clothes and Joan looks in the direction it came from in disbelief. The gaoler moves towards them to remove the chains and, as he does, the others start to undress slowly, unwillingly as, one by one, their hands are freed. As the gaoler gets to Joan, she screws up her face and curses him, hissing her foul breath at him as he removes the rough heavy chain. He jerks back in surprise as his face tightens and she knows it is a mistake, that he will be revenged, but she cannot help herself. The women wash as best they can and the water is freezing, but clear and reviving. And then, when they are all standing naked and freezing, when they think the humiliation is done, the gaoler spots his opportunity. Joan sees him lift the nearest bucket, turn to her and she cannot stop it and the water is icy and spiteful as it hits her, sharp as stones, and she shrinks into herself, huddling over, as he does the same to the others and she thinks *this will kill us*.

Then the innkeeper moves over, Joan can smell the ale on her clothes. She can smell her fear as well – she is as frightened as they are, and Joan wonders why. She passes them shifts and they pull them on quickly, finally covering their bodies, then pull on skirts and bodices. Catherine helps Joan with the fastenings as her fingers are stiff and clenched, then they stand, wrapped in someone else's cloaks but warm for once, and Joan closes her eyes to the feeling.

They are pushed back into the cell, which has been cleaned and smells sweeter, and Joan thinks that this will not be too bad, for if they are to die soon it will not be for long. But then the Howldine woman starts to lord it over them, telling them that she is to provide more food, water to wash in, and Joan is angry that she did not think to do this before, for she could have, if she had any spark of humanity in her bones. Anger courses through her, even though she is powerless and cold and afraid.

So when the innkeeper turns to her, she spits.

33. MARY

I am not here to be spat at, not when I am trying to help, and I am angry as I wipe the yellow glob from my shoe with one of the discarded cloths. The gaoler is clearing up outside, the Town is beginning to stir and I realise that it was all over in minutes, that the sun has barely risen; no one has seen what we did, and that was the plan all along. For the Captain did not want to remind the townsfolk of those imprisoned here, for fear that they will become disruptive. We have already had the lower sort, shouting through the windows at them, children lobbing mud and worse at the walls, but all that stopped when the weather closed in, and it seemed as if people had forgotten. But with the Witchfinder due any day it is going to start again, the crowds, the shouting, the anger and fear, and, all of a sudden, I wish that it would go away as if it had never happened. For I am no longer content, my mind is constantly on edge and I cannot stop thinking about the witches. I am not afraid of their curses, for I know God is protecting me, that this is His mission and I am doing His works. But a tiny part of me wonders if the women truly are what they have confessed to be for sometimes, when I think on it, they just seem so ordinary.

. . .

WE WERE EXPECTING MASTER HOPKINS ON THE THIRTEENTH, THAT'S what his message said, so I am surprised to hear hoofbeats slowing and the sound of his voice in the courtyard below a day early. My mind goes into a spin, but his room is ready, all is prepared and I have plenty of food in. I straighten my apron and coif and go down to greet him. As I open the door, sleet stings my face.

'Come in, come in, Sir, you must be freezing cold.' I hold out my hands for his hat and cloak and he passes them to me with a nod.

'Thank you Mistress Howldine, it is certainly bitter out there.' I look up into his face. It is pale and translucent, thinner than it was in September, and his lips seem to have a blue tinge as he holds a kerchief in his hand, pressing it to his mouth as he coughs gently. I show him up to his room. The fire has not yet been lit and the room is chill.

I hastily move to the bed and turn the covers down.

'Sir, we were not expecting you until tomorrow, else the fire would be hot and the room ready.'

'My business in Yarmouth was concluded quicker than I thought. A trial of twelve sinners. Some reprieved but six witches hanged. A good result.'

'You look as if you need some rest, Master Hopkins. Are you well?' He is changed since he was last here. His clothes seem to hang large on him, but fervour and intent still shine in his eyes.

'There is no resting when you are doing God's work, Mistress. My rest will come when I am received into my Lord's welcoming arms, my sins cleansed from me. Then I may be still. There is much work yet to be done, and Aldeburgh is no exception I fear.'

'It is true that there have been mutterings, Sir, more accusations.'

'And I will hear them all, Mistress, let them come. But what of those already seized? How do they fare?'

I have been waiting for this question so do not hesitate.

'Sir, they are in good condition and make little trouble now.'

'It is as I have found elsewhere. They soon recognise that God has found them out and accept their fate.' He coughs into his kerchief and swallows loudly. 'Some wine or brandy, Mistress, if I could.'

'Of course, Sir, I should have thought.' I move to the door and call to the pot-boy who hovers at the foot of the stairs for his orders. 'A glass of metheglin, boy, quick as you like.' I turn back to the Witchfinder. 'The spices and honey will sooth your cough. Shall I order a hot stone for your bed?'

'That will not be necessary, Mistress, I must begin my work, but the wine will be most welcome. This cough is irksome.' He pulls the long oak table to the window as he did before, and begins to unpack his bags, laying out quills, paper and ink. The pot-boy runs up the stairs with a mug and I take it, setting it on the table before the Witchfinder. He looks up at me, and suddenly I see a small boy behind his eyes, grateful for the care, and I wonder of his mother, his family, wonder how ever he came to a task such as this. 'Thank you.' He sips at the wine and closes his eyes as it seeps through him, for it is a warming and heartening drink, popular with the sailors when they return from the ice of the Northern Seas. Then he is all business again. 'Send for the first complainant.'

I do as he bids.

It is late in the afternoon and the weather has closed in, sleet battering the panes of the windows, thrown up by an easterly wind straight off the sea. It grew dark not long after midday in this, the depths of winter, and candles have been lit. Fires blaze in all the hearths and I have made sure that the one in Master Hopkins room is kept high. The last of the complainants has found his way down into the inn and pulls hard on his ale as if seeking solace from that which he has done. The Lion is full, despite the weather, for all have heard of the Witchfinder's arrival and wait to catch a glimpse of him, keen to see what he will do next.

Master Hopkins sends word that he will need Goody Phillips,

so two men are sent to fetch her from Manningtree. I do not envy them, for the weather is harsh and the sky threatens snow, but I daresay they will be well paid. I hear that Captain Johnson, on behalf of the Town, has agreed twelve shillings and sixpence for them although their master is like enough to take a cut of that. I add the charges for the additional night, wine and meals, to my accounts and go to make up a bed for her.

I am just preparing a tray to take some soup and fresh bread to Master Hopkins when he surprises me by coming down and knocking on the door of my kitchen.

'Mistress Howldine. I am all prepared for the morrow and I wondered if you were in need of company, to chase away the noise of the wind howling, for it sounds like the very Devil himself.' He must have seen my surprise for he hesitates. 'I see you are busy . . .'

'No Sir, I was just bringing you some broth to take the chill away. Please, sit here . . .' I hurriedly sweep my hand over the kitchen chair. 'It is a poor room, but warm.'

'I will, Mistress.' He lowers himself stiffly and clasps his hands around the bowl of soup I proffer, drinking it slowly. 'This is good soup, thank you.' I push the plate of bread towards him and he puts the bowl down and breaks off a portion. His manners are impeccable.

As I pour him a glass of the wine I keep for special occasions, I search my mind for something to say.

'Have more come forward to accuse?'

He chews thoughtfully.

'Yes, indeed. It seems that there are more witches, as I thought. It is surprising how many are drawn out by my visits. And one is being brought here from Dunwich.' I am surprised at this, for the rivalries between that place and this are long-standing and fierce. But, as Dunwich's fortunes have waned, ours have grown and we must be magnanimous, I suppose. I expect they do not want the cost of inviting the Witchfinder for themselves – it is an expensive business – and I suspect that Aldeburgh will have come to some pecuniary arrangement.

'And what of you, Sir? Where do you come from?' I am emboldened by the warmth and the wine and his familiarity.

'I am the youngest of four sons born to the vicar of Great Wenham.' He sees my expression 'Just off the road between Ipswich and Colchester.' I nod, but am still none the wiser. 'I worked for a time as a lawyer in Ipswich but found my calling when I moved to Manningtree.'

'How did it begin, Sir?' His eyes hold mine and I cannot look away. I can feel the zeal and energy spinning from him as he leans in, clasping his hands on his knees.

'I had heard tell of witches who held their meetings near my house in Manningtree, of their activities. It was on a night such as this that I watched for them, and heard one sending imps to another of her kind. She was an evil hag, Mistress, and I had no alternative but to report her to the authorities. And then other accusations against her began. Elizabeth Clarke was her name. She had bewitched the wife of a neighbour who had gone to her in good faith, thinking her to be a cunning woman. Well, they seized her and I questioned her on behalf of the authorities. She was searched, then watched for three days and nights and when my colleague, John Stearne, and I went to note down her confession, she promised to conjure her familiars for us if she was not harmed. Well, I refused, for these are the creatures of Satan himself and I wanted no dealings with them, but she said there was nothing to fear, so we sat. And then Master Stearne asked her if the Devil had used her body, for we needed to know the truth, and she said he had.'

Master Hopkins is sitting forward on his chair now, his eyes gleaming, his face pale and beaded with sweat. He wipes his hair from his forehead and takes a sip of his wine. I can only sit in shock as his story unfolds.

'She was old, one-legged and why Satan would come to bed her

I cannot imagine, but she confessed that he did and that she became his creature. But when I asked her what the Devil looked like she said . . . she said . . .' he takes another pull at the wine and I see his hand is shaking '. . . that he was a tall, proper black-haired man, more proper than I, and when John Stearne asked her who she would prefer to share a bed with she replied 'The Devil'. And she looked at me and she laughed.'

HE SITS BACK AT THIS AND HIS CHEST HEAVES AS HE COUGHS INTO HIS kerchief. He sips more wine and stares into the fire and I sit perfectly still, unable to break the spell, as he recovers himself.

'She told us such things – that Satan had first come to her some seven years before, saying he must lie with her, and, each time, they enjoyed each other's bodies for half the night. Told of things that should not be spoken of in polite company, saving your presence, Mistress. And then she started to make a kissing noise with her lips, and we feared she was making mock of us, but she was summoning her imps.' He frowns deeply and moves his head as if to shake off the memory but I can see it is burnt into him.

I lean forward.

'And then. What happened then?' I keep my voice low and even but inside my heart beats hard against my chest as if it would break out.

'She called out the name 'Holt'. Nothing came for near half an hour. But then we saw it, creeping to her, a small white thing, bigger than a rat but not as large as a cat, and it went to her and then disappeared to wherever it had come from. Then she called 'Jarmara' and another imp came, a short fat dog-like creature, not of this world. She summoned others and unnatural creatures appeared; one like a hound, one like a polecat, another as a toad. And, as she told us of other witches and their familiars, I felt God move my hand to purge this evil from His lands. I heard his voice in my head, Mistress, telling me to do this thing. So we sought them all out and I interrogated them and such stories came out as you would not believe. How feeble old women came to cause the death of horses, cattle, made a woman lose feeling in her side. They lamed men, conjured children to die.' He sits back in his chair, calming himself. 'The Devil is all around us, Mistress Howldine, and I would free this country from his grasp, bring it back to peace and prosperity and goodness.' He closes his eyes now, the telling has clearly tired him. I should fill his glass, ask if he would like more bread, but I can only sit and stare. For I have never heard such horrors and I know that, if this is what the witches in our gaol have done, and if they are such as he describes, then they deserve all that will come to them. But the thought also comes to me that it may not be true. That one old woman may merely have been trying to save herself by telling such tales.

34. JOAN

Mistress Howldine looks different this morning. She is unkempt, her coif askew, her apron smudged. She is not the person she was yesterday, and Joan is sure that her spitting was not the sole cause, for the change is too great. She brings stale bread, dusty ale, and no meat.

'That will not keep us alive.'

She looks at Joan.

'That is all you will get this day.'

Alice Gardner rises to her feet, pointing her finger at the innkeeper, who pulls back in real fear, and Joan wonders what has happened to her to frighten her so, what she has heard.

'We were to get more until the Witchfinder comes ...'

'And he is here. And this is all you will get.' They look at each other in horror.

It is coming.

35. MARY

I watch from the inn as a fifth woman is unloaded from a wagon, babbling and moaning, lashing out against her captors with feeble hands, enraging them further.

'Get inside – filthy witch' The guard's face is twisted with malice and spite as he pushes her into the gaol, but his voice tells more – it tells of fear. I have already taken over the morning meal for the others but I am charged with providing this new one with bread and ale as well, so I gather some leftovers from last night's dinner and cross the square.

This new woman is very old, small, and her face a net of lines. She is clearly not in this world for she has the blank look of the brain-sick. And she stinks. I suspect she has not bathed for some long while, although her clothes seem fairly clean. She huddles herself into a corner of the cell and lies on her side, holding a grey apron, dark with stains, over her face, and rocks, small movements, backwards and forwards. Her coif has gone missing, and thin white hair falls around her face from a mottled pink scalp as she plucks at her apron, crying; a soft keening that pulls from the very depths of her, echoing the call of the sea-birds which wheel and dive outside. I move towards her and hold out the food on an old cloth, as if to a stray dog. The others look at it with starving eyes but they do not move.

'You. The Dunwich woman. Is that where you are from? What is your name?' The rocking stops and the apron is lowered. Pale eyes, one clouded and unseeing, fix on mine and I see for an instant her mind is clear.

The gaoler leans over her and spits.

'She's Widow Clarke, that's all they told me.' The old woman's head turns to him but then I see her mind slip away and the crying resumes.

'Can you not shut her up?' Joan Wade's words are over-loud. 'Her noise cuts through me.'

'She is frightened, as you were when you were brought here.' Alice Gardner's voice is cracked but soothing.

'That noise will get her nowhere.' Catherine Butts sits up in her corner. Isbel stays lying, facing the wall. She, at least, is silent.

Alice puts her hand out to the newcomer, who shrinks away.

'I do not think her mind is right.'

'Well, at least if she was quiet we could all rest. God in Heaven, she smells.' Widow Wade's spite has burned itself out and she sits back in silence. I push past the guard and outside where the wind is blowing in from the sea, wrapping the flint walls in damp brine.

THE NEXT MORNING I DO NOT HAVE TIME TO TAKE THE FOOD TO THE prisoners. The early arrival of the Witchfinder has kept me busy, and the inn filling each evening, with people wishing to catch a glimpse of him, means more clearing up, so I send the pot-boy in my place.

He returns with the empty tray, a look of disgust on his face.

'Did you feed them?'

'No Mistress, the gaoler took the tray from me, said them witches weren't a sight for me. But I wanted to see them, Mistress, I ain't never seen one before. I wanted to see what they look like. I

tried to look through the bars but the gaoler came after me so I ran
…'

I box him firmly round the ear.

'Must I do everything myself? Get on, those pots won't get scoured on their own.'

At least Master Hopkins keeps himself to himself today, our intimacy of the previous evening dissolved, he just calls to me to ask for his meal to be brought to his room. The only noise I hear from him is at night, as I pass his door and enter my bed-chamber, the intoning of prayers, the creak of the bed as he gets in. I wonder how he is able to sleep with such things as he has seen running through his head.

I HAVE AVOIDED GOING ACROSS TO THE GAOL ALL DAY, BUT I CANNOT delay any longer. I do not wish to see the witches, do not want to be reminded of their plight, but I have a job to do so I must put my feelings aside. The Town will not pay me if I am not seen to carry out my orders.

As I enter, a sweet rank smell hits me. The gaoler sees my expression.

'Stinks, dunnit! It's that new one, the Dunwich witch which smells bad.' He laughs at his own wit, then catches my eye and looks down. I enter the cell with my basket and and unload the bread and ale onto the floor. There was a little meat left over in the kitchen from yesterday, it was going over so I cannot use it in the inn, but I can add the cost to my ledger so it will not be wasted, and the women will be grateful. Joan Wade leans over quickly and grasps a crust, greedily stuffing it into her mouth. The mother, Catherine, snatches bread and a piece of meat and passes them to her daughter, then grabs some for herself. Alice Gardner takes her time, waiting for the others to finish before reaching for her share. They all chew fast, eyes lowered, faces scowling.

The new one doesn't move and I look at the gaoler.

'Is she well?'

He nudges her with his foot.

'She was well enough when I brought the food in this morning.'

'You lie . . . you lie!' Widow Wade has raised herself and is looking at him, her eyes narrowed in fury. 'You never brought any food to us. We have had nothing since yesterday.'

I look at the gaoler.

'Is that true?'

He shuffles his feet and looks away and I know he is about to lie.

'No, they had what you sent over for them. Look at them, do they look as if they remember?'

Joan Wade clears her throat and hawks forcefully at him, yellow wetness splattering his britches.

'You are a liar.'

I look down at her.

'That is enough. Is the new one ill?'

Alice Gardner looks at me with hardened eyes.

'She was awake earlier. Perhaps it is lack of food that ails her.'

I look hard at the gaoler. I must be careful, I should not be seen to support them.

'I'm sure these women are mistaken . . .' Widow Wade glares at me, readying herself to spit again, but decides against it. 'But in future you are to ensure that all food and drink paid for by this Town is given to the prisoners. All of it. Every last bit. Is that clear?' He nods sullenly and I turn again to the Dunwich woman. The smell emanating from her is like rotting meat and suddenly I recognise it. It is infection, I have smelt it before, and we cannot afford to let these women die, especially now the Witchfinder is here, it would not reflect well on the Town, or on me.

'She does not look right. I will ask Captain Johnson for advice, Gaoler, and we will see what he thinks best to do. We must not risk an outbreak of fever, for these women must stand trial.' The gaoler nods and I move to the door. I glance back. The Dunwich woman lies as if already dead on the packed-earth floor.

36. JOAN

Joan had decided to help the new prisoner feed herself, for she is clearly demented, just lies on the straw and moans, but the food never came. She heard someone outside, a boy she thought, arguing with the gaoler, but the door never opened. They have sat unattended all day, the stench rising with their hunger; a bitter-cold draught comes through the window, but it is not enough to cleanse the room. And now there are five of them who have to use the one pail. Catherine and Alice have put it in the corner under the window to try and mask the stink, placed a piece of cloth over it, but it needs emptying and Joan doubts that gaoler will bother unless he is told. She vows to tell the innkeeper when she next comes. She resents having to ask her for anything after what she has done, but this cannot go on, they will become ill – it may be that the Dunwich one has brought some fever in with her, she smells so bad. Alice tried to feel her forehead for heat but the old woman just batted her hand away as if it were an insect set to bite her.

And the noise. She just moans and moans. It's enough to make anyone angry.

Finally the innkeeper comes. Joan tells her they have not been fed and she can tell Joan does not lie, and takes the gaoler to task in front of them. Joan hides a small smile for it is such little triumphs that make life bearable. After she has gone the gaoler sullenly changes the pail, but she knows he will remember. He will bide his time. And the women settle and wait as another long night draws in and the Town quietens, until the only sound is the thrum and brawl of the sea and the pebbles and the keening of the Dunwich witch.

37. MARY

The Captain has given permission for me to ask the midwife to return and attend the Dunwich woman. I sent a message summoning her this morning and I am ready when she strides through the inn door this afternoon.

'Mistress Howldine. Is something wrong with the girl, Isbel?' She looks concerned, as well she should, given what she did.

'No, Midwife, she is as can be expected but there is another requires attention now. I do not think there is much involved. One has been brought here from Dunwich and . . .'

'I thought I made it clear that I am merely a midwife?'

She is angered and I hasten to soothe her as I need her skills – admit them or not, she has them.

'Midwife – Rose – I would deem it a great favour if you were to look at the woman who has just been brought in. Her wits are half-gone anyway but she is in some pain and she is causing a disturbance, upsetting the others. They must be kept settled, in good condition and you have a way with you.'

Rose looks at me. She knows I am placating her and she also knows I need her.

'Very well, I will look at her, but I make no promises as to whether I can help her.' She hoists her battered leather bag onto her shoulder, I bundle my cloak around me and we step out into the freezing December evening.

'This wind is bitter. I think there is a smell of snow in the air.' I hug my cloak closer, pulling it over my head. Ice stings my face and I wonder if it is sleet, or if the sea spray has indeed frozen, for it is cold enough.

THE CELL IS STILL FAIRLY CLEAN, BUT THE STENCH COMING FROM THE Dunwich woman is greater than ever, and her voice is one constant moan of torment. I take a lantern from the gaoler as the midwife moves swiftly towards her and crouches down, speaking softly to reassure her, but as she reaches a hand to touch the old woman's ankle, the witch pulls her leg back and kicks out, hard. Her feet are yellow, gnarled with age, her heels are black; deep cracks curve around them, dark with dried blood. She has no shoes.

'I am Rose. What is your name?' There is a gasp and, in the darkest corner, I see Alice Gardner shuffling quickly back into the shadows. The midwife's focus is on the old woman and she speaks slowly and calmly to her, putting her face close, seemingly unaffected by the stench. The old woman turns and her pale eyes, one unseeing, fix on her, then sweep to me and I see terror in them, pain. 'Are you hurt? Did they do something to you?' Rose speaks softly, not wishing to frighten the old woman further, but I can see her mind slip again and the crying resumes.

Catherine speaks from the corner.

'She has been like that all night.' Her voice is cracked and croaked through lack of sleep.

'Most know better than to make a noise like that. It achieves nothing.' Joan Wade must have her say and I glare at her.

She looks back at me steadily as Rose leans again towards the old woman and reaches for her hand.

'She cannot help it, see how old she is and her mind is not right. What is your name, Mistress?' The keening stops and Rose's hand remains held. 'Your name, can you tell me?' The woman's face clears, and I think she will speak, but then the gaoler coughs, the spell is broken, and she huddles back down into herself, mumbling softly. 'I am going to look at your leg.' Rose reaches out and slides the woman's grimy skirt up her calf and we cover our mouths with our aprons as the source of the stench is revealed. The woman's shin is bloody and hollowed, the bone palely visible. The skin around it is reddened and sore, and in the lamplight, I can see it writhe with the white bodies of maggots.

Rose opens her bag and ties a clean cloth around her mouth.

'This is an old wound, it has not been kept clean. It must have been like this for weeks. She will be in agony . . . the jolting of the cart alone to bring her here . . .'

'Midwife, remember why this woman is here. Your sympathy is misplaced and would be best preserved for those who are more deserving of it. It is very unwise, in these times, to show sympathy for such as she.'

My voice gives a warning, but Rose turns to me with silver eyes blazing.

'Mistress Howldine, you have asked me to care for these women and I will do this regardless of what you believe them to be. After all, only God, in a court of law, will decide their guilt or innocence.'

I nod in surrender. I need her services too much to want to offend her now.

'You are right, Midwife, you must help her as best you can. Is there anything that can be done for her?'

Rose looks down at the wound.

'The maggots have eaten away the rotten flesh which is good. I will need to remove them and bind the wound with honey and a clean cloth. It will make her more comfortable, but I have seen this before. She may need a surgeon.'

Joan Wade pipes up.

'There is a surgeon – he has removed legs before, there was a servant a few years ago, a lame girl . . .'

I turn to her.

'No one asked you.' I say, 'Be silent.' She curls back in on herself with a sulky frown and mutters something at me under her breath.

I close my ears to her mumblings and turn to Rose.

'The Town will not pay for that, not for one such as she. You must do what you can with what you have. Dunwich sent her to us. The carter who brought her said they did not want her upkeep, that she was a drain on their resources, and that when she was accused as witch they thought to have the Witchfinder examine her along with ours.'

Rose looks at me in disgust, but I am only mouthing what I have heard.

'I will need to fetch some honey and cloths. I will come back in an hour and dress the wound.' Rose stands. She looks sick to her stomach and her shoulders are hunched, but she pushes past the gaoler who looks at her with a light in his eye. I have seen that light before and I know to put it out and quickly.

I glare at him.

'This is God's work we do here, Gaoler. You would do well to remember that.' I pin him with a look such as I use with my most difficult customers. 'God's work.'

WHEN I RETURN TO THE LION, MASTER HOPKINS IS WAITING FOR ME and I see he has heard of the midwife's visit. He misses nothing.

'Are the accused in good condition? I hear the one who was brought here was injured.'

I drop a curtsey.

'I have just checked on them myself, Sir, and a midwife is tending to the one brought from Dunwich.'

His gaze flicks to my face.

'Midwife? She is a woman of faith? Of good character?'

I can see where his mind is going and I hasten to reassure him.

'Yes, Sir, a very godly woman, who has attended the births of this town's children for many years. Although I have had to bring her from Saxmundham, she is known in these parts and respected. The Town has employed her to care for the prisoners until they stand trial, and she will be dutiful, I can assure you of that. And I will be with her at all times – when my business at the inn allows.'

His brow furrows.

'Make sure you keep a close eye on her, Mistress, a very close eye. It is known that witches will easily seduce others into the Devil's work.'

'Oh no, Sir, I am sure this midwife will remain devout and do her duty. She is not the sort of person who would be corrupted.'

'All can be corrupted, Mistress, the Devil is everywhere. We must all take a care not to fall into sin, and it is known that women are more weak and susceptible to his entreaties than men, which is why men must lead and govern. Aldeburgh will be made clean and pure. It will be swept of evil and destruction and this is only a beginning.' His eyes gleam. 'We seize another witch tomorrow.'

ROSE KNOCKS SOFTLY ON THE OUTER DOOR OF THE INN AND I STEP out to join her, closing it behind me as we cross to the gaol. I watch her carefully as she enters and pushes her hood from her head. She is a striking woman and no mistake. Her pale hair is tied neatly under a scarf and she is clean and well-dressed. She has a way with her, and I can see why she makes a good midwife.

The prisoners stir and sit up, even the old one, although Alice Gardner remains slumped in the darkest corner, her cloak over her face, and I am grateful, for she always upsets the others.

As the midwife bends to her bag the old woman speaks.

'Dorothy Clarke, widow, of Dunwich.' Rose gazes at her.

'Mistress?'

'You asked my name before. I am telling you what it is.' Her voice is cracked from lack of use, her Suffolk accent strong, but these are the first words she has spoken and we all listen.

'Thank you, Mistress Clarke.' The midwife smiles at her warmly. 'I am called Rose and I have come to dress your leg, if you will allow me to?' The midwife sets out cloths, a thin sharp knife and a small jar, as the old woman nods and pulls at her skirts. The wound is even redder than before, the smell worse. 'This will not cure your leg, but it will help to ease your pain. I can give you a tincture ...'

I start at this.

'No, no tincture. She must be in her wits when she is examined. I have been told that these women are to have only the barest of treatment, and that only when strictly needed. The Town is not made of money, and the Captain has said it would all be wasted if they hang, as surely they will.'

Rose is removing the maggots one by one with the tip of the knife, dropping them onto a cloth, but she pauses at my words and looks up sharply.

'Mistress Howldine.' Her face is sharp with anger. 'Do you not think that they are women, the same as you or I?' I resent the suggestion – despite my wondering, they are not as I, never could be. They are witches, the Devil's own brood – Master Hopkins has told us so.

I cannot allow her to voice such thoughts, for they are dangerous. I speak up.

'But surely we have a duty to God to search out evil in our midst, Midwife. Does the Bible not say *'Thou shalt not suffer a witch to live.'* Do we not, in these Holy words, have God's own command to put such women on trial and, if judged guilty in a court of law, to sentence them to death and the everlasting torments of Hell? Is this not what is said? Is that not what is taught?' My voice is rising now, I feel as if I myself were on trial. 'I am a God-fearing woman, I go to church, I follow the true path and I pray for redemption when I eventually go to my Maker. Men teach us and lead us, they know what should be done, they understand the teachings of God, as we do not.' The midwife looks at me – I can feel my face is red and shining, feel the heat in my body. It is the heat of the righteous, I know it. I am not as they. I cannot be.

'But, Mary.' Her voice softens. 'Does the Bible not also say '*Love thy neighbour as thyself*'? Does it not say '*Turn the other cheek*'?' She is pouring golden honey from a small jar into the wound, reaching for a cloth to cover it, her patient silent as she works. I wonder at the old woman's courage for, throughout, she has not made one sound, despite the pain it must be causing. But the midwife is wrong, so wrong, and I bend towards her and my words come out in a hiss.

'Be careful, Rose, for what you say will be seen as heresy. My advice is to do your duty, give the care required of you, nothing more, and then hope, pray, that this will pass you by. For I believe you to be a good woman, and the Town needs good women now, to help it back to the Lord.' She bites her lip, looks at me and nods. She will learn. The only way to get on in this life is to follow without question. It does not pay to think.

38. JOAN

I t seems the midwife is able to think, has opinions of her own, but Joan, too, could have told her this was dangerous. She knows Rose is merely seeing which way the land lies with Mistress Howldine, feeling her way through the situation, but she is vulnerable. Gone are the days when cunning folk and healers were held in esteem, treated with respect. These are bitter times, when all are mistrustful of their neighbours, wary of their friends. These are the days when the smallest word will have the constables knocking at your door. Joan knows. For she has not been cautious, not kept her silence. She has cursed and sworn and riled against life and look where it has got her – held in a stinking cell with a mad child, her frightened mother and two more just like her, who have fallen foul of their emotions.

Joan sinks back against the wall and watches the midwife's deft fingers cleanse the wound then reach out for the honey. An ancient custom, brought back from Jerusalem by the crusaders all that time ago, a remedy used for centuries. But now, as men begin to call themselves surgeons, the old ways decline and fade and women are pushed aside, their powers feared and they begin to be called witches.

Just then the lantern-light catches the gold glow of the honey trickling from the jar. Joan cannot resist and, as the midwife begins to wrap the wound, she reaches out. The midwife freezes, watching every movement, alert for danger, but then her face softens as she sees Joan stretch her hand to the jar of honey, dip in her finger and put it to her mouth. Rose watches with sadness as Joan closes her eyes against its sweetness, leans back, and lets herself slide down on the straw.

39. MARY

Now the Dunwich one is settled, the others seem calmer. I wonder if Alice Gardner is well, for she was full of opinions when she was first brought in, but now you don't get a peep out of her. I didn't think that the watching would break a spirited one such as her, but maybe three months in that place has drawn her pride out and made her see the error of her ways. Either way, she says nothing and I am grateful. There are five of them in there now, and I dread to think what they will get up to between them if they are not kept quiet. I ask the gaoler to keep an extra watch on them, for sometimes there is strength in numbers. I am sure that these prisoners are all too beaten down and cowed to begin their devilish work now, but you can't be too careful.

I AM STOOD TALKING TO THE GAOLER OUT OF THE ICY WIND IN THE LEE of the Town Hall when we both look up in surprise. Captain Johnson is sat high on his horse, riding down the hill. He has a rope halter in his hand and tied to the other end of it, stumbling, is a girl.

We both lower our heads in deference but I know that the gaoler, like me, is looking under his lashes at the sight. For Captain Johnson has not sullied his hands in this matter so far, keeping his distance, leaving the dirty work to others whenever he can. A great leader of men he may be, brave and forward in battle, the scourge of Parliament with his demands for men and artillery to guard our section of the coast, but he has no stomach for this task of witch-finding, and it comes to me that it is the women who make him nervous. I think he is a cold man, although he has had two wives, three children. There are stories about his eldest, but the Captain himself is respected hereabouts, feared, but known to be fair, and I wonder at the sight of him riding towards us with a girl.

Master Hopkins strides across from the inn to greet him as the Captain reaches the gaol – he has been waiting, or else he knew. I wonder these days at his skills.

'Captain Johnson, I bid you good day. Is this is the one?' The Captain nods. 'Very well, she will be put in with the rest, for she must be removed from your household immediately. You cannot have such evil affecting yourself and your good family.'

'My wife is distraught, Master Hopkins, for she thought highly of her. We are shocked, Sir, shocked to find how she has treated our family and I hope that your investigations will find the truth of the matter.'

'Oh, indeed they will, Captain, my methods rarely fail. Leave the matter with me.' He nods at the gaoler who takes the halter from Captain Johnson and pulls the girl towards the door of the gaol. I cannot see her face clearly as she is wrapped tight against the cold, but her cloak is good, for all that it is muddied by the journey, and brown hair falls from her hood. She is clean at least. The gaoler unties the halter and pushes her inside and I see her flinch as she sees what is before her.

THE CAPTAIN TURNS HIS HORSE AND SPURS IT AWAY. HE HAS NOT looked at me, at anyone save Master Hopkins.

The Witchfinder turns to me.

'Please provide food and drink for this one as well. I intend to question her later today, along with the Dunwich woman, for it will be easier on them if I can gain their confessions and make them see the error of their ways.' His speech, as always, is precise, his voice soft, but I see the cruelty running through him now. Under the kindly exterior runs a sewer, foul and noxious, which no one seems able to stop.

I curtsey and turn away, waiting until he returns to his room, humming a hymn under his breath, before I go back to the gaol with some bread. The others have made room for the new one, but her head is bowed low, and in the silence I can hear her sobbing.

'Here – bread. You will be cared for here, you will not starve.' Joan Wade draws a breath but I catch her eye and the words die on her lips. 'They will return for you later. You and the Dunwich one over there . . .' I touch her with my boot. '. . . are to be interrogated by Master Hopkins. It will go easier for you if you confess.' Her sobbing stops and her body stills. Then her hands go up to her hood and she pushes it back from her face and her eyes fix on mine and will not let go.

I SHUDDER UNDER HER GAZE, FOR I KNOW HER. SHE IS THE MAID AT Captain Johnson's, a pretty girl with the sort of looks that were always going to get her into trouble. When I first went to the Captain's house, she was the one who opened the door to me. And then I remember that I had also seen his son, Francis, that day, standing behind a pillar, watching. I thought at the time he was looking at me but now I think he was not – he was watching her. I have heard rumours about Francis Johnson. The first-born son, spoiled and pampered as eldest sons often are, but not a preening man full of airs and graces. No, Francis Johnson is another type of man altogether. He is dark and angry, coiled like a spring, watching all that goes on. He is married, but in the three years since that grand occasion there has been no issue, no one to inherit the Captain's wealth. Some say Francis is cruel to his wife, a quivering little thing, prone to shakes and cries, who pushes herself into the corners of their box at church so as not to be seen. And there have been murmurings in the Lion of his liking for a house-maid, some say his obsession, how he will not leave her be.

And now here she is, slumped before me in the gaol, seized as a witch.

40. JOAN

Joan sees the glimmer of recognition from the Howldine woman as she passes the bread to the new girl. Her head is lowered, and she is not sure that the knowledge of what is happening to her has sunk in yet. When the innkeeper has gone they all move closer.

Alice comes out from the shadows and is the first to speak.

'What is your name?' The girl's hood is down, so now Joan can see that she is pretty in a country sort of way, the type of looks that cause men to gaze. Green eyes, dark waving hair and her clothes are good too. She is not like the rest of them and when she speaks Joan knows why, for her voice is soft with innocence.

'I am Sarah. I am a maid in the household of Captain Johnson.'

'But that is a good position, how did you . . . ?' Sarah's tears start up again and Catherine reaches for her hand.

'It was the Master's son, Francis . . .'

'You will not be heard, the walls are thick, the gaoler outside.' Catherine's voice is soft with understanding.

The girl looks at her and around at them, her face earnest.

'He has a liking for me. He follows me, has done for a long time. I do nothing, Mistress, nothing to encourage him, I swear to it. But he is always there, looking, standing behind me, too close. His eyes are always on me. And he started to speak to me, such words that a good girl should not hear and I told him, I said he should not say such things. But he kept on, he never stopped, and so I . . .'

'You surely did not curse him? Not in times such as these?' Alice's face is shocked.

'No, no, I would never do such thing, for it is wrong in the eyes of the Lord and I know what is right and what is wrong. But I had to stop him, for it was making me ill with worry.'

They all wait, expectant, as she rubs her eyes with the back of her hand and draws a deep breath.

'He came upon me in his wife's bed-chamber, when I was cleaning, pressed himself against me. It was not for the first time, but this time he forced his hand down into my dress and I slapped him away. I knew I should not have done it, but what he was doing was wrong. He has a wife to tend to his needs and I am a servant in his father's care.' She is sobbing again now, the tears flowing faster.

Joan leans in to her, all curiosity.

'So what did you do?'

'I told him that if he did such a thing again I would speak to his wife. I would have told the Captain, but he dotes on his son, so I knew I would go unheard. But Mistress Johnson is kind, although weak and fragile in health, and I thought she at least would listen. But I was not able to, for the Captain seized me and brought me here, without a word. He tied me to his horse . . .' Her voice breaks and she shakes her head in disbelief, her shoulders heaving.

Joan sits back on her heels, her bones aching along with her heart. For the servant-girl has done a foolish thing. She has trusted.

41. MARY

I am present in the courtroom when Master Hopkins interrogates the two new prisoners. He has demanded I be there, to ensure all is done correctly, so there can be no suggestion of wrong-doing. Goody Phillips has not yet arrived, and I think he must expect to gain confessions without her. I think that any woman, imprisoned with those who have been there for three long months, seeing their condition, would wish to shorten their ordeal. And they will talk, they must do, for the others will have told what happens to those who do not confess. This will be over quickly, he is right.

He asks for the woman from Dunwich first, thinking to get the easier one out of the way. He thinks she will readily admit her sins, but it is clear from the start that her wits have gone. She is trembling and mumbling to herself, clutching bony fingers at her grimy skirt.

'What is your name?' She does not even look up, just continues her noise with head down. Master Hopkins nods at a guard who grabs at the old woman's scalp and pulls her head up sharply. She lets out a scream and the babbling gets louder, but it still makes no sense. He looks down at his papers, arranged neatly on the table before him. 'You are Dorothy Clarke, a widow, from the town of

Dunwich. Is that correct?' She looks at him through wide, reddened eyes, mouth slack and drooling, her head held tight in the grip of the guard. He continues, not looking at her. 'The papers from Dunwich say that you sent an imp to torment a Master Spatchett when he refused you aid. That you were begging door to door, and cursed him when he set his dog on you, and that this imp gave him such pains in his head, tormenting him day and night, so he knew it came from the Devil himself.' I look down at my hands which I find are twisting in my lap, my palms damp. Surely this charge will not be believed. All folk get sore heads, you should see the men in my inn after the fair has been through. It seems to me that it is more likely that the old woman has become a nuisance and a drain on the parish and they want rid of her, for no town likes the new law that says they must provide for their poor – it also seems to me that the coming of the Witchfinder to Aldeburgh has given them a perfect excuse to remove her.

AT LAST MASTER HOPKINS LOOKS UP AT HER. WIDOW CLARKE IS rocking in place now, looking as if she is about to fall to the floor.

I step forward, my head lowered.

'Begging your pardon, Sir.' Master Hopkins turns and nods for me to continue. 'Her wits are gone, she has been like this ever since they brought her in. The midwife has tended to her, as her leg was injured when we got her. She does not cry so much now, but she has not spoken in all the time she has been here.' I cross my fingers under my apron at the small lie, then realise how this could be seen in this place and hurriedly straighten them again. So easy it is to fall into the path of wrong-doing.

'And she has said nothing at all, nor confessed her guilt?'

'No, Sir, not in my hearing.'

'Then she must be examined for witch marks. There will be proof and we will find it.' I pray he does not expect me to do such thing and it is as if he reads my thoughts. 'Do not worry, Mistress,

Goodwife Phillips will be here shortly, I am sure. I would not expect you to do this and I have no doubt her experience will prove fruitful.' He turns away from me and waves at the guards, who take up Widow Clarke and carry her, moaning, outside and down the steps. I can hear her through the glass, her cry weakening, carried away by the wind that is now blasting off the sea.

It is not a cry of anger, it is a cry of fear. She is right to fear.

It is but a few moments before the guards return, pushing the servant-girl before them. She stands in front of the table and her head is held high. My heart sinks.

'Your name?'

'Sarah Parker, Sir, servant to Captain Johnson.' She curtseys. She thinks that speaking his name, showing respect, will take her from this place.

'Girl, you have been accused of bewitching Francis, son of Captain Johnson. What say you?'

A look of horror widens her eyes but she composes herself quickly.

'I never did, Sir. I am a God-fearing person. I go to church every Sunday with the family. Ask the Captain, he will tell you.'

'I am sure you think you are God-fearing, Sarah, but claims have been made against you and I want your confession.' The Witchfinder's voice is soft, wheedling. He is lulling her.

Her head goes up. I wish her caution but I see she does not have it.

'Claims, Sir? I know not of any claims. I do not know why I am here, save that I told Master Francis that if he touched me again ...'

'Enough. You are accused of threatening Francis Johnson, saying that you would curse him and his line.'

She blows out a laugh through pursed lips.

'If you consider pushing him away when he came too near, touching and fondling at me. He does not stop, Sir ...'

The Witchfinder holds up his palm and she pauses.

'It is clear you do not know your place, girl, for it is not for you to say what your betters can and cannot do. He claims it was you that wantonly pursued him, that when he rebuked you for it, you cursed him so that he is no longer able to lie with his wife as a husband should.'

Shock sears the girls face and I can see all her pride leave her in a breath.

'Sir, that is untrue, I did not! I know nothing of such things . . .'

'Quiet!' Master Hopkins glances around the room. We all stand silent, eyes averted, faces stony. We have heard the rumours. But such things are never spoken of, should never be said in place such as this.

'Do you confess to the sin of witchcraft, girl?'

She stands proud again, too proud for a servant, but she cannot afford it now.

'No, Sir. I have done nothing wrong. I will not confess to something I did not do.'

Master Hopkins nods.

'Take her down.' He is a ball of fury as he drops his eyes to his papers and scribbles in his book. I can see the quill bending under his fist, black ink spattering, until a sharp crack and the nib splits.

The Witchfinder is incandescent with anger, it billows from him like smoke, filling the room. I have never seen him like this and even the guards are shuffling nervously. When he speaks his voice is tight, clipped.

'No confessions. I thought to have this matter done by now. But I see we will need to take further steps.' He bends his head to the pile of papers and pulls over a clean sheet. He throws the broken quill to the floor and reaches for a new feather, pulling a blade from his pocket. He scrapes its edge against the quill and I watch as white threads dust the air like snow, soft and gentle. The action is softening his humour too, he is containing his temper with the methodical task, and by the time he has finished to his satisfaction I can see he is himself again.

'Sir, may I fetch you some ale, wine?' I seek to restore him further in the best way I know how. He looks at me as he creases the paper in his thin fingers.

'No, Mistress, that will not be necessary. I will return to my room to wait for Mistress Phillips, for there are preparations to be made. Perhaps a little supper?'

'Certainly, Sir, I will arrange it.'

'And there is a room ready for Mistress Phillips?'

'Of course.'

I look down at my hands. More expense – the Captain will not be happy, the Town even less so, but they brought this thing to our door and they must see it through. And more coin will be chinking its shining way into my coffers. But I am wondering at what cost.

42. JOAN

The girl, Sarah, when she is brought back, looks confused and angry. Such a pretty thing, face flushed, hair swirling around her head. But innocent, Joan can tell by her manner that she is still untouched, still not wise to the ways of men.

'Did you confess?' Catherine is alert, and Isbel, close by her, just stares at her.

'No, for such is the thing that I was accused of . . .' She falters and Joan sees that, underneath her bravado and high manner, a seam of fear has stitched itself into her guts.

Alice Gardner moves from the shadows to sit by her.

'Tell me what they said.'

'They said I had bewitched Master Francis. That I . . . that I had pursued him and cursed him and caused him to be unable to lie with his wife.' Her face reddens and she puts her hands to cover it. 'I do not know what they mean. I do not understand. Why would they say such a thing when it is not true?'

Alice reaches out ands pulls her in to an embrace.

'It is God's will that we produce children, child, some say it is the true purpose of matrimony. I would say that it is a way to give men power over us, to make us their creatures, and men are frightened of losing this power, and it makes them angry when they do. There are many reasons why this happens.'

Sarah looks up.

'But I should not be blamed for that.'

'No, you should not. Master Francis is older, his wife is always ill and fragile. It is likely this is to blame, but he is a man, he will not admit to frailty. You have refused him and so he has put the blame on to you.'

Sarah rubs her eyes.

'But it was the other servants that said this, it was not me – am I to be condemned for mere gossip?'

'In this case you may be.' Alice's face saddens. 'There is little you can do.'

'But I told them how he pursues me, how he pushes himself against me, touches me, surely they can see that he is to blame and not me?'

Alice bites her lip.

'They do blame you. They have said that you tried to seduce him. That is the way with masters and servants. He has failed, been refused and his pride is dented. He seeks to hold someone responsible.' Sarah looks blank and Joan thinks it is only now that she begins to realise her position.

And then, a miracle. Isbel, so long frozen and still, stands, and slowly moves to the girl's side. She bends and, lifting a corner of her grubby apron, wipes Sarah's tears away, then sits beside her and takes her hand. She lays her head on the servants shoulder and begins to croon, and tears prick Joan's eyes for the sadness of it all

43. MARY

I t is the next morning when the search-woman arrives with her escort. I pass the men mugs of ale for their troubles and they gulp gratefully. The horses steam in the frosty air, their breath gusting out like smoke, as the yard-man helps Goody Phillips from her horse. She staggers a little as her boots touch the ground.

'Are you well, Mistress?'

She does not look herself, as she did in September. She seems smaller, shrunken somehow, but she pulls herself up, brushing her cloak with her hands.

'I am, Mistress Howldine, but I am cold and stiff. It is not the weather for riding, the horses slipped and slid, for the ground is rutted and sharp with ice.'

'Then come in before the fire, sit and take a glass of metheglin to warm you, or I can heat some mead?'

She looks at me gratefully.

'Mead would be most welcome, Mistress, for I am cold as death.' I move closer to take her bag from her, and look into her face. Her lips are blue-tinged, her features sharpened with the cold, and I usher her inside as quickly as I can, for I do not want her ill now, not when she has just arrived. I show her to a seat before the fire in the bar. The Lion is still empty, it is too early even for the hardiest regular, as I take the poker from the fire and plunge it into a stone jug of mead which I have saved from the summer's making.

'Here, this will restore you. Shall I tell Master Hopkins you are here?'

She slurps at the hot drink loudly then sets the cup on the table beside her.

'I will take a moment to gather myself. So, Mistress, how do the witches fare?' This is the first time she has spoken to me in such a normal, civil manner and I wonder at the change in her.

'The witches are kept well and fed but some have been so long incarcerated they are not in the condition they were.'

'That is to be expected, it is the way of things. And I understand you have more who require searching?'

I pause. It seems endless.

'There are two, Mistress Phillips, one a servant girl but the other – well, she is aged, her wits are gone, she is not of this world. She was brought here by cart from Dunwich, accused of sending an imp to cause a bad head to a man who refused her aid. But . . .' I hesitate to say, but the moment seems right, Mistress Phillips relaxed. '. . . I find it hard to believe that such a thing is caused by witchcraft.'

Straight away I realise my error.

Mistress Phillips' face snaps shut and tight like a farmer's trap and I am caught. I let my guard down, I was not quick enough.

'Mistress Howldine, I am shocked to hear you say such thing, and you a God-fearing, Christian woman. These witches summon imps in any shape or form to carry out the Devil's wishes. Surely you cannot think that this woman, however frail and old, could be innocent of such a charge, brought, I understand, by a respectable yeoman? I do hope your time with them is not causing you to feel sympathy?'

I back down as quickly as I can, for I have fallen into a monstrous snare of my own making.

'No, Mistress, of course not. I know them to be daughters of

Satan, that is why they are seized and that is why they must be tried, and by better folk than I.' She is placated a little, but I must seek to remove the seed of doubt I have planted in her mind. 'I was only wondering how it is that these women come to fall into sin. I have low people who stay here in the summer, when the fair is here, but none such as they.' I pause, choosing my words with care. 'My visitors are not always as refined as yourself and Master Hopkins.' Surely she cannot be immune to flattery – she is not.

She nods and her mouth curves into a small smile that does not reach her eyes.

'Indeed, it must be hard for you at such times, although I'm sure the increased trade makes up for any inconvenience.' She has the measure of me now, things are as they were before.

'The fair brings in plenty of trade, yes, but the type of people who stay . . . they are not like us. I frequently have to replace the straw in the mattresses, for the lice and vermin they bring in are the very Devil to get rid of.' My heart stops as I speak the words, my mouth has run away with me, but her smile stays fixed and I breathe again. 'It is a pleasure for me to be able to entertain guests such as Master Hopkins, and yourself, Mistress Phillips.'

'And we are grateful for your hospitality, Mistress Howldine, although I am sure you are being well paid for it.' The old Goody Phillips has returned, shrewd and sharp as a blade. Sharp as the pricker she uses.

THE WITCHFINDER COMES DOWN FROM HIS ROOM AT MIDDAY, Mistress Phillips in tow. I am serving customers and the bar is noisy, but all stop as he enters. Faces drop down into flagons, but all ears are pricked.

'Mistress Howldine, we go to the courtroom to search the two new prisoners. We will require supper when we have finished, if you would be so good. I do not think it will take long.' I curtsey at their departing backs as slowly the talk returns, getting louder. But under the conversations and comments there runs a tide of unrest. The men in the bar are unsettled. They have seen many things at sea and on land, travelled to far-off places, to countries of heat, of ice and snow. They have farmed the land, harvested the seas, drained the marshes hereabouts, caught eels and fish, trapped birds and animals. They are set in their ways but now those ways are being questioned, disrupted, altered for good. The coming of the Witchfinder is breaking the Town apart.

THEY SAID LATER THAT YOU COULD HEAR THE SCREAMS ACROSS THE Town. The deeper moaning from the old woman, the high-pitched cries of the girl. The men who came into the inn that afternoon were subdued, morose, intent on drinking away all that they had heard.

I did not listen, I closed my ears and busied myself with work. I could not dwell on it. I scrubbed tables between serving customers, not spending time with them in conversation as I would ordinarily do, for I did not want to hear about the witches, I did not want even to think about them.

And when Master Hopkins and Goody Phillips returned an hour or so later I took them their food without a word. I tried to shut the talk away, like it was a rabid dog, but, like that dog, it escaped, and I heard that the servant had confessed to witchcraft but the old mad woman had not and would therefore have to be watched.

44. JOAN

The women clean the two of them up as best they can. The servant girl, Sarah, is sobbing and limp as Alice runs the damp cloth over her. Joan rinses it out and passes it back as the water in the bowl gradually turns red. Such little marks to cause such pain – she and Alice have both felt their bite, know how they sting and ache. But they also know they heal and, while they are washing the girl, Isbel speaks quiet words of comfort, while Catherine sits across the cell, holding the hand of the old woman. When Alice and Joan turn to tend her it is clear whatever wits she had are completely gone. Her eyes are blank and hollow, as if the person behind them has been snuffed out like a candle, and she makes not a sound when they wash her wounds. The searcher has tried harder with her, they can see it – her thin, frail body is a mass of holes and tears, already bruising as the old are wont to do.

When they have finished Sarah clutches at Joan's hand. Joan does not pull away.

'Mistress, I couldn't bear the pain. I am so ashamed . . . it was so bad, I said yes to whatever they asked me.'

Alice is standing, stretching, rubbing bony knuckles into the small of her back. They have all become stiff and sore in here. She looks down at the servant.

'There is no shame in it. They have seized you, have twisted a tale around to suit their purposes, and it is best to save yourself pain where you can.'

'But I am no witch.'

'None of us are, girl, they just want us to believe that we are, make us cry for mercy, beg their forgiveness, admit to anything so that they can feel power over us. You are not to blame.'

Sarah rubs at her bleeding arms and Joan reaches out to still her.

'Don't, you will invite infection.'

She cannot bring herself to tell Sarah that this is not the worst of it.

45. MARY

The inn is packed with customers that night, but the mood is sombre. There are no cards played, no dice thrown. Men stare into their mugs with downcast faces and they do not joke and tease such as they are used to doing. I serve the ale as fast as I can as the pot-boy runs around clearing tables, and I think all will be well until the back door opens and Master Hopkins comes in. The silence is immediate.

He looks around at the crowd as he stands tall above them on the step.

'I am in need of three men.'

No one looks at him. It is as if they think he can reach into their souls and know they are lacking. He sees their fear and reads it as sullenness, so he raises his voice and speaks again.

'I am in need of three men. To sit with a witch this night.' Some glance at their companions under furrowed brows but still no one speaks. Master Hopkins sighs.

'The Town will pay one shilling to each man for a night's work.' The room shimmers with movement. This is a lot of money. Men work long and hard in terrible conditions for such a prize. Master Hopkins knows he has them, I can see it in his eyes as he smiles thinly 'And Mistress Howldine here will supply ale.'

Slowly a hand rises at the back of the room. I cannot tell who it is for the man's cap is pulled low over his head but I see from his dress he is a sailor. This winter is the harshest in memory and times have been hard. I cannot blame him for taking an opportunity, for this will keep his family fed until he can put to sea again. He clears his throat.

'I will do it, Sir, but what about payment? I cannot wait until the Town sees fit to open its purse.' Master Hopkins slants his head to one side, looking as if he is sympathetic.

'If you carry out this task I will ensure payment when it is done.' Others nod in agreement and two more hands rise. The Witchfinder licks his lips in satisfaction and I wonder if he has ever experienced failure, for all seem to fall to his will. 'Come with me to the courtroom. The witch is prepared.' There is hesitation, but desperation too – no man can afford principles in these days of hardship and want. The three shuffle to their feet, heads bowed, not catching the eyes of their companions, as they shrink through the door behind Master Hopkins and out into the cold night, leaving behind them the smell of shame.

I HAVE NO OPTION BUT TO TAKE ALE TO THE WATCHERS, FOR MASTER Hopkins has told me that they must have some at the start and the end of their task. I wrap up against the cold and carry a jug and three mugs across the square. I can feel the ice freezing my face, my skin tightening with the salt. We are two streets back from the sea here but tonight, as the winter wind howls around the buildings, it is as if we were standing on the very pebbles before it. I climb the stone stairs to the courtroom slowly, my tray as heavy as my heart, and I knock on the door with the toe of my boot.

Master Hopkins himself opens it.

'Ah, Mistress Howldine, good.' He turns back into the room. 'Men, here is ale as I promised.' I step in to the room and look around. It has been cleared, the large oak table pushed against the side, and four chairs are arranged around a central one, where the Clarke woman is sat. They have already stripped her to her shift, which is piss-stained and soaking. Her hands and feet are tied to the chair with coarse rope and she lolls with head down, panting. Her shin is bleeding where the dressing has been lost, and I think I will need to ask Rose to return, as it does not look right. I take the tray to a side-table and set it down and, hearing the noise, she looks up. Her face is still dotted with dried blood from the searching, although I can see attempts have been made to wash her. But her eyes are blank, the one curtained in white making her look unsettling, otherworldly. I draw in my breath sharply and Master Hopkins comes over to me, all solicitous.

'Mistress, is all well? Is it the witch?'

'All is well, Sir, it is just the way she looked at me.'

'Has she cursed you Mistress? It may be done with a look, I have seen such things before.' I do not want to be party to this so I hasten to reassure him.

'No, no, Sir, nothing like that. It was just that she seems to have completely lost her wits now and I wonder how she will know to confess, if she is guilty of that which she is accused?'

'That is for God to judge, Mistress, for this work is carried out in His name. If this prisoner wishes to confess her wrongdoing, to forsake the evil she has invited in, then God will find a way for her to do so. We watch for imps and familiars this night and if one comes to her then that is proof of her guilt – we will need nothing more.' I bob a curtsey and move to the door for, truth be told, I cannot wait to leave that place. 'I intend to stay and watch with the men this night.'

I halt at the Witchfinder's words.

'I will fetch another mug.'

'There is no need, I need no sustenance when doing God's work. His joy in my deeds is sustenance enough.' I curtsey again. As I straighten, the old woman looks around and her gaze finds me. I stand transfixed. Her face has cleared and I can see that she is back in her mind. Her expression softens as she spies me and she opens her mouth to speak, but as she does so, one of the men scrapes his chair on the floorboards so I do not hear. But I am used to watching lips in a noisy inn, hearing words unspoken, I can make out what she says.

And what she says is 'I forgive you.'

SHE DOES NOT TAKE AS LONG AS THE OTHERS. IT IS JUST BEFORE DAWN when I hear the clatter of footsteps and the inn door click shut. I am already awake, preparing for the coming day, so I wrap a robe around myself and go to the top of the stairs. In the hallway below, the Witchfinder stands, looking up at me, his face flushed with cold and satisfaction.

'You have her confession, Master Hopkins?' I think of that old woman, unable to move, sitting in her own mess with no food or drink, shivering in the cold room despite the bright light of the candles. I wonder how long I would last.

'No, Mistress, better than that.' I hear a door open behind me and Goody Phillips looks out. She is fully dressed and I wonder if she has slept at all. Her face, too, is full of anticipation. 'We sat for many hours, but then, a noise. A scrabbling and scritching in the walls and a clicking sound from behind the wood. There was a tapping there for many minutes then it came. A huge brown beetle, not of this world, it crawled towards the witch, over her foot and up her leg. And she wriggled then, you can be sure, for it was the Devil's servant sent to suckle from her. All saw it. And there we have our proof. The men will speak against her when she is tried and will tell of what they saw. She is condemned, there is no escape for her now. God has pointed her out to me and asked me to carry out his commands. She will be punished now, as all such evil is punished.' His face reddens and he begins to cough, but he is triumphant. 'Mistress Howldine, please take more ale to the men as was agreed. I will go to Captain Johnson and obtain coins to pay them. It is good work we have done this night.'

I turn back to my room and close the door. I am so weary. But I must see this thing through so I pull on my apron, settle a clean coif on my head, and go down to the bar and fill a jug from the barrel.

46. JOAN

They are still asleep when the watchers carry the Dunwich woman back to the cell. Joan takes one look at her and fears they have killed her, for she is so pale and thin she looks like a phantom. Her shift is filthy and wringing wet, her face closed, and Joan sees her wits have left her again. The men drop her heavy to the floor and Joan gives them a look, for they should not treat an old woman like that. But she is not that to them – she is a witch and to be treated worse than a dog.

'No confession, no need. Her imp came.' Joan looks up at the voice. It is one of the sailors from Slaughden, she remembers him. She never thought him to be a cruel man and wonders what has changed him.

'Imp?' Catherine peers from the shadows.

'A brown beetle, the like of which we had never seen. It was tapping in the panelling then it came to her and suckled. We all saw it, even Master Hopkins, who watched with us.'

He is puffed up with pride at being part of this and Joan's anger overtakes her.

'A beetle? Such as are found in old buildings? A beetle? How can such a thing suckle?' She tries hard to keep the contempt out of her voice but he hears it and leans towards her, his long nose wrinkling in disgust.

'It went to her, you can see where it pierced her skin with its jaws. Be silent, you old hag. The sooner they hang the lot of you the better.'

All Joan knows is that it was the pricker that pierced Dorothy's body, and her leg is damaged and bleeding. But men will build such things out of the very air, and they are helpless in their grasp. All they can do is keep watch, so they sit around the old woman as the sun slowly rises and, from somewhere other, comes a hum. They hold each other and sing, comforting her with their voices.

47. MARY

There is a strange low sound coming from the gaol as I cross the square. The gaoler is outside, rubbing his arms briskly to try and warm himself. The morning cold feels thick and heavy and I sniff it. No snow yet.

'What is that noise, Gaoler?'

He sighs dramatically.

'They have been at it since the old one was put back in there after the watching. Singing and humming, enough to drive you mad. You wouldn't think they had the strength, but who knows what goes on between a gathering of witches such as they. Need to get rid of them I say, and quickly, before they start to conjure up their magic and damn us all.' He turns and opens the scarred door of the cell.

Six pairs of eyes glare at me as I set the tray down in the centre. They used to grab at the food, stuff it into their mouths, but now they are slower, uninterested. I nod towards the Dunwich woman.

'How does she fare?'

'What would you care, Mistress? We are just creatures to you.' Joan Wade's tongue is as sharp as ever, but I see the others nod in agreement, and a shiver runs through me. They are banding together, becoming one, as Captain Johnson's troops do in battle.

I do not know why I feel I must explain, but I try.

'I am charged with your care.' Catherine Butts snorts at my words. 'I am as imprisoned in this thing as you.' As I say this it strikes me that it is true. Like them, I am unable to escape.

'I doubt that, Mistress, I doubt that very much. I don't see you dining on stale bread and ale left over from the pots of others. Do you collect their leavings up, Mistress, or do you leave it to that poor boy that you run ragged?' Alice Gardner seems to have found her voice again and she struggles to her feet to confront me. She is swaying slightly and I can see that the months of imprisonment have reduced her, for her once young-looking body is thin and wasted. She may be all bones, but her spirit is still there. I go to deny her accusation, but shame makes me pause. For I do send in the leftovers, I do ask the pot-boy to save the dregs, but I have a living to make and the money they are paying me for this would not go far if I was to serve good food to witches. So I choose to ignore her, but she knows the barb has sunk deep.

'How is the Dunwich woman.'

'Her name is Dorothy Clarke. She has a name.' Catherine's voice comes sharp out of the dark corner. 'How would you be, Mistress Howldine, if you were of her advanced years, to be treated so?' I turn to her and I see that Isbel is sitting with the servant girl, Sarah, their arms linked, their faces pale. They could be sisters, they too are bonding. This is a dangerous thing. They are looking out for each other, feeling each other's pain and I realise the gaoler is right, such comradeship must be cut off before it grows monstrous.

I GO STRAIGHT UP TO MASTER HOPKINS ROOM AND TAP GENTLY ON HIS door. I am wary of waking him after his night of watching Widow Clarke, but I fear I must tell him about the women before he hears it from someone else. I cannot afford to anger him.

The door opens so quickly he cannot have been asleep, and he is fully dressed.

'Mistress Howldine, is there news? Is there a problem with the accused?'

I bob a curtsey.

'No Sir, not a problem, more . . . a difficulty.' He opens the door wide and waves me in, leaving it open, for decency. 'I thought you would be asleep, Sir, after your long night.'

'There is no sleeping when the Lord's business is being carried out. I need little rest. I will have all the rest I need when I meet my Lord, and he welcomes me into his fold. Now, what is this difficulty?' I hesitate, for, under his gaze, I am not sure how to proceed, and a part of me wonders if I imagined the witches bonding. I should ask him if it is safe, find out if he thinks they could hold a coven and damn us all. But he stands before me, his eyes radiant with zeal, his face expectant, and suddenly I see the latent cruelty in the man, the obsession that has taken him over, and it is all I can do not to cry out.

'Mistress – this difficulty?'

He tilts his head in that manner he has and I am so close to telling him all. But then . . .

'I need the midwife.' It comes out fast, unintended, and his brow furrows in confusion. I plough on. 'Master Hopkins, the old woman from Dunwich who has just been watched. Her leg is infected and is getting worse. It should be tended again, so I would like your permission to send for the midwife.'

He is suspicious, I can tell, he knows that this is not why I came, but he says nothing, considering my request.

'But the witch is to hang, Mistress, that is certain, given that her imp appeared, and in front of witnesses. To employ the midwife again would not be best use of Town funds – they keep telling me how these are limited.' He laughs, soft and harsh, then coughs into his kerchief. When he brings it down from his mouth it is flecked with blood.

'But Sir, the old woman may die in the gaol if her leg is left. She will not survive this winter, nor the journey to the Assize.'

'They will not be going to the Assize, Mistress, they will be tried here.'

Shock rips through me. I had thought that this deed would be done elsewhere, that it would be taken away from here so that we did not have to think any more on it. All have heard about witches who are questioned, then imprisoned in Colchester, Bury and Ipswich, and held in those foul places, pending the quarterly Assize. We know that in Bury St Edmunds, such an Assize had been held in this August past, with a hundred and fifty men and women accused of witchcraft, many brought in from the other areas. That, in the stinking heat of summer, they had been packed into a barn to await their fate. We were told how witches from the nearby towns and villages, from Halesworth, Dunwich, Westleton and Yoxford, were among them. The Witchfinder has been diligent.

'Tried here, Sir? But I thought . . .'

'This Town has a Royal Warrant and so can try its own cases. Magistrates will be summoned. Francis Bacon has been named by Westminster as a Commissioner and he will preside. The Town Bailiffs will attend, and these witches will be tried within the due process of the law. All will be carried out as it should, but here, in Aldeburgh.'

'And if – when – they are found guilty? What then? Will they stay imprisoned here or go to elsewhere?' I think of the weeks, months, that I would have to provide for them. See them. But part of me is torn. A trial will bring people flooding in, for they are like holidays; there will be street vendors and people will want food, ale, rooms. Much as I want the matter ended, a trial could make my fortune.

He has turned away, intent on his paperwork, and I think I go unheard, but then he looks back over his shoulder as if remembering my presence.

'Send for your midwife, Mistress. It is right that she should be

summoned.' I pause, for there is something else in his voice, something that makes my neck start to prick. But then he continues so
smoothly I think no more on it. 'And, no, they will not be imprisoned here or anywhere else. They will hang, Mistress. God will
order it. I will ensure it.'

48. JOAN

The Howldine woman tells them she has sent for the midwife. It is just as well, for Dorothy Clarke is clearly in pain. Although she does not speak, she moans and cries, little whimpering noises like a puppy, keeping the others from their rest, what little there is of it here. Once the women talked amongst themselves, but that seems a lifetime ago. Now they can only sit, each with their own thoughts, as the days slowly pass and the nights crawl by. None of them have the stomach for food but they force it down by habit. They use the pail when they have to, and at least the gaoler empties it each day now, and the cold makes it stink less. But the cold. Bitter, it has crept into their bones, even the younger ones feel it, Isbel who has been there since the beginning, Sarah who has only been there a week. Those two are like sisters now, always together, and Joan is glad, for they had their lives in front of them, and now this has been taken away they find solace in each other. Isbel has stopped her constant preaching, thank the Lord, and it is only occasionally Joan sees her lips move in prayer, for Sarah's presence seems to have calmed her. This place has changed Alice too, she who seemed so strong and alive when she was brought in. There is something amiss there, for she is not a silent person by nature, but now she pulls back into the shadows at every sound. No, there is something, but the cold has addled her brain and Joan is unable to put her finger on it.

49. MARY

The midwife's knock on the inn door is so quiet I only just hear her. She stands shivering on the doorstep in her red cloak, her worn leather bag on her shoulder.

'You wish me to tend to the women again? Is something wrong with Isbel?'

'No, nothing like that. It is the old one from Dunwich, whose leg is ulcerated. The wound looks worse, and Master Hopkins has asked that you attend her.'

Rose looks hard at me.

'He asked for me?' Her voice is strung tight with tension

'It was I that suggested you were summoned, do not fear. He has not mentioned you himself, but he wishes the women to be kept in good condition. It seems they will be tried here, not in Bury.'

'Here? Is such thing possible? Does the law not say . . . ?'

'It is arranged.'

'So when will this be? How long are they to stay imprisoned?' I do not answer but throw on my cloak and escort her across the square.

. . .

HAIL COMES SIDEWAYS IN A STIFF EASTERLY BREEZE AND CATCHES AWAY our breath. The gaoler is huddled around a small brazier, wrapped in several cloaks, a broad-brimmed hat pulled low over his face. He pulls himself away from the heat reluctantly and unlocks the cell door, passing us a lantern, for winter has made this place dark as hell. Inside, nothing moves, so I announce our arrival.

'The midwife is here to tend to Widow Clarke.' I make sure to use the witch's name, I do not want any more arguments. There is a shuffling as the bundles of rags separate and become human. After the clean cold air, the stench takes my breath away.

'I will tend to any who need me.' Rose puts down the lantern and opens her satchel.

Joan Wade is quick to see.

'Do you have more honey?'

She reaches out a grubby claw to the bag, but I smack it away.

'Leave that, it is not for you.'

Rose has pulled up Dorothy's skirt to her knee and, although she masks it quickly, I see her recoil in disgust.

'This wound is far worse, it is full of dirt again . . .'

'She was watched, last night. The cloth you put on was lost when they took her away.' Widow Wade's voice is full of pity – I had never thought she had such feeling in her the way she has behaved here, but this place is changing them. First that girl Isbel looking halfway normal again, not babbling on, now Joan Wade, who has always been known for her sharp tongue and spiteful ways, showing kindness.

Rose looks up at me.

'I will dress this wound again as best I can.'

She works swiftly, cleaning and wiping and I see Dorothy Clarke relax under her touch. She binds the wound tight and then looks around.

'Isbel, are you well now?'

The girl nods.

'Her courses are stopped again.' Catherine reaches for her

daughter and puts an arm around her. 'Does she need your tincture?'

Rose keeps her face lowered.

'No, I think not. That will likely be caused by the lack of food and care in here.' She looks around her, holding the lantern up little higher. 'Sarah, is it not?'

The new girl nods.

'Yes, Mistress.'

'And are you hurt?'

'They took her and pricked her, how do you expect her to be?' Joan Wade's voice is sharp in the darkness.

'Do your wounds still bleed, Sarah?'

The servant shakes her head. Her prettiness is still there, but exhaustion and pain have worked their spell on her already, and she looks older than her years.

Rose turns.

'And you, Mistress Wade, how fare you?'

I expect the witch to laugh, or spit or curse as she is wont to do, but instead she softens under the midwife's question and with a shock I see, beneath that harsh exterior, a terrified old woman.

'As well as I can be, in such a place and after such time.' Rose reaches out and pats her arm then holds the lantern up high, looking around. In the corner Alice Gardner's frozen shape and white face is caught by its rays and in that moment a look passes between them. It flashes there only for an instance, but I see it.

They know each other.

My brain races backwards to when I helped search Alice Gardner's house. Her carved wooden chest, the pale blue silk bodice and clothes, too many for one woman. I remember the clouts, remember how I thought that Alice Gardner was too old to need such things, how I thought there was a second one. It is all clear now. This explains why Rose was so reluctant, why Alice has kept herself small and quiet in the cell. They know each other.

The midwife turns quickly away, thinking I did not see. But I

192 | L M WEST

did, and my mind is in turmoil with what I should do with this new knowledge. For I believed Rose to be a good person, skilled in healing, I thought her willing to help me. But she was not – I forced her into it, and the reason may be that she knows this witch, knows her well.

And I have promised to protect such a one from the Witchfinder. I gave her my word.

WE HUDDLE AGAINST THE WIND AS WE CROSS BACK TO THE INN, OUR heads down, not speaking. My mind is racing. If Rose does know Alice Gardner then she may also be one of them. I think of her fear of the Witchfinder, the potion she gave to Isbel, and what that may have done. I need to know the truth.

I make up my mind.

'Midwife, will you sup with me? This wind is bitter, it will help to warm us.'

I can feel her hesitation.

'That would be welcome, Mistress, but I cannot stay for long. There is a babe due in the houses by the sea and the mother will need my assistance.'

'Just for a few moments then, come in.' I show her into the back room and to a chair, then I leave her to settle while I fetch some wine. When I return she has loosened her cloak and is holding her hands out to the fire. Her bag is on the floor beside her.

The poker is red hot in the blaze and I plunge it into the mugs of wine and pass one to her. It smells hot, burnt, and sweet, and she takes it gratefully. We sip in silence but then she puts down the mug.

'You saw.'

It is not a question and I do not lie.

'Alice Gardner is known to you.'

Rose flinches and lowers her eyes but not before I see the terror behind them.

50. JOAN

Now she has it. Joan may be old but she doesn't miss much. The midwife, Rose, who came and tended them all, Joan had not expected her kindness – she hasn't seen much kindness in recent years. But it was as the midwife turned and the light fell on Alice, that she knew, saw the look that passed between them and it all fell into place. The reason Alice has held back, pushed herself into the shadows – Joan realises now it happened when the midwife first came to tend Isbel, for Alice was well enough before.

That look. It flashed between them like lightening, and Rose moved the lantern away quick enough, but Joan saw history between them – love even. She could see it in their eyes. They are both good women who deserve to be saved.

Joan tried but failed to protect Alice at the watching. And she now wonders if there is anyone who can protect Rose?

51. MARY

The midwife reaches for her wine, taking a long pull for courage before looking up at me.

'I do know her. It was she who brought me up. My mother had died, my father long gone and she took me in – I am not sure what would have happened to me if she had not done so. She was kind, and I owe her a great deal.' I say nothing, waiting for her to continue. 'I was eight years old then, and I lived with her until I was seventeen. She taught me her skills, and that enabled me to find my own way in this world. She had been selling herbs and potions for many a year, giving comfort to the sick and dying, helping the young maids and lads, and she showed me what to do. People used to go to her for help, but not for a while now.' She takes another sip of wine, her face furrowed. 'For as you grow old people do not want you. They no longer trust you with their children, and they begin to wonder where your knowledge and skills came from. They forgot all that Alice did, the wise woman that she was, the people she tended; now they have nothing but contempt and hatred for her. A witch. That is what they call her these days.'

I can no longer keep silent.

'But she made a poppet for Catherine Butts, and the men saw

her familiar come to her when she was watched. How can this be anything other than Devilish work?'

Rose rubs her face with her hand and I can see exhaustion leaching out of her.

'It is so easy to fall into such things . . .'

'So you know her to be a witch?'

The words come out harsher than I meant and Rose recoils.

'No, never. She was a wise woman who helped people, she was valued and respected. Never a witch. But when you see such things as we do, hear stories – well, it is easy to give in to superstition, to do as people ask, if you think it will help them.

'Isbel Butts said . . .'

'I have heard what was said, but she is a child, young for her years, with a father who . . .'

I hold up my hand.

'Do not speak against Master Butts, for he is a godly man. I know he once was not, for he frequented this inn as he did many others, he was known as a drinker, but the Bible preaches forgiveness and, however hard, that is what we must do.'

'He was also known for his temper.'

I nod reluctantly. Martin Butts was ready with his fists from a child, always picking fights. I was glad when he found God and stopped coming to the Lion. I know it to be a sin to speak ill of people, but he was a nasty piece of work and all pitied his wife. But he is changed, reformed and I hasten to his support.

'He was quick to anger, that is true, but all changed when he was brought to the Lord. He attends church, has stopped his drunken ways, everyone can see what a new man he is. And he has brought his family up in the new ways too.'

'You were not there though, when Catherine went with Isbel to see Alice. You do not know what that *godly* man was doing.' She spits the word out with contempt. 'That *new* man forced himself on his own daughter. Then he twisted her mind to make her believe it was Satan himself come to purge her from evil. The girl was innocent, she did not know, so she believed his words when he told her how evil she was. And her mother could do nothing to stop him, for the first time she did he punched her to the ground so hard she was in fear of her life. So Catherine took Isbel to see the one person she believed could help them. Alice Gardner. The wise woman who was known to help others. And Alice told me that she did the one thing that she thought would stop him. She . . .' Rose drops her head, considering whether to continue, then looks straight at me. '. . . scraped wax from the candles, softened it in the fire and moulded it to make a figure. Catherine had taken a piece of her husband's shirt to wrap it, a shaving from his fingernail to press into it, and they tied it with cord to bind the spell. And then they gave Isbel a thorn and told her that the next time the man visited her she was to show him the image and tell him that he would be pierced by Christ's own thorn if he were to touch her again. Alice knew it was wrong, knew how such things are seen. But these are the old ways, those who bless may also curse, and she thought it would help. And it did, for Isbel said that the sight of that poppet was enough, and that the man dissolved into the night and never troubled her again. I know you cannot imagine such desperation as Catherine and Isbel felt . . .'

It is as if a hole had opened up in the pebbles on the beach and I was being sucked down into it, with the sea flooding over my head, drowning me. My hands are shaking so much I can barely hold my mug.

'I do understand. More than you could know.' The words that come out are not what I intend. It is as if something takes me over. 'For so many years I have wished her ill but she was trying to do good . . .'

'Who?'

'Mistress Gardner. All these years I have cursed her, and now she is accused of witchcraft.' I look up at Rose. 'But once she tried to help me too.' I cannot go on. I am too stricken with guilt.

Rose sees my plight for she leans forward and takes my hand.

'Mary . . .' I look up into her pale eyes through my tears. 'What I have told you this night is the truth. I had nothing to do with it, I swear to you on all that is holy. Alice did wrong, I know, but for the right reasons. I have told you of this because I trust you, because I think you deserve the truth, but in doing so I am endangering myself. I am in your hands now, you must do as you see fit.' She squeezes my fingers and sits back. 'I know for a godly woman, such as yourself, these things must be hard to comprehend, but now you have had the whole of it. Alice Gardner did a kindness for someone, and is now seized for a witch. I too could be seized for knowing of this, but that is in your hands. I promise you that the poppet was made for the right reason, to do good, not ill. To save a child from further harm.'

The fire crackles and flares and I glance behind me, but nothing is there. We could be two friends, spending an evening quietly together, but something between us has shifted and we both feel it. I have been so certain of the righteousness of what is being done in this Town, and the evil of the women seized, that I failed to remember how it had been before. How the old ways were relied on, trusted, for generations, until men came and made it a sin. We used to worship in churches that were painted and decorated, so that all could see and understand the word of God; His word was once brought to us by a priest who was sent by Him to watch over us. There were robes, incense, prayers, and Saint's days. Celebrations of harvest and springtime, Christmas and the Twelve Days. But all that has gone, men are allowed to read the word of God for themselves now, and this has raised them up, good and bad. I have been convinced that Satan was in our midst, that to invite the Witchfinder here was necessary to bring the Town back to godliness. I thought Master Hopkins to be a wise man, that his methods were fair. I have been blinded. But Rose's revelation has undone all that.

'Thank you for trusting me, for making me see.' I squeeze her hand.

'And you, for trusting me.' She squeezes back. Her face is gentle and earnest but I hear the tremor in her voice. "And now I must go, for there is a babe who will not wait.' She smiles and stands, reaching for her cloak, then the fire flares again and she freezes, her face turning as white as a ghost. She claps her hand to her mouth and I rise, too quickly, spinning around to see what has startled her so, my chair overturning, my mug tipping.

The Witchfinder is standing, black and unsmiling, in the doorway. He says nothing, just snaps his fingers and two men appear beside him. The blood rushes from my head, the room swims into darkness before me, and I sink to the floor.

It was quick. Wordless.

When I open my eyes my cheek is pressed cold against the flagged floor and there is a roll of dust by the fallen chair. Drops of wine splatter slowly, pooling beside me. My waking thought is that I must make sure the room is cleaned properly, then I see the worn leather bag, pushed deep into a dark corner beneath the table, and terror rips through me as I remember. I feel vomit burning my throat, my stomach roils. As I reach out to the table to pull myself up I feel a hand grip my arm.

'Let me help you.' His face is concerned and it is as if he cannot feel my shaking. I feel his strength as he part-lifts me to the chair, still warm from Rose's body. My mouth shakes too much for me to speak and I cannot look at him. 'You are unhurt, Mistress? That witch did nothing to harm you?' I gaze dumbly at him. His grey eyes have the look of a serpent and I cannot tell which way he is going to strike. 'I have had my eyes on that midwife. Such women are known to be vulnerable to the enticements of Satan. Well, she will be dealt with.' He leaves go of me and I slump back into the seat. 'You were not to know. I do not blame you.' The Witchfinder pours me a mug of wine and I cannot tell him that this was Rose's mug, that mine lies empty under the upturned chair. With shaking hands I raise it to my lips and the taste is bitter on my tongue.

52. JOAN

The night has set in icy cold and full of winter, and there is no warmth to be found in the gaol, even huddled tight, even with both windows blocked by rags, so it has taken them a while to settle.

It is the footsteps Joan hears first, soft but heavy, several men. She thinks they will go past, that they are sailors returning from a late night at the inn, but the footsteps stop outside. Then, the grumbling and cursing of the gaoler, the ring of the key in the lock and a blast of air. The door is flung open and moonlight shafts the darkness.

The women are frowsy, befuddled with sleep. Dorothy Clarke and Catherine barely stir and Isbel and Sarah stay fast asleep, wrapped into each other for warmth and comfort. But Alice is awake and Joan can sense her sudden fear.

'Make room. Another one for you.' Joan starts to shift to one side, but Alice is already on her feet and, in a flash, Joan knows that she was expecting this. Alice sways like a grey grave-wraith, newly risen from the sandy soil, her arms outstretched, as the midwife falls into them.

53. MARY

I spend that night with eyes wide open, and I cannot stop trembling. I am unable to find warmth, and the terror in me ebbs and flows like the tide. Rose's admission, the realisation that I once sought the help of a cunning woman, who is now held as a witch and likely to hang, has shaken my conviction that what is being done in this Town is right and good. I think of Rose, her kindness and skill, her understanding and forgiveness, and I am undone again. For it is a miracle that I too was not seized but perhaps not so strange, for the Town still needs me. They have to go through with this thing that they have started, and I am the one employed to provide their sustenance and comfort. Important men will come to this place for the trial and Aldeburgh must be at its finest. I am a cog, a wheel on this cart, and they need me in place, steady and firm. If the Witchfinder was intending to seize me, I'm sure I would have been taken with Rose. I may still be safe. But at what cost?

I WASH AND DRESS AS IF IN A DREAM. I CLEAR THE TABLES FROM THE night before, wiping and cleaning, for it is only doing such tasks that keep me from sitting in a chair with my apron over my face and weeping. The pot-boy works in silence, but I see him glance across from time to time as if wondering what has changed in me. My hands still shake and I cannot eat but I try to hold on to the person I was.

'Mistress Howldine.' I had not heard Goody Phillips' footsteps on the stairs and I jump when she speaks. 'Are you well? I understand there was some trouble here last evening.' I do not know how much she has heard. 'Master Hopkins tells me that there was another witch seized, here in your parlour. That you seemed to be entertaining her?'

Her eyes are narrowed and I know I must tread carefully. Like her master, she is shrewd, this one, and misses little. I must be cautious.

'You are correct. The midwife returned with me after visiting the witches in the gaol. The Town had asked her to look them over and, as it was such a cold night, I invited her to sit by the fire and sup with me, as any Christian woman would, to warm us.'

'She was employed on your recommendation, was she not?'

'No, Mistress Phillips, I was asked to find a midwife as the young girl, Isbel Butts . . .'

'Witch.'

' . . . witch, was suspected of being with child, and Master Hopkins wanted someone with experience to look at her. The child had admitted to lying with the Devil and Master Hopkins was keen to find out if this was true. I had to send to Saxmundham, I had never seen her before, had no knowledge of her or where she came from. I only heard that she was skilled and well respected in that town and in Aldeburgh, and that she was willing to travel here.' I know I am speaking too much, too fast, but I am like a fly caught in a web, struggling for my freedom, before the spider can pounce. Goody Phillips looks at me – she is unsure. I hold my breath as she considers what I have said.

'Well, Mistress, she has been found out now.'

'But how is she accused? What is her crime?'

'Master Hopkins has deduced that the accused witch, Isbel

Butts, was bearing a child, fathered by the Devil, and that the midwife gave her a potion to be rid of it and that the girl, knowing this, took it and so deliberately murdered the babe.'

I go cold.

'But to do such thing is a felony . . .'

'Yes, Mistress, and if it is judged against her she will hang for it, they both will.'

'But R . . .' *(careful, careful)* '. . . the midwife, is well thought of, respected.'

'Which is why we must have proof or a confession.' My blood runs cold as my heart stops. 'And that is where I go now, Mistress. She is to be searched for witch's marks and if none are found, she will be watched.' She shoulders her pack and opens the front door of the inn. Icy air blasts round me and I am frozen to the spot.

It is dark by the time she returns although it is only three of the clock – the shortest day of the year. The inn is only half full, the weather being too cold for some to venture out, even for ale, and there is no jollity; the atmosphere is tight and subdued, and people mind their business and keep their heads down.

Goody Phillips enters by the back door to avoid their gaze, and I pause in the hallway, a dish-clout in my hands, gripping it tight to stop the trembling.

'Mistress Phillips. What news?'

She pushes back the hood of her cloak and brushes the damp from it. Pinpricks of ice melt and meld and she brings in with her the salt smell of the sea, the earthy smell of snow.

'Your friend . . .'

'No friend of mine as I explained. A midwife, a hired help only.'

'The midwife had many witch's marks that did not bleed when pricked.' I suppress a shudder. 'There will be no need to go to the expense of watching her. This proof is sufficient.'

The back door opens again and Master Hopkins stands there, banging his arms against his sides for warmth.

'I truly believe the Devil has sent this weather to hinder our work here, the cold is so great. But he is outwitted, for we have one more of his servants imprisoned now.' He turns to me 'Mistress Howldine, I trust you are recovered from the shock of last night?'

I nod.

'Yes, Sir, I think so. And Goody Phillips here has been telling me that evidence has been found on the midwife?'

'She has the signs of the Devil yes, where her familiars will suck. Teats and marks that do not bleed.'

'So what will happen to her?'

'She will be tried with the rest.' His speech is clipped and precise, his mouth snapping shut on the words. 'Mistress Phillips here will be returning home to Essex for Christ-Tide, I will leave today, my services are required elsewhere, but I return home to Manningtree to spend the day in prayer, as all Christian souls should.'

A vision of Christmases past flashes through my mind, the feasting and dancing – the inn full, the ale flowing. The day is a poor thing now, with shops and markets open and fines for anyone who celebrates, but it is the law and a godly one at that. And my soul has become too heavy for dancing.

'I will return here in January for the trial of those held. I trust you will keep them in good condition, Mistress, as you have done so far. And now they have a midwife to tend to them. The Town will be pleased to be saved any further expense, I am sure.' He laughs wryly. 'I will pack my few possessions and take my leave of you.' He bows, and Goody Phillips and I drop a deep curtsey in return, then she follows him up the stairs.

I keep my head down until they have gone. For I am thinking of the Holy Book, remembering the story of Judas Iscariot. And my promised coin feels just like thirty pieces of silver.

54. JOAN

Tears spring to Joan's eyes at the condition of the midwife when the men bring her back from the searching. Catherine clasps her hand to her mouth in horror and Alice sobs uncontrollably as she takes Rose from the gaoler and gently helps her to the straw by the window. Sarah and Isbel just stare, their eyes round.

'Are you bringing water and cloths?' Joan's voice is cracked and hard, it does not sound like hers. The time in this place is diminishing her, but the gaoler sees the look on her face and goes off to find some. He does not want trouble, not now when all is nearly done. He is frightened of her – she still has that power.

Rose is even paler than before, well, in the places you can see. For there is blood everywhere. Catherine passes over her cloak and the women make a bed for her as best they can while they wait for the gaoler's return. And all the time they wait Rose does not cry, but a single tear snakes down her temple and into her hair from her closed eyes. It seems to take an age for the water to arrive but when it does the women set to. Isbel and Sarah soak and wring out the cloths and Catherine, Alice and Joan sit her up and pull off her shift. Rose's body is blue in the freezing air, a mass of dried pinpricks, so many that they can all see the malice that has been employed. Even Dorothy Clarke senses her pain and leans forward, reaching out crabbed and skeletal fingers to hold the midwife's hand in hers.

They work silently, cleaning her face and head, washing her front and turning her gently over, working down the bony spine which pokes through pale skin. But as they get to her buttocks there is a sharp intake of breath for they are red-raw, bleeding, and between her legs blood is running. It is as if she has been whipped. Alice uses the cloth gently to remove the crusts of dried blood and Rose gasps under her touch, but she stays still. Dorothy Clarke keeps hold of her hand for comfort.

Joan reaches down to her own clothing.

'Use my underskirt. You can tear it, she will be more comfortable if you pad her.'

Alice smiles gratefully.

'Thank you. If you will not miss it?'

Joan thinks of the cold, of that small layer of warmth, but then thinks of Rose. She fumbles with the ties of her overskirt and lets it drop to the floor, then takes off the underskirt and passes it to Alice. She puts the overskirt back on and returns to her place against the back wall. Alice uses her teeth to tear a start in the fabric and then pulls it apart with a sharp rip. She makes squares with it, tears a long piece to tie them up with and, passing a clout between the midwife's legs against her wounds, she ties it around her waist. It is not enough but it will suffice.

When they are done, Rose opens her eyes and looks at the circle of frightened faces around her.

'It is I that should be tending you . . .' She smiles cautiously through thickened lips then closes her eyes and drifts into sleep. The witches sit around her, keeping vigil. The darkness thickens. It is the longest night of the year.

55. MARY

Even the gaoler seems to have softened, for when I carry the prisoners' food across the next morning I see he has taken the women some washing water. I look at him in inquiry, but he keeps his head lowered as he carries out the bowl, avoiding my gaze. The bitter wind lifts the corner of the cloth as he passes me, and I see its contents – the water is blood red.

They have tended the midwife as best they can in this place, for she looks better than I had imagined, although she does not move as I put the tray on the floor. The rest are sitting in a circle around her and all look at me with contempt.

I flush red, my face burning.

'This was not of my doing.' Suddenly it is important that they know. 'The Witchfinder overheard her speaking.'

'Did you not think of this when you invited her in. Are you sure you were not seeking a way to incriminate her as well?' Alice Gardner's voice is harsh.

'No, no, I wanted her company.'

As I speak Rose lifts her head and starts to push herself upright, pain shadowing her face.

'I am well enough.' She waves Catherine's helping hand away.

'It was not the fault of Mistress Howldine. Mary and I were talking and I spoke unwisely. I should have had a care for who may have been listening.'

Even in this she is still kind but I still seek to reassure them.

'They have gone – Goody Phillips and Master Hopkins – gone until after Christ-tide. There will be no more witches seized for now.'

'What is one more in all this?' Catherine is shaking her head. 'We are already seven and they would be hard pressed to fit more into this cell, but what would one more be?'

I watch as Joan Wade takes her hand.

'You must not speak like that, Catherine. We have been here for three months, they have done their worst to us. We must endure this now. For this is all.'

Alice Gardner sees my face.

'You have more news?'

I nod.

'You are to be tried when the year has turned. Master Hopkins is to return then, to bear witness. You are not to be taken to the Assize – your trial will be here, in Aldeburgh.' They all look up, startled, and I wonder if they thought this imprisonment was to be their lot.

'What will happen then?' A small voice croaks from the dark and I see Sarah Parker's face peering through the gloom.

The older women shush her, but she is trembling hard, so Isbel goes to her side and holds her tight, speaking softly to her.

'Whatever happens I will stay by you, for you are my friend now. I will hold your hand and we will go to meet our Lord together, if that is what they say.'

Sarah sobs loudly and thrusts her fist into her mouth.

'But I have done nothing wrong.'

Isbel strokes her shoulders in small round movements.

'Have faith in the Lord for does He not forgive sinners and bring them to His side in Heaven, where they can find eternal peace?'

I wonder at the blindness of her faith, but I do not begrudge her for it. For it calms and encircles her, encircles them all, as they reach for the bread I have brought them and slowly, resignedly, begin to eat.

THE INN IS A POOR PLACE THIS CHRIST-TIDE DAY OF 1645. BANNED IS the singing and carousing, instead time is spent in worship and prayer. The celebrations of previous years are now said to be wasteful, a remnant of the old Roman faith, and the word 'mass' is removed – the godly men have ordered that we must no longer call it Christmas but Christ-tide, and that, as no such festival is mentioned in the Bible, it is no longer to be celebrated. We are all to be sober and godly as befits good Christians at this holy time of year. And it means that my inn must stay open, as all businesses must, for the law now says that we do not even get this as a day of rest, as we have been used to.

After the morning service in the church on the hill, men trickle in to the Lion and sit down. The mood has darkened further in the Town, it did not lift when the Witchfinder left as I had thought it would. The weather outside continues bitter, ice frosting the trees, the roads glittering and slippery. The wind blows straight from the sea, whistling round the houses, and all who can keep indoors, seeking warmth and shelter. Those who do venture in here do not stay long, and the only talk is of the weather and how this is the hardest winter in living memory. Outside, a heavy sky roils low with bulbous clouds, yellow and brown, and the air smells of snow, but still it does not come, despite our prayers for it to break this raw cold that gets deep into your bones, creeps through all the layers of clothes. But I am thinking today of the women in the gaol, that it is Christ-tide, so I make a tray with fresh white bread and a little meat for them all, find some late apples, slightly wizened, but not yet rotten. And there is a piece of cheese which will go over if it is not used today so I take them this too. I will hide the costs in my ledger where I can but this is my small gift to them, to Rose. To ease my conscience.

At midday I wrap myself warm in my best cloak and, taking care on the icy ruts, walk slowly across the square to the gaol.

56. JOAN

Joan is still not sure that Rose was not betrayed to the Witchfinder, and it seems Mistress Howldine feels guilty, for she brings them proper food, such as they have not seen these past months. Fresh bread, meat, a few scrawny apples. They each take their turn now, they have little appetite, but this meal is to be savoured and they eat slowly. Dorothy has barely a tooth left in her head so they break the bread and cheese into small pieces, soak them in ale, and feed her and she chews appreciatively, her eyes closed. Sarah bites small pieces of apple off with her teeth and passes them to her, and she grunts with pleasure as the sweet sharpness touches her tongue.

The innkeeper watches them for a little while, as if she has something to say, then she turns to go, but looks back at them. Seven pairs of eyes gaze at her.

'I wish you all blessings on this Christ-tide Day.'

Alice straightens up.

'It is Christmas? Christmas Day?'

'Christ-tide. That is what we are to call it now.'

'We have been here so long?'

It is true that time has stood still in this place but Joan has watched the moon waxing and waning, seen the movement of the stars, as she did from her cottage at Slaughden, before all this, and she knows it has been months since she was brought here.

The gaoler locks the door behind the innkeeper, and they are left alone.

'Christmas.' Alice shakes her head at the knowledge. 'I never thought to spend a Christmas like this, in such filth and cold.'

Catherine leans forward, her arm round her daughter, their cheeks touching.

'Do you remember Christmas at home by the beach, Isbel? The feast we would have, the laughter.' Isbel nods and moves deeper into her mother's arms.

'My Henry caught a duck, I roasted it for us over the fire.' The words come out of Joan's mouth before she has even thought them, the memory striking from nowhere like a blade, cutting sharp and sweet. 'He was my husband for seven months, that was all, only one Christmas we had together, and we ate that duck, dripping and golden and succulent, with roots from the garden, bread and honey I had made.' Joan stops speaking, remembering the private times. How, after they had eaten their fill, they had licked the juices from each other's fingers and, when it got dark, how they had gone to their bed, and loved and loved for the sheer pleasure of it.' She closes her eyes to keep the memory in, then opens them again as Isbel speaks.

'Pa made me a sailboat.' The girl's face peers from beside her mother and Catherine's arm tightens round her. 'Wood it was, with a cloth sail and he had carved it himself, just for me.' A small smile lights her face and Joan sees the child that she was.

Catherine sighs heavily.

'One day we had, one day a year when he was at home and happy in our company, for the taverns and inns were closed, and he had to look to his wife and daughter. I made us a good meal and we sat and talked, and all was well for once.'

'Alice, what do you remember?' Joan asks her, for she has kept very silent since Rose was brought in. Alice lifts her head and Joan sees some of her old spirit return.

'When Rose lived with me we would play games and I would kill an old hen and roast it on a spit and the whole house would fill with the smell of it.' She smiles at the memory.

'You made me a doll once, of cloth, with hemp for hair and a skirt and apron and a little bonnet, do you remember?' Rose's voice is soft with the past.

'I remember. You loved that doll so much, took it everywhere.'

'I have often wondered what happened to it.' Rose looks at her fingers – it is as if she could feel the shape of it again in her hand.

'I kept it in the chest. I could not bear to part with it after you left, for it reminded me of our times together.'

Rose takes Alice's hands and squeezes them, then leans in and plants a gentle kiss on her cheek.

'You were as a mother to me, and I love you as such.'

'And now I have brought you to this.' Alice's voice cracks as her pain bursts through.

Rose hugs her close.

'No, no, we are here together and it is Christmas. We should be glad we have this time.' She looks around her 'We all should. Sarah, what of you?'

Sarah lifts her head. Her face is grimy and tears have dried salty on her cheeks but she is pretty, even now.

'We servants are always given a rest from our duties, other than to serve the family. We eat the remains of their feast for our supper and the Captain gives us all a coin and blesses us and it is a good day. We play games and we laugh.' She looks into space, smiling at the thought of it, escaped from this place for a moment. They all sit, full of memories, until a cracked voice breaks the silence.

'My father set me high upon his horse.' They all turn to look at Dorothy Clarke. She is sitting up, her face shining, the memory clear for all to see. 'I was so little, my legs stuck out and he sat me in front of him and rode out towards the heath. We trotted up the main street and everyone looked and waved at me and I felt like the Queen. And my father held on to me so tight, for fear I would fall.' She smiles beatifically then, all of a sudden, the light goes out of her again and she settles back down into the straw and it is the saddest moment clothed in happiness. They huddle back and dream of better times.

57. MARY

They did not even know it was Christmas Day. Time has so stretched and thinned that they did not know. And the shock in their faces when I told them they were to be tried in January, I do not think they had expected it. But the Town will not allow them to remain in prison forever and we cannot go on with this. People say that the coming year will mean a fresh start for Aldeburgh, that it will be cleansed and godly again, free from Satan's grasp, but I cannot let myself think about what must come before that. I go about my duties and speak little, and the pot-boy bears the brunt of my low humour as I scold and shout at him. Customers come and go and time drags heavy as the hours pass.

Two days after Christ-tide, when I lay down the tray of food on the gaol floor, Rose reaches out and clasps at my arm. I jump, pulling away in fright as I brush her hand off me, and she sits back, but her eyes hold mine.

'Mistress Howldine – Mary – I have a boon to ask of you and I beg you, for our past small friendship, to grant it.' My heart stops in my chest and I hold my breath, waiting. This cannot be a little

218 | L M WEST

thing she wants. The others sit expectant, the very air crackles. 'My midwife's bag . . .'

I remember the soft brown leather folded and hidden under the table in my parlour. It is still there, I dare not touch it. I have waited for Master Hopkins or Goody Phillips to ask for it, but they have not, so it stays out of sight in the rolls of dust, unseen.

'I cannot bring you that, it would be more than my life is worth, for I would be seen and Master Hopkins would be sure to find out . . .'

'No, no, not the bag. But something it holds. A small pocket of herbs.' She looks at me beseechingly. 'They will be needed, Mistress, for some of us,' she nods towards Isbel and Sarah, 'for what is to come. It is a tiny thing, it could be secreted in your apron.'

I shy back in horror when I realise what she is suggesting.

'I cannot do such a thing. You are all to be tried as witches under the laws of this land and I dare not interfere, for the law says you must face your reckoning in full mind and body. I cannot provide herbs for you!' I am startled at her suggestion, that she even saw fit to ask. It was dangerous enough for me to turn a blind eye to the potion she made for Isbel but this – to provide solace for condemned witches – I cannot. 'Rose, you must not ask this of me, you presume on our friendship too much and I have to look to my own safety. I will forget that you even spoke the words. Here, eat your meal, for there may not be many more of them.'

Fear makes my voice harsh and they shrink back as I walk heavily out of the gaol. I do not go straight back to the inn, but instead walk the short path through the houses to the beach. I step onto the pebbles and they crunch against my boots, grounding me, as I walk towards a pale sea. I have never known such cold. From the east wind that blows against my face to the blood that thumps through my veins, I am frozen. To be asked to do such thing, to interfere with nature, with God's work, with the laws of this country. It is against everything I have ever known, all that I have been taught. Cunning women may make spells and charms, but it was only once that I lapsed and did not keep away from such things. Since then I have read my Bible daily, and attend the church on the hill each Sunday. I listen to the sermons. I even spoke against the curate Violet, so that his poison would not infect our Town. I do not know why she would ever think I would do it.

JANUARY COMES IN AND THE COLD SHARPENS EVEN FURTHER. THE SEA-foam freezes on the beach, and the boats cannot put to sea. Ice stiffens reeds and grasses, and the marshes are an elf-land of white and silver as the Witchfinder rides back from the lowlands of Essex to Aldeburgh. Captain Johnson has not been idle. The trial is set for Wednesday, the seventh day of January. It will be the biggest thing that our Town has seen for many a year, and he wants to have it right. So Francis Bacon of Shrublands Hall, that lofty landowner, will be acting as Recorder and standing in judgment. Captain Johnson and Master Thompson, who saw the rock come down from heaven and told us the Town was cursed, are brushing off their Bailiffs robes of office. The talk in the Lion is all of a notice pinned up in the market square, seeking six men to act as guards for the trial, and they will not be short of volunteers, for the pay is a shilling each a day and all the ale they can drink, provided by myself. Rooms have been reserved for Master Hopkins, and a man has already been sent to Manningtree to fetch Goody Phillips, for she will be required to give evidence. I have taken the liberty of putting aside the small back room for her. I have ordered in meat and cheese and barrels of ale from Saxmundham, and I have even bought the pot-boy a new jacket, which makes him strut around the place like a peacock, until I catch him, and box his ears for his vanity. Yes, all is prepared as far as it can be, we just wait now for Master Hopkins. I say little to the witches as I take their meals for I am still wracked with guilt by the midwife's request.

· · ·

BUT THERE IS ONE MORE PREPARATION I MAKE. LATE ON THE NIGHT before the Witchfinder returns, I creep downstairs and sit in the parlour, watching and listening. I can hear the sea thudding on the pebbles, its endless chant soothing me. When I am certain all is silent, and I am alone, I fall to my knees and put my hands together in prayer. I thank the Lord for all that He has given me and I pray that He keeps me safe from harm. But, as I speak the words, I reach under the table and slowly, carefully, so as not to disturb the dust, pull the leather bag towards me, opening the flap with trembling fingers. The air thrums in my ears as I reach in and fumble about, my heart in my mouth. There are small pots, sharp objects, a knife and cord, bunches of herbs, and I feel around the shape of them with my fingertips, searching. Then I find it. Deep in the bottom of the bag is a tiny linen pouch. I pull it out slowly. Its surface is coarse and slubbed under my touch, about the size of my little finger, fastened with a fine cord, and I can feel leaves and seeds inside. It smells of herbs but something else too, something musty and dark, as I pull it to me. I slowly, carefully, replace the bag and then stoop and blow gently. Motes of dust settle over it and it looks as if it has never been touched. Then I sit up, reach for my workbox, take needle and thread and sew the linen pocket into the hem of my skirt.

58. JOAN

Joan knew she would not do it. She already knew that the innkeeper was all for herself, and she was surprised that Rose had even asked, she thought she would have been a better judge of character. Well, she has her answer, and so they can only sit and wait. The Howldine woman barely speaks when she brings their food and they can all see that she has drawn back from them again. Joan thought she would still feel angry, as she did when they first brought her to this place, but all the anger has left her and she finds she is only filled with a gnawing fear and a growing sadness at it all. So the women shiver and eat and use the pail when they must, and all the time they look for warmth. The cold envelopes the gaol, seeping into their bones, freezing their joints, and they push tighter together, unspeaking.

But they listen too, for there is a clattering now, a bustling outside. The sounds are changing, people are moving around, it is different. They dare not look out of the window for fear of being seen and spat at, or worse. But they know that the change is because of them, and they can only sit and wait in the dark and cold of the cell.

59. MARY

Master Hopkins clatters in to the yard on the sixth day of January, his mount slipping and sliding on the icy cobbles, his cloak splattered with mud. He drops from the saddle and calls to the yard-boy to tend his horse as he pulls off his saddlebag and strides into the inn. I am waiting for him at the door in my best apron and coif, and I smile as is expected of me, but my heart is as cold as the day.

'Welcome back, Sir. I trust all is well with you?'

'Indeed it is, Mistress, indeed it is. For it is always well to carry out Our Lord's work. Is all prepared here?'

'Yes, Sir. I have been told that Captain Johnson will be here to see you shortly, and I have prepared a good fire in the parlour for you both. Your room is ready.'

'Is Goody Phillips arrived yet? The road from Manningtree will be most icy and uncertain.'

'A man was sent yesterday to fetch her and they are expected to return shortly.'

'You have done well and I thank you. I will unpack my bags and then spend some time in prayer. You will let me know when Captain Johnson arrives.' It is not a question. I drop a curtsey in reply, all the time looking at him. He is changed again, larger, more confident and puffed up. For he is in his element now – his searching and watching are done, his prey is cornered. He waits only to pounce.

It is a while before the Captain arrives, breath smoking deep into the evening air as he removes his cloak and passes it to me as if I were his maid. I shake the ice off it and silver droplets spin through the air, wetting the floor and walls.

'Tis bitter cold, Captain.'

He looks at me, distracted, as if seeing me for the first time, and nods.

'Mistress Howldine. The Witchfinder, Master Hopkins – he has arrived?'

'Yes, Sir. Come through to the parlour and I will send the pot-boy to fetch him from his room. He is in prayer. Some wine to warm you?'

'That would be most welcome. And the witches in the gaol, are they – well?' I see he relies on me to tell him. It would have been a thing of a moment for him to go and see for himself and I wonder if this man, who is one for action and control, always in charge, is already trying to distance himself from what is to happen. Well, he is too late for that – all know it was him that started this, with his rock from heaven, and tales of hellfire and damnation, lamenting our ungodly ways. He has made enough from it too, for I have seen the pamphlet he published in London about the events of that day, and it seems that all eyes are now looking to this Town to see what will happen.

I bustle through to the kitchen for wine and mugs, and by the time I return to the parlour, Master Hopkins has come down and is making himself comfortable in a chair opposite the Captain. I step behind them and reach down for the poker, heating the jug of wine with the red-hot tip. A smell of sweet burning fills the room, as it hisses and spits and, just for a moment, the sound conjures in my head an image of the Ipswich woman, burned for her crimes, and I shudder as if a ghost has walked over my grave.

THE MEN SIP AT THEIR WINE CAREFULLY AND EXAMINE EACH OTHER under lowered lids. The Captain, tall and fair, is normally commanding, but tonight somehow seems diminished. The Witchfinder is small and dark, but in this low light, on this evening, he fills the room with his presence.

'Captain Johnson – the preparations are made?'

'They are, Master Hopkins. Recorder Bacon will arrive early tomorrow from his estate. He has made it clear that he hopes the matter will be settled in the one day, as he has important business to attend to elsewhere.'

Master Hopkins nods.

'It will not take long, Captain, for the evidence is clear. Have you arranged for men to guard the sessions in case of any disturbance as I requested?'

'You expect disturbance?' They have forgotten my presence as I step forward and refill their mugs.

The Witchfinder narrows his eyes.

'Your town will be busy, for a witch trial always brings a crowd, and it is best to be prepared. In any case, guards will add gravitas to the occasion, show the populace that such evil will not be tolerated. We must show that the full force of the law will be brought to bear on those who threaten the godliness of this place.'

Captain Johnson nods in agreement.

'The guards have also been retained for . . . afterwards.' He is hesitating, but we all know what he means, and Master Hopkins looks him full in the face.

'Captain, there is no doubt of the witches guilt. The witnesses are bound over to appear, and Mistress Phillips and I will be there to give evidence of all that we saw and heard. The prisoners are all guilty, every last one of them, we have obtained either proof or a confession, and it is merely for the jury to provide a favourable verdict. And if they do – when they do – the witches will be punished.'

The Captain looks down at his boots, and I stand and stare at the pair of them, discussing the taking of lives so simply. Thomas Johnson is a military man, used to death, but this is not a war; these women cannot fight back, and I wonder at how he is able to sit there so calm. A candle gutters and Master Hopkins' face is suddenly bathed in firelight, red and quivering, as if lit by the flames of Hell itself, and I see that his expression is one of power, of satisfaction at a job well done – and of pleasure. Yes, he is taking pleasure in this. Gone is the gleam of zealousness, of the desire to carry out God's word, that was there when I first set eyes on him. Money and pleasure have overtaken this. In a few short months he has become a little man made big by power.

And all know such men are dangerous.

60. JOAN

It is Isbel who puts a voice to it. She has stopped her incessant muttering and bible-ing that drove Joan mad in the early days, it has been sucked out of her by these months of imprisonment, but she still carries the light of God in her eyes, still prays at the drop of a hat and Joan hopes now only that her faith will sustain her.

'What are they going to do to us?'

Alice Gardner looks up. She is another changed by this, as if the seizing of Rose has taken her soul. She seemed strong and brave, so full of courage when she came here, and Joan feels sorrow to see her brought so low. But they are all low in this place, and set to go lower.

'They will try us, child. There will be a judge, a jury of men who will hear all who speak against us. They will listen and they will decide whether we are guilty.' It sounds a simple thing as she tells it, of little import, but it is a heavy thing, the only thing, and they all dread it.

'And what will happen then?'

Catherine's voice is shaking and sharp as she holds her daughter to her.

'Hush, child, do not think on such things. God will judge us and no one else.'

Then a voice, croaking and harsh, from the corner of the room. Dorothy Clarke, her wits gone more often than not, chooses this moment to be a part of them.

'They will hang us, girl. That's what they want, and that is what they will have.'

Isbel drops to her knees.

'And I will meet my Maker, at last, and be in his presence. The Lord is my Shepherd . . .' Her eyes are lit, her face shines, but her words are drowned by a sound from Sarah Parker, whose mouth slowly shapes into a square. Her eyes close and a noise, that starts as a gurgle, rises to a piercing scream which sears through them, on and on, until they think their heads will burst.

61. MARY

I t is the gaoler that alerts me, for I am busy trying to get the last customers to go home to their beds. He leaves his post and runs across the square to the Lion, hammering on the front door. At first I think he is a sailor, trying for a late drink, so I ignore the noise, but then I hear my name called. I slide the bolts back and open the door a fraction. The gaoler stands there, puffing and blowing.

'Mistress, you need to come.'

In the distance I can hear screaming, as if people are being murdered in their beds.

'What is it? Why are you here and not calling the constables?'

'It is the witches, Mistress. One screams and screams and will not be quiet. I thought that you . . .'

'Very well.' I reach for my heavy cloak, sighing, and step out into the frosty air – it feels as if the very weight of the skies pushes down on us.

'Quick, Mistress, she must be made to stop, before she wakes the Town.' I follow him as fast as I can after a busy day on my feet, tiredness dogging my every footstep. I wish only to be in my bed, far away from this, sleeping in peace.

We reach the gaol and he unlocks the door and the shrieking scorches through me.

'SILENCE! BE QUIET!' I use my best innkeeper's voice and it seems to take them by surprise, as the little serving-maid stops her noise and drops her head to her hands, sobbing loudly. 'You must be silent. It is late, the Town sleeps.'

She looks up at me with white, tear-streaked face, and I wonder how a girl can be so pretty even with red swollen eyes and a streaming nose. For a moment I am envious, and then I remember why she is here, who I am, and the envy melts away.

Sarah's voice is wobbling and hoarse.

'They are going to hang us. I cannot do it. Let me go back, let me return to the house, and I will do all that Master Francis bids, I will do anything he wants, just . . . just let me live.'

Tears stream down her cheeks and Isbel moves to her side and takes her hand.

'But, Sarah, in death you will be received unto the Lord, taken into His presence, bathed in His light. Is that not a glorious thing?'

Sarah pulls her body away and looks at Isbel. They have been so close but this thing looms large between them.

'Do you not want to live, Isbel? To run free on the beach, feel the wind in your hair. Hear the seabirds, the foam crashing, the rack of the pebbles? To go home?'

Isbel's face falls.

'No, not home. Bad things are there – the man in black . . .' We watch in pity as she begins to rock from side to side, hugging herself, and I see she has gone back as she was before. Catherine tries to hold her, but she pulls sharply away and, to my dismay, starts to moan.

'Bad girl, evil girl, you must be cleansed for the Devil has taken you . . .'

Sarah watches in horror as her friend disappears and becomes a damaged child again.

Rose moves forward and takes Sarah gently by the shoulders.

'You must listen to me. Isbel has been harmed, and this is what she does to hide herself. You did not see her before, for you were not taken then, but she has been badly hurt, and this is what happens to her when she remembers that hurt. Your screaming has taken her back to a bad place, and she thinks she must hide away, inside herself. Do you understand?' Sarah nods. 'She needs quiet. She needs help. You must stop screaming.' Then Rose turns to me, the question hanging in the air unspoken, and the packet of herbs in my skirt hem sits heavy in the dark.

I LOOK AROUND THE CELL AS IT FALLS SILENT. ALICE GARDNER AND Rose move together and sit with heads lowered, as do Catherine and Isbel, who is still rocking, but less so. No one speaks. The midwife's words seem to have calmed Sarah a little, but I can see she is on the edge of madness, that it will not take much to tip her over, and that Rose continues to hold her hand to keep her steady. Dorothy Clarke lies on the straw looking at me through her one unclouded eye and it is hard to tell if she is in her wits or not, for she just mumbles and sucks at her thumb.

It is Joan Wade who gazes at me, her black eyes glistening, as if she knows what I carry, as if she can see inside my very soul. It is uncanny, and I feel naked and exposed under her stare, as her eyes slide down from my face, over my cloak, to where my boots peek out under the dusty bottom of my skirts.

'Mistress Howldine?'

She knows. I cannot tell how, but she knows. The linen packet seems to crackle and thrum, I can feel its presence weighing me down, and I know it is she doing something. She is making me choose.

Then I feel it. It is as if her hands have grasped mine, moving them to part my cloak, reach down, and pick up the hem of my skirt. It is she, not I, that makes me bite the stitches in the hem loose with my teeth, she that causes me to tear the seam apart with shaking fingers and pull out the linen packet. My hands are trembling as I feel its roughness, every warp and weft of its making, the cord encasing it twisted and fine, feel the dry crispness of the leaves through it, the hard roundness of seeds. It is she, Joan Wade, that makes me lean forward and silently pass the packet to Rose, who stuffs it into her bodice with a brisk nod.

And when it is done the old woman sits back with a sigh, as if exhausted. And, as her power leaves me shaking and cold, I know I have been touched by witchcraft.

62. JOAN

Joan had known the innkeeper would take the packet in the end, for she can see such things, always has been able to. She knew she wouldn't be able to resist looking in the midwife's bag, knew also that her conscience would tell her that such things were wrong, that she would be no better than them if she were to help. She saw her fear, and understood it, for they all felt it, and the fear of being accused is sharper and more bitter than most.

Joan's own fear had faded into a dull throb during the months of imprisonment, but now she does not care. She no longer needs to hide the sight and the powers she has always had, for she has already confessed her guilt. To do such a thing before was to prove that she is as they accuse her, but she has nothing left to lose now. Those two young girls, they are the ones who need help, for their terror is great. Sarah, with her flowing hair and rounding body, who has tried to be good, despite the presence of men who wish her ill. She should have been allowed to live her life, to be loved by someone good, to marry, live out her days. There were babies waiting to be born. But the word of one man, privileged and proud, has ruined her without cause. For Joan has looked into the future and cannot see a life for her beyond this winter. Her chord is to be cut soon.

And Isbel – poor, sad little Isbel, who is certain that death will redeem her, who believes that the Devil came to her; another child abused by the very person she should have been able to trust, her own father. A godly man they say, church-loving, inn-hating. Pah! Joan knows that behind such godliness can lie wickedness and foul abuses. Isbel is not the first, she will not be the last, but the girl is not strong and her abuse has caused her mind to weaken and fly, like a butterfly rising from a summer flower.

For the two girls she did it. For the children she never had, for the husband that was taken after such a short time. For all those who had felt the sharp end of her tongue when they reviled and despised her for being old and poor, called her witch, hag.

Her efforts have caused Joan's fear to return now and it is great, but at least she has done some good, in this, the darkest of times. It has exhausted her, such concentration. But she had to do it. And she is glad.

63. MARY

I wake the next morning after a fitful sleep. For a moment there is quiet, my mind is still and all is well, and then fear floods through me like a storm surge. For today is the day of the trial. The inn will be full, the Town packed, and all day I will be busy and rushed and hot. But inside I am still frozen. For I have been touched by the hand of a witch and I am full of fear. So I will stay in my inn and work hard and push the women from my mind.

IT IS MASTER HOPKINS WHO CHANGES IT. I THOUGHT I WOULD BE able to stay here and see to my customers, but he has other plans. When I take him his bread and meat to break his fast he tells me I am needed to attend the court. That he may require me to speak.

'Sir, I had not thought . . .'

'Mistress Howldine, you have visited the prisoners on a daily basis since August, you have seen how they are. If any witness should falter, or the jury seems disinclined to believe certain testimonies, it would be most valuable to know that you were there, that I could call upon you to bear witness as to the prisoners foul persons, their evil words and deeds. After all, you were with the

Captain when the first witch was seized and you helped search the house of another, did you not?'

'I was, Sir, I did, but I do not think . . .'

'Mistress, your presence is required.'

His eyes are darkening now, I must take care.

'I think only of the inn, Sir, of my business, nothing more. For the custom will be great today and I should be here to see all is as it should be.'

'You have employed more helpers though?'

'I have, that is true, but I cannot trust . . .'

Master Hopkins smiles his snake-smile.

'Then the matter is settled. And, remember, you will be able to run your inn as it should be, for the hangings.' My eyes widen. Surely the trial would not demand such a thing. I had imagined imprisonment, hoped it would be elsewhere, so our Town could go back to how it was. He sees my horror.

'Did you not realise, Mistress? I will be asking for any who are judged guilty to face the full force of the law of this country, for how else will we be rid of the horror of witchcraft? And a town fills for a hanging.'

THE SUN HAS BARELY RISEN AS I CROSS THE SQUARE TO THE courthouse, my cloak flapping, my steps slow and reluctant. I make myself think of the inn, of how well it will run with me absent, but my thoughts keep being torn to what is to happen today, how it will be. I follow others up the stone steps and move inside.

The room is transformed. Benches have been arranged on three sides, and an ornate carved chair with a cushion has been placed in the centre, against the far wall. Candle-flames gutter and sway in the draught from the open door, and the leaded windows are pulled tight shut against the bitter wind which howls outside. Men are assembling, great men, ones I have only ever seen in church on Sundays. Amongst them are the Bence brothers, wealthy landowners who seem to hold this side of Suffolk in their thin white palms. I should not be surprised, for nothing passes here which they do not know about. I recognise their lawyer, a man with fingers in many pies. They are all well-to-do aristocracy, the eminent of Aldeburgh. They have never known poverty or hunger, fear or hatred. You can see that in their gloved hands, their long white faces that have not seen a days labour in the sun, their white collars that some maid somewhere has scrubbed and bleached with her hands cracked from the lime and her back aching from stooping over the wash-tub. Twelve good men, here to act as jury.

As I step into the room a constable moves forward, holding up his hand to stop me.

'Mistress Howldine – the public are not yet admitted to the hearing, you must wait outside.' I know him, he is often in my inn and usually the worse for drink.

'You know full well that I am not the public. I am here on the instructions of Master Hopkins to act as witness. Where should I sit?' He looks at me intently then nods.

'My apologies, Mistress. Of course, please sit here, the other witnesses are expected.' He bows to me and I think he is best not to overdo it, for the occasion has clearly taken him up. He is not normally this polite. I sit on the bench to the left of the door, as close to the window as I can, hoping not to be noticed.

There is the rumble of many footsteps now. More men troop into the room and are shown to their seats, as befits their status. The man who accused Joan Wade. Behind him comes Master Butts, husband and father, abuser turned accuser. A sailor I recognise, but do not know the name of, sits beside me, woollen cap in hand, turning it between his fingers. A stranger lowers himself onto the bench next to him, eyes fixed ahead.

The sailor nudges me.

'Mistress Howldine, I had not thought to see you here, what

with the Town being so busy.' His voice is a coarse whisper, I can barely hear him above the throng.

'I had not thought to be here, but I am summoned to attend as a possible witness. What is your business in this place?'

He shrugs.

'Witness, like you. The wife bought a potion from the hedge-witch for our son, but he died, and now we are sure it must have been her doing. All we wanted was to ease his pain, for he was creased up with it in one side. The Gardner woman told us that her herbs would help, but that she could not be sure of the outcome. He died in such agony, Mistress, screaming and crying fit to tear your heart out. The wife said the herbs had helped, that our boy was lost to us anyway, but now there is all this talk of witchcraft, we think that it must have been the Devil's work. See him?' He nods at a man seated on the bench next to us. 'He's the one who accused the Dunwich witch, here to give his evidence. The one next to him accused the first one, that they brought in from Slaughden. And that there is Martin Butts.' He nods again. 'He has accused his own wife and daughter, I hear.' His eyes are rounded in horror and I open my mouth to reply but then there is all commotion, a hammering of wooden staves on the floor and the bailiffs enter. Master Thompson and Captain Johnson, their black, lace-edged robes of office padded with fur, that the Town had paid highly for some years ago, spruced and immaculate, heads held high, faces fixed and solemn. And behind them the Recorder, Francis Bacon of Shrubland Hall. There is more power and money in this room than has even been seen in this Town and we bow before it as the room quietens in respect and awe.

Below us, in the gaol, a scream is quickly stifled.

64. JOAN

They can hear the noise going on in the courtroom above, boots clattering, shoes pattering. Benches scrape and crash, and the sound of many voices rattles through the silence. The boards overhead bend and creak, and dust floats down through the air to settle on them.

Isbel clutches her hands to her ears. They are not used to such a sound, it has been quiet until now, only the everyday noises of the market square outside, people coming and going, carts rolling, dogs barking. The honking of geese on market days, the braying of cattle. Natural sounds, such as they are used to, living as they do in the deepest countryside. Sounds that die down as the daylight fades into a star-lit black that they can no longer see. But this is different, a mass of sound, harsh and loud. It is man-made and all they can do is look at each other, unspeaking, eyes wide, shaking.

It is here.

65. MARY

From our benches we listen as they bring the prisoners up from the gaol below. The clatter of the guards, the clash of their staves; the murmur of the crowd outside in the square which rises to a pitch, then shouts, catcalls, the screams of women, the howling of men. All in the courtroom sit silent and expectant as the noise outside intensifies. Then, a thumping, a shuffling of feet, and they are here.

I cannot believe how they look. Their clothes are grime-laden, like shrouds hanging off their wasted bodies, and the smell of them causes kerchiefs to be raised to mouths, nosegays crushed between shaking fingers, so a summer smell of lavender and sage mingles ineffectively with the stench of shit and filth that fills the room as they move slowly to the front. I shudder, for I had thought they would look better than this, I had made sure they had water to wash, food and drink, as I was instructed. They are chained together with iron shackles that weigh them down, forming them into a grey cloud of bodies, barely human. The room fills with whispers and the constable bangs his stave on the floor for order.

Master Bacon rises, straightening red robes over bony shoulders. His face is narrow and sharp with a fierce intelligence. He is not one to be dabbled with as he brings his gavel hard down on the polished oak table before him.

'Clerk, read the indictment.'

A young man to his left rises, his black gown shaking as he steadies the parchment clutched in his hand, peers down at the document held before him, and starts to read. The words are unintelligible and I see the women raise their heads in confusion, and then I realise – it is a legal document. It is in Latin.

THE CLERK DRONES ON, HIS VOICE BUZZING LIKE A BEE CIRCLING A flower, and my mind drifts. Then, words I can understand.

'*The Kings sworn officers maintain upon their oaths that Joan Wade, widow; Catherine Butts, net-maker; Isbel Butts, net-maker; Alice Gardner, widow; Sarah Parker, maidservant, all of Aldeburgh; Rose Gardner, midwife, of Saxmundham; Dorothy Clarke, widow, of Dunwich, all in the County of Suffolk, in the twenty-first year of the reign of our lord Charles, by the grace of God Kind of England, Scotland, France and Ireland . . .*' I cannot pull my eyes from the women, who are looking around in confusion. '. . . *being common witches and enchantresses, not having God before their eyes, but moved and seduced by devilish instigation . . .*' Dorothy Clarke is mumbling and dribbling as Joan Wade supports her. Catherine holds tight to Isbel and they both grip Sarah, who is shaking so hard I fear she will fall. '. . . *at the aforesaid Aldeburgh in the aforesaid county, wickedly, devilishly, feloniously, willingly and from malice aforethought did imploy divers evils and wicked spirits . . .*' Alice Gardner and Rose stand slightly apart, their heads held high, their faces blank, but I watch how their fingers touch now and again, and I can sense them drawing courage from each other. '. . . *used, practised and exercised certain evil and devilish crafts called witchcrafts, charms, enchantments and sorceries on Thomas Lamb, cow-man, Martin Butts, fisherman, Thomas Spatchett, yeoman, Francis Johnson, landowner, and Isbel Butts, accused, against the peace of the said lord King, his crown and dignity, and contrary to the form of the statute lately issued and provided in this regard.'*

The clerk stops and the room is so quiet that the only sound is of the boom and hiss of the sea, forcing the shingle back and forth on the beach. He sits down and picks up his pen, pulls a paper towards him, and look expectantly at Master Bacon.

'Prisoners in the Court, how do you plead?' The Recorder's voice is deep and full of authority. The women look startled, glancing at each other. For a moment none speak. Then . . .

'Not guilty.' Rose's voice is low and clear. The others gain confidence from her and mumbles of 'Not guilty' echo around the room.

All but Isbel. Her eyes are blank, I can see that, but she pulls herself up, her face lit, and steps forward.

'Guilty. I am guilty. For I am full of sin and deserve to be punished.'

Catherine stifles a sob with her hand and the women close in together as if to stop her falling.

'Clerk – note six pleas of not guilty, one of guilty.' The clerk bends his head over his parchment and the sound of his scribbling scratches into the silence.

'Call the first witness.' The clerk looks into the room and the men on the bench stir. I sit like a statue on a tomb, cold, frozen in time.

'Call Thomas Lamb.' The man rises and moves to the space at the front, not looking at the Recorder, but twisting his greasy wool cap in his hands ceaselessly. The Recorder gazes down his long nose as if something unpleasant was beneath it.

'Master Lamb. Your occupation?'

'A dairyman, Sir.'

'You are here to bear witness to an act of witchcraft? Well, speak, man, whom do you accuse?' The Recorder is impatient, clearly keen to do his duty and leave.

The man before him peers at the tight mass of women before him and his brow creases. He sniffs and wipes a dribbling nose on his sleeve, then spits onto the floor and I see Master Bacon's nose wrinkle in distaste.

'I can't quite be sure, Sir . . . they all look the same.' The Recorder looks to the back of the room, frustration written on his face.

'Constables, remove the chains from the accused and put them in a line.' Two constables rush forward and a key is produced. Together they pull the heavy iron chain back through the hoops in the shackles so the women stand free, rubbing their wrists and moving their shoulders to ease them, standing a little taller now some of the weight has been lifted from them. The constables push and prod them into a semblance of a line and then stand at either end, staves at the ready, for any signs of trouble.

Master Lamb peers at the group again and recognition dawns in his eyes. He raises a grimy hand and points.

'That one there – Widow Wade. She bewitched my cow so her milk dried, an' later she fell sick an' died. An' she cursed me too, an' I fell ill an' thought also to die, such was the strength of it.' He seems to have sprung tears to his eyes. I had not thought him to be of a sentimental nature. I always found him to be a careless and conniving man, oft in my inn, oft evicted for his coarse words and nature.

The sailor sitting next to me leans into my ear, his breath hot and stale.

'We have her now. She cannot deny this.'

I do not know why I reply.

'I hear the beast was poorly treated.'

'That's as maybe, but it was bewitched, sure as eggs are eggs. For it was tethered on the common this summer past and no harm befell it afore she came near.'

'But the summer was dry, the common turned to dust. Could the cow not have starved?' As soon as the words leave my lips I realise my mistake, for the sailor looks at me and scowls.

'Surely you do not defend a witch, Mistress?'

'No, not at all, I was merely thinking . . .'

'Best not to think too hard, Mistress, not these days, for fear your thoughts are heard.' He edges away from me, watching as Master Lamb sits, then fixes his eyes on the red robes of the Recorder. I sit, still as the grave, in my corner, whilst all the time my leg jolts under my skirts in fear.

'Next.' The Recorder is abrupt, growing angry. The stranger rises and moves forward. 'Name?'

'Thomas Spatchett of Dunwich, Sir.'

'Occupation?'

'Yeoman, Sir and member of. . .' The Recorder cuts him short.

'And which one do you accuse?'

'Her, there, at the end. The Clarke witch. That one.' The man is puffed up with pride now his moment has come.

'And what did you see, Master Spatchett.'

'She was begging, see, coming from door to door muttering and cursing. Her eye is crooked, marked by the Devil like as not. Well, she is always wanting something, saying she is hungry, moaning on at her fate, has been for years, so this time I refused. She banged on my door and asked for a cup of clean water or a crust of bread and, I tell you, she was stinking and foul, and I had had enough of her. So I said no. Then she looked at me with her good eye and a chill went right through me and I wanted rid of her quick, so Brandy . . .'

'Brandy?'

'My dog, Sir. I was holding him close as I had thought it was a murderer or worse, hammering like that on my door, so I let him loose and he went for her. Ran like the very devil, she did, not much wrong with her then.' He snorts with laughter and rubs his nose. 'Well, when she got to the lane she turned. The dog couldn't reach her there, his rope wasn't long enough. She saw it, turned and waved her fist at me, and shouted such profanities that I was shocked, Sir. Then she said, and it's as clear as a bell still, she said "It's not only that dog that will be halted soon." And she went.'

'And? What happened, man?' The Recorder is clearly in no mood for such a lengthy tale and his face is stony.

'Well, twas but two days later that I fell to the floor, Sir, with a pain in my head such as I could not bear, tormenting me something shocking. I managed to get to my chair but I could barely sit, the pain was so great. And when I glanced over at the fire I saw a black imp looking up at me. His eyes were red as coals and he was laughing. He was not of this world, Sir, and I know it was her that sent him, to punish me for not giving her aid. Sir, I have some little experience in matters of witchcraft and I know what I saw. She is as guilty as the others.' He deflates a little, his words done, and looks again at the cap in his hands as if surprised to see it there.

'Very well, you may sit.' The Recorder nods at the clerk. 'Note – imp.'

Then Master Hopkins stands.

66. JOAN

The women huddle together, secured in their irons and chains, as if the men think they will be able to conjure a devil and fly away from this place. It took a while to get them all up here, as Dorothy Clarke had refused to move. The guards had to push and shove her up the steps, but now she is here she is calmed. That or terrified, it's hard to tell the difference. Joan knows how they must look, for in the daylight, as their eyes clear, they can see their clothes are black and filthy, their faces streaked with grime. Pomanders go to noses, hands are put to mouths, as the good and the great of Aldeburgh look in horror at what stands before them. Joan is faint with fear and she can feel the others shaking, they are so close that the vibration runs through them all, joining them together.

Then the man who accused her stood up. All she had asked for was a cup of milk, for she had not eaten for two days and she thought he would not miss it. At first he does not know her and hope threads her heart, but then the constables come and take the chains off. The iron is still heavy and bites at her wrists but it is easier to stand with the weight of the chain gone, a relief.

Then he points straight at her, tells some tale about how she ill-wished his cow. He lays it on thick and she can see they believe him. Then he sits back down and the next one stands up. Joan does not know him but Dorothy stiffens beside her, her face dropping in fright. Joan reaches for her hand and squeezes it and Dorothy knows she is there, for she squeezes back. This one is full of himself, goes on and on, and Joan can see the judge getting cross, as he keeps shuffling and clearing his throat, but then he tells the man to sit back down and she thinks it is all over. She takes a deep breath and her shoulders drop, loosed of their tension.

But her heart stops as the Witchfinder steps forward.

67. MARY

The Recorder stiffens as Master Hopkins rises from his seat, but he waves him forward.

'Master Hopkins?'

'May I suggest something, Sir, to speed these proceedings?' Master Bacon scowls but nods. 'I and my search-woman can bear witness, for we obtained confessions from most of the accused and saw imps and familiars come to the others. Your time is valuable . . .' The Recorder softens – another one fond of flattery it seems. '. . . so, with respect, could I suggest that I provide evidence of their crimes, with Mistress Phillips' assistance? It may help events along and be clearer. But I bow to your learned opinion.' He bends low, sweeping off his hat in deference, and I can see the Recorder considering. The sailor next to me huffs in disapproval as his moment of glory disappears like a sea-fret, and the room shuffles and whispers.

Then Master Bacon bangs his gavel on the table for silence.

'Very well. Master Hopkins, please state the accusations against the next prisoner and tell this court of your evidence.' The Witchfinder stands tall in his heeled boots, replacing his high black capotain hat as he moves to the front of the court. His eyes are shining and his presence fills the room and suddenly I can see why he was chosen for this job, why people flock to him, and why towns such as ours employ him. He commands the courtroom. He is like a fish in water here – this is his natural world. He opens the black book in his hand and begins to speak.

'I was invited to Aldeburgh by the Burgesses and Bailiffs to seek out witches in their midst. They had seized one already in gaol, the one that Master Lamb has already given evidence against.' I see Master Lamb from the corner of my eye – he is preening himself at the mention of his name. 'Widow Wade, of Slaughden. She had confessed nothing, so she was searched by Mistress Phillips here.' He stretches out his hand to the search-woman and I see it is still. He does not shake as I do, but is calm and assured. Goody Phillips is all efficiency, nodding in acknowledgment. 'As you know, Sir, the procedure is to search the bodies of any accused and then, if no witches marks are found, to watch them and see if their imps and familiars come to them, as they often do. No such marks were found on the Wade woman, and she still refused to admit her crimes. I prefer to have proof or a confession, for it would be wrong to falsely accuse some poor woman of such a terrible crime were it not warranted.'

He pauses and looks around him. He holds the room in the palm of his hand and even the Recorder is transfixed. I watched the King's Players when they came to this Town, saw their performances and it comes to me that he is as skilled as they, for he makes the unreal seem real.

'I also seized Mistress Butts, and Isbel her daughter. They were both accused by Master Butts of serving the Devil and, under my questioning, the girl freely confessed to her sins. I felt there was no need to examine her further, given her tender years and the fact that she had admitted her crimes. She told us that her mother had procured for her a poppet . . .' He hisses the word through clenched teeth as if the very saying of it would defile him. '. . . made by another of the other accused witches, Widow Gardner. The girl

Isbel also said that the Devil had visited her in her chamber and used her for his pleasure.'

The men sit up as one at this and look expectant.

Master Bacon holds up his hand.

'Master Hopkins, let me be clear, this girl claims to have lain with the Devil?'

'Yes, Sir, I have her full confession.'

'And how do we know that it was Satan? How did she describe the deed?'

The Witchfinder turns to his notebook, flicking through sheets of paper.

'Ah, here it is. Isbel Butts confessed to me that *"he used me, Sir, most cruelly, not just once but other times too, that he was cold, that his"* . . . I beg your pardon, Sir, for the profanity . . . *"his yard was icy cold. It hurt me and I burned and his seed was cold too."* She said that she had taken the Devil to her bed numerous times and there she did his bidding.'

The room is hushed but eyes narrow and glitter. I can see heat and lust on the faces of many and I turn away in disgust, lowering my eyes to my hands which tremble fast in my lap.

The room quietens as Master Hopkins continues.

'As we had the evidence of the girl, Isbel, I had the mother searched, and she confessed quickly and freely. I fear she was also instrumental in causing the death of her husband's mother but, sadly, I could find no evidence of this, and the girl denies it, says she died of natural causes. I think otherwise.'

The Recorder turns to Mistress Phillips.

'And you witnessed this confession?'

Goody Phillips curtseys deeply.

'I did, Sir, as God is my witness. I also fear that others have suffered at the hands of these witches.'

'Very well, Mistress Phillips, you may return to your seat. Master Hopkins, continue.'

'The very next day we sent out a party to seize this Widow

Gardner, the one accused by Isbel Butts. She was taken after some struggle.'

'And was any poppet found?'

'No, Sir, despite a thorough search of her house and garden, and so I felt it appropriate to have her searched. Mistress Phillips was again on hand to do this.' The Witchfinder clicks his fingers and Goody Philips rises to her feet, smoothing her skirts, then looks up at the Recorder.

'What form did this searching take, Mistress?'

Goody Philips clears her throat. Like her master, she is confident and assured.

'She was stripped, Sir, to her shift. I pricked her all over with my bodkin, in an effort to find those places that a witch has that do not bleed. She was a hard one and I had to prick her many times. But each time she bled and I could find no teats or wens on her that were in the form of witches marks.'

'And you were thorough?'

'Oh, yes, Sir, as I always am. I searched every inch of her, even her private parts and her fundament . . .' Master Bacon holds up his hand, his mouth crinkled in distaste.

'Enough, Mistress. I am satisfied you carried out your work correctly.' The men's eyes still shine. I feel sick unto my stomach and breathe in deeply to calm myself.

The Recorder turns back to Master Hopkins who moves again to the centre of the room, lifting his book as he continues.

'As we had no confessions I had Widow Gardner watched, along with Widow Wade. And I, and the men who watched with me, all saw an imp appear. It was in the shape of a mouse, but one not of this world. It went to Gardner in a most familiar way, but then, just as we were about to see the imp suckle from her, Wade confessed. We had all seen the imp go to Gardner so I took this to be God's sign that she was indeed a witch and that no further confession was necessary. Having noted the details of Wade's confession, both prisoners were returned to the gaol. And there they stayed, Sir, awaiting trial, and I was asked by Captain Johnson to return, as the Town felt there may be further witches in their midst. So return I did, just before Christ-Tide. And they were right, there were more.'

I sit, stilled with horror. There is no mention of the long weeks the women were imprisoned, the cold and hardship they endured. The Recorder does not know how they were confined, how little they were fed. He was not there on the day when they were brought forth to be cleaned off, in the bitter cold, so that no one would see how badly they had been treated. He knows much but he is not being told the whole of it.

The Witchfinder clears his throat and continues.

'I returned to Aldeburgh on the twelfth day of December to find that another witch had been sent by cart from Dunwich, Widow Clarke. As you have already heard, she was accused of sending an imp to a neighbour to harm him. I also questioned a servant girl, who had been employed by Captain Johnson himself, who was accused of bewitching an innocent man, of causing him to be unable to lie with his wife in the normal manner. Neither confessed. The old woman does not always have her wits about her – I suspect her of being able to change them at will – and so I had them both searched. The servant confessed quickly but the old one said nothing, and so she was watched. At the watching, the men and I all saw a large black beetle go to her and climb up her leg and suck her blood. Proof indeed. So I have all the evidence required, seen with my own eyes, noted in my own hand.'

The Recorder looks up.

'And this is all?'

'No, Sir, not all. Then there is the midwife.'

68. JOAN

It is so fast. The women deny their guilt, knowing it will not make a difference, although Isbel confesses, so maybe she will be spared. But Joan can tell there is little point in this trial, for their guilt has already been decided, it just has to be justified before the court.

So fast. The words they speak, the evidence they have, it all washes over her like a tide. Master Hopkins speaks for all, and his word is law it seems. Joan sees how this Town has fallen under his spell, and thinks that this makes him as much witch as they are. For all have skills, knowledge, it is just that some choose not to use them. It is the way people are made, in God's image, for did Our Lord not also have the power to heal, to change water into wine, to bring back the dead? Who is to say that was not witchcraft? She doesn't not understand why the small things they have done are different.

She tries to listen as Hopkins goes through it, pretending that all he and his search-woman did to them was good and right. The men sit up straight, hanging on his every word. He has them, she can see it; she watches as their faces light up when he peppers his speech with the sort of detail godly men should not put their minds to. But Joan knows that men are men regardless of their robes and station in life. They are the hunters, and women such as her, their prey.

It is all over in minutes. But then he speaks of Rose.

69. MARY

My blood runs cold. I made a promise to protect Rose, for I thought that she was an innocent in this, a midwife carrying out her role within the bounds of the law. But, although it was her own words that betrayed her, I wish I had the courage to speak up for her. And now I am helpless in the face of it, the fear for myself too great.

Master Hopkins pauses only to cough rapidly into a white kerchief. As he brings it away from his mouth I can see the spatters of red.

'Master Recorder, we have found that this midwife was brought up by another witch.' He pauses and points a thin finger at Alice, and his nails are clean and shaped. 'We have no knowledge of her true parents. The accused has plied her trade for these past ten years in the surrounding area, but I believe her to have been corrupted in her youth by the woman she calls mother, Alice Gardner, who stands here before you accused of making a poppet and other foul devices. It is known that such witches will lure and seduce their offspring into the ways of Satan, by kind words and favours, teaching them to glory in his power.'

I glance around the room. The men sit alert and eager, waiting for the details, while Rose stands tall and proud, her face pale, her eyes full of sadness, as she holds on to Alice's hand.

Master Hopkins coughs heavily again and I can see how much it troubles him now, for his chest heaves with the effort but, as it leaves him, he pulls himself up to his full height.

'The midwife was first hired by the Town to attend when it was thought that the accused, Isbel Butts, may have been with child. The midwife swore that this was not the case. She was later employed to tend to the prisoner from Dunwich, who was damaged when she reached us. I was persuaded by another that this was the Christian thing to do, that the Dunwich witch, being old and infirm, could die before standing trial, and so I agreed.'

I cannot think straight, my mind whirls so. Will he accuse me now, in front of the court? I am overcome with terror and push back on the bench, making myself small, wishing to be anywhere but here. But he does not look at me, does not call me, and I keep my eyes down and listen hard as he continues.

'I considered it likely that the Butts girl *was* with child, for, as you have heard, she readily confessed to lying with the Devil on many occasions, and I believe the said child was that of Satan himself.'

As one, the room takes a sharp indrawn breath. This scandal had not reached their ears.

'I also believed that Rose Gardner used her devilish skills and enchantments to rid Isbel Butts of this child, against the word of God. An horrific crime, Sir, and one that should be punished in the most severe fashion. So I kept her in my sights, watched her every move and she made a mistake. For she came to the landlady of the inn where I have lodgings . . .' My heart stops. It has come. '. . . a godly and Christian woman who has done no harm, and there this midwife boasted of her powers. I heard her myself, from outside the room, and she was seized immediately before she could bring another good woman over to her abominable views.'

I am weak as a kitten, I dare not move or even make a sound. I am praying I am overlooked, forgotten. My hands will not stop shaking and I sit on them so as not to attract attention, for the sailor is already looking at me strangely. I cannot bear to look at Rose.

'Although I had sufficient proof to hold the midwife, I felt it best to search her, so Mistress Phillips was sent for, as she has vast experience of these matters. The accused was searched thoroughly.'

The Recorder looks up, his face pinched.

'And?'

'Marks were found on her body, marks and wens that did not bleed when pricked, the signs of a true witch. And she did not cry, no tears were seen, although the pain must have been great. It is well known that witches do not bleed and they cannot cry. A truer witch I have never seen.'

THE COURT IS SILENT. THROUGH THE WINDOW I CAN SEE THAT EVEN the seabirds circling in the leaden sky have ceased their calls. The roiling of the sea sounds far away, muffled and echoing, as if we are all underwater.

The Recorder looks at Master Hopkins and then across at Goody Phillips.

'And you swear to the truth of this?'

Goody Phillips curtseys.

'Yes, Sir, I do. I found the proof myself.'

'Then I accept your evidence and thank you for your clear and concise giving of it.' He looks to the jury sat to one side, and then to the line of women who stand, shaking and pale, before him.

'Prisoners, do you have anything to say in your own defence? Any of you?'

Alice Gardner stands tall.

'I wish to call a witness.'

'It is not allowed. The accused are not allowed witnesses – where would the court be if that were allowed to happen?' He smiles grimly. 'However, under the law you are allowed to have

260 | L M WEST

someone speak for you. So. Do you have anyone? Are there any present who will speak up?' He looks around the room in mock-amazement. 'I see no friends here. Clerk, note that no one speaks for the accused.'

The scribbling fills the silence then the Recorder straightens in his chair, pulling his robes over his shoulders self-importantly.

'Members of the jury, I have no need to direct you to your judgment for I fear it is clear. Please consider your verdict.'

I expect the jury-men to leave the room, hoping that there will be a pause in the proceedings, for I find I cannot breathe. I am in need of fresh air, to be outside in the icy cold, for my chest is painful, my head spinning. It has all been too fast. The evidence, the witnesses. It has been done with a precision and efficiency that Captain Johnson would be proud of and I lift my head to look at him. He sits next to the Recorder, bowing his head and smiling as they exchange words, as if they were sitting in my inn over a glass of wine. He is pleased with what he has done, I can see it in his face, whereas I feel only shame and horror. I did what I thought was right, understanding that this was the path that God himself had dictated. I believed we were all following His Word in searching out this evil in our midst, and that Master Hopkins was truly righteous. But I see it now. I see him. He has found how much money can be made, vast quantities of it pour into his coffers, so much so that he and Goody Phillips can sleep secure in their beds.

And I am no different. The thought stabs through me that I also looked to make money on the back of this, that my coffers are now full to brimming. My mouth fills with bile and I reach into my pocket for my kerchief, pushing myself to a stand to leave this place, then I look up and swallow hard for the jury have come out of their huddle.

70. JOAN

She already knew the way it would go, when Master Hopkins rose to his feet. No second sight needed there, no hedge-witch scrying. Now the jury-man stands and she can see in his face what is to come before he even speaks a word.

71. MARY

One man speaks for the jury. Those twelve good men and true say the witches are guilty of all the indictments brought against them.

Guilty.

The word hangs heavy in the air as the Recorder clears his throat and stands.

'And you are all satisfied with the verdict?' Twelve nods of agreement. 'Then I will pronounce sentence.' He turns to the women huddled before him. 'And the sentence of this land is that you will all be taken from this place to the gaol and thence to a place of execution, where you will be hanged by the neck until dead. And may God have mercy on your souls.' He sits back in silence.

I had expected noise; cheering and clapping, raised voices, but the room is quiet. It is as if they have only just realised what they have done. Seven women have been condemned to hang here, in Aldeburgh, a sinful Town that was to be made more godly. I had thought the women would be imprisoned, taken to the gaol at Colchester or Ipswich. I never thought . . . But this was my error – I never thought. If I had not stood and given evidence against that curate, Maptid Violet, and he had not been removed from office

264 | L M WEST

along with his Vicar. If the Town had not experienced that first sweet taste of power. I try to tell myself that I am not the only one to blame, that my part in this is small. That it was Captain Thomas Johnson, with his talk of rocks from heaven, his conviction that it was the voice of God telling him to mend the Town, and William Thompson, his friend and fellow Bailiff, giving credence to it all. It was they that persuaded the Town to invite the Witchfinder, they that said we were corrupted by such women and needed to be cleansed. They have spent endless time and money on this and look where has it brought us.

To a hanging. Guilt hangs heavy on my shoulders.

THE CONSTABLES MOVE FORWARD WITH THE CHAINS AND PASS THE heavy links back through the shackles and I wonder why, for the women are too stunned to make their escape. They are looking at each other in dumb horror as they are pulled and pushed to the door. It opens to a flood of fresh air which fills the chamber, taking the heat and stench and the witches with it, as it sweeps round the room and out again. The clerk, gathering his papers, fumbles, and a sharp gust scatters them. Parchment spills and drops as the sheets fly to the floor. Candles gutter as men pull themselves to their feet, fastening cloaks, placing hats on heads, trampling the fallen papers under heavy boots, careless, the words smudging and blackening beneath their tread. The Witchfinder is master of all he sees, patting the jury-men on the back, shaking hands with the Recorder who rushes away, to his dinner no doubt. Merely a mornings work for him. Master Hopkins' face is a mask of stately pride, and satisfaction shines from him. Mistress Phillips gathers herself and moves towards me as if to speak, but I cannot face her. I fasten my cloak hurriedly around my shoulders and push through the throng to the door, taken by an urge to run, get away from this place. Someone calls my name but I take no notice. The need to feel cleansed is overwhelming, so I push through the crowd assembled outside, and swerve around the back of the gaol, through the streets to the beach, walking as fast as I can. I take great gulps of air and my body shakes, not only with cold but with horror at what has just happened. I crunch onto the pebbles, steadying myself against a fishing boat that is hauled up there. My hand brushes the rough wood and I feel a splinter spike into my palm, but I carry on, staggering towards the sea, the sharp pain welcomed.

It is unnaturally calm. I glance behind me and see the sky blackening overhead as the afternoon progresses, what little light there is sinking behind the dark houses and the church that looms over the Town from the hill. I turn back. The sea is pewter, the line between ocean and sky melded into one, so I cannot tell if I am still on the earth or have left it. It is only the stones under my feet that ground me, for my mind is whirling and spinning so, then my legs give way and I fall to my knees. The pebbles are solid and damp under me, rough and hard and I feel their cold seeping through my joints. The sky is full of snow, but still none comes, and the clouds push down on our Town, heavy and thick, like an icy blanket, grey-brown and smelling of metal and brine. No tears fall. I am too full of horror for tears.

It is the voice of Master Hopkins that brings me to.

'Mistress Howldine, are you unwell?' He is pacing across the shingle towards me, Goody Phillips by his side. As they reach me he puts out a bony hand under my elbow and lifts. The search-woman takes the other side, and I lean into them as I stand, for I can do nothing else.

'Are you ill, Mistress?' His face is all concern and kindness, as if his words had not just condemned seven women to die.

'A temporary fainting, Sir, the heat of the Courtroom . . .' I hope this will be enough, that he will not press me further. 'I needed air, that is all.'

'Well there is air enough here, but you must return inside

before you catch a chill or worse, it is bitter cold. Not even at home in Manningtree have I felt such cold.'

'It comes straight from the east here, Sir, straight off the sea. Too cold for snow I think.' Ordinary words. I listen to myself pass the time of day with this man and it is as if I inhabit another body, as if someone else is speaking.

They help me back to the path and through the streets to the Lion. I tell the pot-boy to send up their food as I wave away their attentions and go to my parlour, where I fall into the chair by the fire, only then remembering to remove my damp cloak. I drop it to the floor and reach down to untie my boots. My whole body aches and shivers with cold and I wonder if I will ever be warm again, for my heart is turned to ice.

72. JOAN

They are to hang. The terror that had left Joan has returned with a force and she shakes ceaselessly. She cannot imagine what it will feel like. Sarah is sobbing, and she thinks how it is unfair that the girl has been made to take the blame for all that happened to her. That the Witchfinder, by not allowing witnesses other than himself and his creature Phillips, has covered up the actions of Captain Johnson's rake of a son so no harm or insult will fall on his head. The rich have protected themselves, nothing new there. But no one protected Sarah, and now she will hang, they all will, and none of this is fair, none of it deserved by any of them.

They are numb, each slumped back in the gloom of the cell, drowned in their own thoughts. The only one who seems at peace is Isbel, who at least is a comfort to Sarah.

Then Catherine speaks.

'They did not say how long it would be, when we will . . .'

'We must be a comfort to each other now.' Rose speaks clearly but her voice is gentle. 'We must find our courage and our dignity to endure this thing in the knowledge that we will soon be far from our pain and in a better place.'

Alice puts her arms around her.

'I am sorry, love, that I could not protect you. I hoped against hope that you would be spared.' She buries her face in Rose's hair.

'It was not your fault. I was not careful as I knew I should be, I spoke without thinking. The fault was all mine.' She lays her head against Alices' and closes her eyes. Catherine clings to Isbel who is back to muttering her litany and it goes right through Joan, for her nerves are shattered like ice under the plough.

'Can you not stop her row?' All her old spite comes back, she cannot help herself. It is the fear.

Rose opens her grey eyes and looks at her. Her face is pale, her eyes reddened.

'She is but a child, her wits are going. We should feel sorrow for her, not anger.'

Joan turns and her face crumples.

'I know, I know, I was too sharp. I am sorry. It's just that . . .' Her voice breaks. After all these months of imprisonment and hardship it is only now that tears come. She cries, muffling the sobs that wrack her, and she is angry with herself for her weakness. Rose leans across and takes her hand and her touch is a comfort.

'We are all frightened, Joan . . .' The sound of her name in Rose's mouth is like a blessing. '. . . but the only way through this is to help each other, not to give way to anger and rage.' She is right, Joan knows it, but rage has been her fellow for so long it is hard to let go.

Then Dorothy Clarke opens rheumy eye and pulls herself to a sit. She gazes around at them and opens her mouth to speak, and this is so unusual they all sit forward to hear, watching as she dampens her mouth with her tongue, licks her cracked lips.

'Is the food here yet?'

The women look at each other and slowly smiles crack their faces through the dirt and tears, then they are laughing, all of them, so hard they cannot stop. Tears are cleansing their cheeks and their ribs ache under their thin clothes, and each time they look at one another it starts again. And it is joyful and rapturous and takes them out of that place and what has just happened, and what is still to come. The laughter goes on and on until they fall, exhausted, against each other, warmed and smiling.

And this, the last time Joan laughs, is when the hammering starts.

73. MARY

I have the pot-boy deliver their morning meal for I cannot face them. My whole body is weak and my stomach roils, and I often have to rush to the chamberpot as my bowels fail me. It is as if I were condemned with them. I feel hollowed out with fear and disgust, my mind flitting to and fro, like a black bat on a warm summer night, and I cannot settle to anything. All talk in the inn is of the trial and the hangings to come, and I can only go through the motions of my daily tasks, for my thoughts are elsewhere, with the seven women in the gaol. I could so easily have been with them. I should be with them. The long-ago visit to Alice Gardner, my knowledge of how Rose helped Isbel, would be seen as collusion, the packet of herbs I passed them. But even my thoughts must be contained in case I am discovered, for Master Hopkins can scry into your very soul, I know this now, and I must give nothing about myself away in case I, too, am damned.

He and Mistress Phillips will be on their way today. They do not stay to see the results of their cruel work tomorrow, as if by leaving they are able to absolve themselves of all responsibility for it. We who are left must bear the weight. But they must hear the preparations for it. Since dawn there has been sawing and hammering, as the carpenter, another close friend of the Captain, builds a scaffold.

But as I consider the timbers needed, the nails, the ropes for the halters, I realise that this was what was always intended. It was already planned. The outcome of the trial was decided before a word was spoken.

EVENING HAS FALLEN WHEN I SCREW UP MY COURAGE AND GO, WITH A tray, to the gaol. I have put extra on the plate, some meat, a little cheese, and it is the best stuff, not the leftovers that I have used before. I want them to think well of me at the last. I want do some little thing for them. The air is bitter still and I wrap my cloak tight as I cross the square.

The gaoler is inside, blowing on his hands, crouched over a small brazier. He is wrapped in a grimy wool cloak and looks for all the world like an imp as he glances up at me with coal-reddened eyes.

'Mistress?'

'Are they . . . ?' I nod towards the door.

'Quiet, aye. Now, anyway. Sounded like they were laughing before but that cannot be. Now it seems like they are already dead.' He laughs grimly. 'Won't be long, at any rate.' Then he looks down at his hands and his voice softens. 'Never seen a hanging, Mistress.'

'Nor me.'

We say nothing more as he moves to the cell door and unlocks it.

'Here you are – food.' There is no noise inside the cell, no movement and I peer in hesitantly.

Then, a voice from the gloom.

'We are still to be fed then? Not dead yet?' Joan Wade's sharp tongue sears through me as the gaoler lifts his lantern and I step inside, placing the tray on the floor in front of them. The cell is freezing, worse than I have ever know and the women are grey with cold. I turn to the gaoler.

'Fetch a brazier.'

'What . . . why? They are to die tomorrow, why waste good money?'

'Because I order you to. If you cannot find one go to the Lion, tell them I sent you. Coals too. Leave the lantern here, fetch yourself another.' He scowls at me, his face devilish in the lamp-light, then shrugs and goes, locking the door behind him. Locking me in.

I KNEEL STIFFLY AND PLACE THE LANTERN BESIDE THE TRAY. LIKE stray dogs, wary and afraid, the women slowly lean into the centre, reaching for food, and we sit in a circle. They say nothing so I search for words to fill the silence.

'I would have you warmer tonight. I have brought some meat, cheese. Look.'

'Warm enough soon, where we're supposed to be going.' Widow Wade's eyes are black and beady, just as they were the first time I saw her, the small, broken thing huddled behind her bed. It seems so long ago.

I see Rose put her hand on her arm to silence her.

'That is kind, Mistress, we are so cold and hungry. Does it snow yet?' I shake my head. Black clouds have been gathering but then they are blown inland by the easterly wind that screams from the sea.

'Not yet . . .'

'Do you know . . .?'

We both speak at once and I nod for her to continue.

'Do you know when they will come for us?' The others stiffen at the question, dreading my reply.

'It is to be tomorrow, Friday.' It was once a day of fasting and prayer, in the days of Popes and priests. Now it heralds their death.

'So that hammering – it is for us?' Sarah's voice is small and trembling. I nod, unable to speak, and I watch as her face folds and creases and sobs shake her tiny frame. A month ago she was free, carrying out her duties, fending off the Master's son, worrying if her work was good enough, fearing reprimand. No doubt dreaming of a young man, a life still to be lived. A month ago I thought that hers was the sin but now I know it to be mine.

And then we all jump out of our skins as she begins to scream and scream. We stop our hands to our ears to try and blot it out as Alice and Catherine seek to calm her, but the noise goes on, and I look at Rose and her eyes are pleading, and I know what must be done.

74. JOAN

The girl Sarah is screaming fit to burst and Joan is about to shout and silence her, when she sees a look pass between the Howldine woman and Rose. Alice is hanging on to her, holding her tight, trying to calm her as Catherine moves her hands over her daughters ears. Even Dorothy Clarke rocks forward and back, arms wrapped round her head, eyes screwed tight shut, moaning.

Then the screams lessen, slowly turning into sobs, and they hear the clatter of the gaolers boots. He is mumbling and cursing as he unlocks the door and drops a small pot-bellied stove onto the floor. Out of his cloak he produces two small pieces of sea-coal.

'Here you are – waste of time if you ask me . . .'

The Howldine woman's voice is sharp.

'I don't. Well, light it, man. Use a coal from your brazier, it will be quicker.' Joan reluctantly gives the innkeeper her due, for she certainly knows how to give orders. He grumbles even louder as he stoops to his task and the women draw away from him, back into the shadows. Then, a red glow, a spark and crackle and slowly, a tiny warmth rises from the blackness.

The innkeeper stands.

'I have forgot the ale. Gaoler, I will be back shortly, no need to lock up.'

'Nay, Mistress, more than my life's worth now. They may turn into toads and imps, flee. No, I will wait outside for you, but locked in they will be.'

75. MARY

I walk swiftly through the dark streets on silent feet, away from the Lion, back to the beach, a crack of moon lighting my way so I can just see. I have little time. The pebbles crunch under my feet as I stoop, feeling around with frozen fingers for the right shaped ones. I find two and push them into the pocket of my apron, then pull my cloak back around me and make my way to the inn. I avoid the curious looks of the pot-boy and find an old jug which I fill with good ale.

'That's not for those . . .?'

'Mind your business, boy, I need not explain myself to the likes of you.'

I go out again into the frigid air and scurry across the square. A wind has risen, sudden and sharp, it moans around the houses like a phantom and I am almost glad to reach the gaol. The gaoler unlocks the door and ushers me inside, then opens the door to the cell and its smell of filth and fear is now fuggy with warmth.

'Your ale.' I set the jug down next to the now-empty tray of food, look at Rose and give a small nod. She moves towards me as Alice Gardner reaches for the jug and pours a little into a mug. The gaoler is outside now, huddled again around his brazier, his hood up, but the door is open. He does not hear me carefully remove the pebbles from my pocket. He does not hear the rustle as Rose fumbles in her bodice and pulls out the small packet. We are both silent as, with broken nails, she picks out four or five seeds that gleam wetly in the firelight. The only sound is of ale trickling into mugs as Alice continues to pour.

Rose places the seeds silently on to one of the smooth flat stones I have brought her, then looks up and whispers.

'Speak, talk about anything.'

Joan Wade is first.

'Is the Town filling up to see our leaving of it?' She cackles grimly into the fire, her hands stretched to its small warmth. 'You must be making good money from all this, Mistress Howldine.' She turns to me. 'No wonder you bring us better food, heat. Shame that was not done three months ago when we were taken. We would have been fatter, made a better spectacle as we drop.'

'That's enough, Joan, think of the younger ones.' Alice is strident now, powerful, as she was at the first. 'Sarah has terrors enough without your words. So, Mistress Howldine, will it snow?'

And all the time we speak I can only just hear the soft sound of stone grinding on stone, seed shells cracking; the tapping as the powder is tipped into a mug, the slight splash as the ale is swirled around. I do not see what they do with it, who is given it. I cannot be part of it, any more than I have already. For what I have done this night is witchcraft and I do not want to feel the hemp around my neck, as they will tomorrow.

I OPEN UP THE DOORS OF THE INN EARLY THE NEXT MORNING, FOR I have not slept. Visions of the witches crouched around the small fire, me amongst them, at one with them, haunted my every dream; images of their hands reaching out to me, embracing me in their midst, filled my head. Too many times I woke, shaking, wet with sweat, cold with horror, and now I am numb with exhaustion.

I stand on the step, fumbling my keys into my pocket, taking a deep breath of sea air, then I raise my head and freeze.

Soaring above me, in the centre of the square, is a gibbet. A long ladder is propped again the side beam and a man I see often in the inn is at its top, fastening ropes over it, his boy passing them up to him. Seven of them, thick and knotted.

He finishes his task and climbs down, wiping his hands on his britches. He turns and sees me standing there with my mouth open.

'Good morning, Mistress. All ready?'

I cannot speak. The halters he has tied shift slowly in a wind that has dropped from last night. The air feels a little warmer.

'Ready?' My mind is frigid, I cannot comprehend.

'For the visitors. I hear there are already carts on the road bringing people to Aldeburgh. This is a big day for the town, Mistress, an' you are sure to be busy. A hanging always brings 'em in, better than a market they say.' He turns and follows my eyes to the ropes.

'Dun a good job with this, though I say it myself. Makes a change from rigging and tackle. Shorter and sharper I think.' He cackles at his wit. 'Got paid well too, and extra for the knots. Eight shillings all told, and how long would it have taken me to earn that, I ask you? No, they are good, strong halters, although they say that the witches . . .' He spits onto the icy ground. '. . . are barely alive now, so no strain there.' He looks at me intently. 'Are you well, Mistress?' It takes all my strength to nod. 'It will cleanse this Town once and for all, we will go back to being God-fearing folk, all trace of the Devil gone.'

'And do you think this – this hanging – will do that?'

He nods rapidly.

'I am certain of it, Mistress Howldine, for is that not what they have told us from the pulpit every Sabbath? That thou shalt not suffer a witch to live? The Captain is certain of it, and he is a godly person, a military man, used to such things, and if he says we'll be cleansed by this, well, that's good enough for me.' He touches his cap, signals to his boy, and strides away, back to his hemp and rope-walk, whistling. Then, through the haze that fills my head, the sound of people; boots thumping, spurs chinking, the patter of lighter feet in leather shoes, the shrill chatter of women, the deeper voices of men. They are coming.

I DO NOT GO TO THE WOMEN. THE INN HAS FILLED WITH PEOPLE, MORE than I ever expected, all wanting to fortify themselves with ale before the hanging. It seems the whole of Suffolk is here – fisher-men, sailors, merchants. The surgeon stands by, and the town scribe, and I think how the ledger he sold me will fill up further today. But that is not why I do not go across to the gaol. No, for Captain Johnson himself comes into the inn with his fellow Bailiff and tells me that it will not be necessary to feed the witches this morning, as they are shortly to die; that the Town has to be careful now with its money as the Witchfinder's bill will be more than they had planned.

'So they are to get nothing?' The Captain scowls at me but I cannot help myself. 'They will have to face this thing hungry? I cannot take them one last meal?'

'No, Mistress, to what purpose? They will be dead within the hour.' The blood drains from my face and my knees weaken. I reach for the firmness of the bar and steady myself.

'So soon?'

'All is prepared, Mistress, we just await the hangman.'

I know who they have employed. A rough sort of man who slaughters the hogs and cows for those too squeamish to do it themselves, who will turn his hand to anything for a ready penny. And who is currently sitting in a corner of my inn, downing ale as if the end of the world is nigh.

76. JOAN

The hammering stopped a while ago, thank the Lord, but a hubbub continues to rise from the streets outside. They can hear it clear as day. The gaoler keeps going outside to see the commotion. The innkeeper does not come.

'We are not to be given food.' The statement, bland and bald comes from a dark corner, from Catherine, who still holds her daughter tight.

'No.' Alice bites at cracked lips. Rose rises and moves to the window that faces east, blocked all these weeks by cloth to keep out the cold, not that it worked very well. She pulls away the filthy linen and a blast of fresh air hits them. It smells of the sea, clean and sharp and salty and Joan pushes herself to her feet and stands next to her. She feels around on the plaster with her fingers, finding the mark she made all those months ago, her mark, scratched there when she imagined she might be freed, and puts her fingers to it. It thrums under her touch and she swallows a pang of fear.

'I shall miss the sea. Of all things, I shall miss the sea.' The midwife's voice is low and Joan turns to look at her, watching as tears trickle their snail-trails down her cheek. She reaches out and brushes them carefully away with her thumb. Rose's skin is soft under hers, the wetness warm. Joan has not thought about missing.

She has been imprisoned here too long now to think of it, but now the moment has come she realises that she will miss birdsong; she will miss spring, the changing of the seasons, the rustle of the reeds deep in the marshes. She will miss everything.

Alice comes to stand with them.

'I will miss my home, my life there. Lighting the fire as winter draws in, the comfort and smell of it. And I will miss my Rose.'

She reaches her hand out and Rose moves into her arms.

'You have been as a mother to me, but soon we will be together in Heaven and our trials on this earth will be ended.' She looks at Joan, glances at the plaster. 'What is that?'

Joan looks at the two of them, standing close, holding each other.

'It is my mark. I made it when I first came here. To show I had been, that I was real. A foolish thing.'

Rose puts an arm around her.

'No, Joan. Not foolish. And perhaps we should all make our mark here, together? To show that we also have been.' Joan nods, her heart full, her eyes blurring. The women stoop and scrabble, searching the packed-earth floor, until Alice stands, a small, pointed, flint clutched in her fingers.

'Here.' She passes it to Rose. 'You first.' Rose takes it, and carefully begins to scribe an 'R' in the damp plaster. She passes it to Alice, who makes an 'A', then nods to Catherine, who draws back, looking down in shame.

'I cannot. I do not know how.'

Joan's eyes fill with tears and she turns and looks around the cell. Dorothy, Isbel and Sarah sit quiet and calm, their eyes full and dark. The poppy seed and henbane have done their work, taken the sharpness and the fear away, and they fly like witches in their dreams.

'No matter.' Rose's voice is soft. 'Make your mark anyway, and one for Isbel. Make a mark for all the others.'

Catherine staggers to her feet and takes the flint. Carefully she marks a row of four crosses, making each one different. The women stand back and look at their handiwork, clasping hands.

Alice's voice is barely heard over the noise outside.

'There. We have been. We are real.'

They stand silent for a moment, the voices from outside fading, then, as the noise rises again, Rose pulls them closer, her voice low.

'We must make a pact. When they come for us we must not speak, nor falter either. We must be brave and strong. For they will abuse us, beg us to repent of our sins, but we have done nothing and we should not be afraid. We must show them that we are fearless.'

Catherine, Alice and Joan nod in agreement and then, as one, they reach out their hands and cleave together and power flows through them and into them and they are made strong.

They need to be. For there was not enough ale to go round; not enough herbs for them all.

77. MARY

The Town is full to bursting now, the noise harsh and deafening. The sounds of hundreds of people feasting and drinking and enjoying the day. There are pedlars weaving through the crowds, selling portions of rope and miniature gallows. One claims to have a witches apron and the small pieces are gone as fast as he can tear them off and snatch the coins into his wiry hand. The ale in the inn flows fast, people push and argue as they try to reach the bar. The pot-boy, kitchen-hand and even my stable-lad are clearing away mugs and splashing ale into jugs as fast as they can. It is hot and busy and I do not get a moment to breathe and for a while the thought of what is to come is blotted from my mind.

Captain Johnson and Bailiff Thompson have already left with the hangman, and I pray that he is steady enough to do his job. I am just wiping up a pool of spilt ale when there is a clatter of hooves, a shout, and everyone in the inn pushes towards the door and windows. Then the place empties as if a dam had burst and I am left, wiping shaking hands on my apron, my breath coming short in my chest and a pain in my heart such as I have never felt.

. . .

I HAD NOT INTENDED TO WATCH. I HAD THOUGHT TO STAY IN THE Lion, clearing up and waiting for it to be over, and the customers to return. But I am drawn to it, like a lodestone seeks the north. I find my hands untying my soiled apron, my arms reaching for my best cloak and I fasten it tight around my neck, as I move unwillingly towards the door. The pot-boy and the others have already left, anxious to get a good place, and the inn for once is empty. The crowd outside is dense and bellowing, so much so, that as I open the door, I realise I will not be able to push myself through them. So I turn back in and bolt the door, pausing in the hallway. I feel weightless, transported, as I did when Joan Wade bewitched me into handing over the packet of herbs, and I feel her presence now, calling to me. I turn and walk slowly up the stairs to the front bedchamber, dropping my cloak to the floor. This was my best room, the room where the Witchfinder slept, where he heard the accusers. It is cold and unwelcoming now – his presence has changed it forever.

I cannot help myself. I glide to the window like a ghost, open it a fraction, and peer out.

BELOW ME IS A SEA OF BODIES, BROWN AND BLACK AND GREY, jostling and shouting. Dark cloaks and jackets, tall hats and woollen caps, white coifs and dusky shawls. Black robes with sparkling white collars adorn the good and the great, who are seated on a platform in the square, raised above the rougher sorts. I can see the town hall to my right, its brick and oak gleaming in the uncanny light that comes from the thick yellow-grey clouds that billow and glower above the Town, above the sea. There are people everywhere, packed like herrings in a barrel, the side streets crowded with folk all hoping for a glimpse of the witches. The scaffold shines wetly above the square; ice has already formed on the ropes swaying there. The constables have employed more men to ward the crowds and I know that they have been paid extra for ale after their work is done. For I am tasked to provide it.

Then a shout, a path begins to open through the crowds, the constables hold the people back, staves at the ready, and the godly men on the platform straighten. All eyes are turned to the town hall and the door below it, as the gaol opens and the women are led out.

THEY SHUFFLE, GREY AND RAGGED IN THE DIM MORNING LIGHT, looking for all the world as if they were already dead and rising from their graves. They huddle together and I can see, over the heads of the crowd, that they are supporting Isbel, Sarah and Dorothy between them. The crowd roars and jeers at the sight of them, stones and muck are thrown and the women bow their heads, protecting themselves as best they can with their arms. Time seems to slow as they stumble through the gap in the crowd, and then a great silence descends as the little group pauses before the gallows. Men move forward. There are sobs and cries, but the crowds are so tightly packed that I cannot tell where the sounds are coming from. The constables tie the women, one by one, hands behind their backs, pushing them into a line, and I watch as Sarah and Dorothy fall to the icy ground which has been churned to mud by hundreds of boots. The crowd goes quiet as the guards reach first for Dorothy Clarke, dragging her roughly to her feet. Her head lolls and I am glad that she is not aware as the executioner mounts the ladder, his boy below, and they half pull, half drag, her to the top. The hangman fits the noose over her thin neck, moves the knot under her ear, and I find myself mouthing a prayer for her soul, but it is lost in the baying of the crowd as he shoves her from the ladder and she falls with a sharp snap. I close my eyes and swallow hard. Outside there is silence; then cries of '*witch* . . . *devil* . . . *whore*' are mingled with urges to repent and be absolved. The noise rises to a crescendo as the hangman swiftly seizes Isbel. The crowd roars, but then falls quiet as they begin to hear her voice rising over their

288 | L M WEST

heads in prayer. She is calm and resigned and, as the rope is placed over her head, her face shines with joy in the thin winter light. She looks like one of the saints in the old paintings that once adorned the church, before Dowsing and the Captain destroyed them, but when the hangman twists the ladder from under her and she drops, it is clear all is not right. For she struggles, choking and gasping, her head twisting, her face going blue, thrashing and fighting, gasping for air, clenching her hands convulsively, unable to help herself.

I gasp in horror, then a voice screams out.

'Help her, help her!' It is Catherine, howling, watching her daughter unable to die.

The crowd, ever fickle, takes up the cry and the hangman moves forward, grabs Isbel's kicking legs and pulls down hard. There is a crack, the small body stills, and, in the silence, all that is left is the sound of Catherine's sobs. I look at the gentlemen sat on the platform – they have their kerchiefs to their mouths and one or two pairs of eyes are closed or raised to heaven, and I will them to look, to see what they have done. Then, movement, as the condemned women put their heads close together, and I see Catherine push herself forward and almost run the few paces to the scaffold. The hangman barely has time to fit the noose, has not removed the ladder, when Catherine turns and leaps into the air. There is a crunch, and she hangs lifeless beside her daughter.

They take Sarah next and I watch in horror, for she seems to wake from her dream as she is manhandled to the foot of the ladder. The crowd roars again and I see her realise what is about to happen and she starts to fight and scream like a wild-cat, her eyes rolling, her mouth in a wide red yowl of fear. It takes two constables to wrestle her onto the ladder and into the hangman's grip, and I want to look away but I cannot for the women draw me to them. I am watching when Sarah is roped and the ladder pulled away. I am watching as she drops and I see that this is all wrong too; her slight frame is not enough to break her neck, the fall is too short, the halter too long, and it has been placed too close to the others. Her hands have become loosened from their bonds, and in her agony she reaches out, grasping at the limp body of Catherine, clutching at her clothes, trying to climb up her corpse to ease her own agony.

The crowd does not like this. It is not what they came to see and some begin to jeer and shout in anger. The hangman wipes his brow with his arm then lunges forward, hauls on her legs and her neck breaks and she is dead. Her body voids itself and he pulls back, swearing, an expression of disgust on his face, as he nods to the constables to bring Alice Gardner forward. I see her step up the ladder, her pride and dignity restored in these, her last moments. She fixes her eyes on Rose as she reaches the top of the ladder and she jumps. And then Rose, tall and etherial, follows her up the steps. At the top she turns and pauses, lifts her head and looks across at my window. She looks straight at me and smiles, and I bow my head to her, to her kindness and her courage. And when I look up she is leaping through the air and the crowd are baying in anger as their entertainment is spoiled.

Joan Wade is the last. She who was the first. She, who has been my trial, my adversary. She walks to the foot of the ladder as if she was going to a wedding and steps up.

78. JOAN

As the women emerge from the gaol Joan looks up. The sky above her is full of pale grey clouds, tipped with pink-gold, and in between are bursts of blue, the colour of blackbird's eggs. It reminds her of a nest she once found in the hedge at the bottom of the lane where she grew up. The weaving of the tiny twigs and sticks that formed it. The care with which it had been built. The perfection of the smooth blue eggs, still warm, the softness of the moss that held them. As she shuffles forward with the others she remembers the green shoots of leaves around it, the smell of sap and growth, the promise of spring, of hope and new life; how she had taken her mother to see its simple beauty.

She looks to the east. Out to sea is a mass of cloud, dark and brown, and she sniffs the air and knows that it will snow. The sea is black, the swell slow, the waves swishing against the pebbles, making them rattle and clatter, as they always have and always will.

THEY HAVE TRIED TO SUPPORT EACH OTHER. ALICE HAS HOLD OF Dorothy, whose wits have gone completely, and Joan thanks God for it. Dorothy is the first, then Isbel, and Joan wants to be sick, she is so terrified. She cannot look up, but she does not need to, for the sounds of the crowd tell her all.

Then Rose's face pushes close – it is blank with fear, the colour of parchment.

'We must jump. Do not let him twist the ladder away, for the halters are all wrong. Jump, and it will be quick.' Joan looks now and, as Catherine leaps, she sees that Rose is right, that this is what they must do. They have made a pact, they will take the little power that is left to them, and decide the moment of their death. First Alice, then Rose and last of all Joan.

She straightens her shoulders and steps forward. It is harder than she thinks to climb the ladder with her legs shaking, her hands tied behind her back, but the hangman shoves and pushes her until she reaches the top. She turns carefully on the last rung and looks out. It is so high she can see the sea beyond the houses, and she thinks of Rose, how she said she would miss it, and Joan hopes she saw it again before ...

The hands are on her neck now, the hemp pulled tight, and it smells of ships and tar, then there is shouting and, as she looks around at these little men with their robes and long noses, at the baying crowd, she is suddenly calm and unafraid. She sweeps her head back to take one last look at the sky, laughing at the madness of it all, and, pushing hard against the ladder, she jumps into the void.

A tightness, a rushing, a cracking, bright white agony – peace.

79. MARY

I do not hear the crack of her neck as she dies. I do not hear the splatter of piss. I am on my knees holding my stomach as it empties, over and over, onto the floor. I kneel in a pool of foul and bitter vomit, wiping my mouth with my hand as tears flood my eyes. I cannot stop myself from shaking.

THE POT-BOY CALLS UP THE STAIRS TO ME, SHOUTS THAT THE INN IS full, that I am needed, and I have to go. I clean up as best I can with a cloth, then pull myself to my feet. I walk down the stairs, steadying myself against the wooden panelling with trembling hand, as I bunch up the soiled and stinking cloth, throw it into the pile for washing, and step into the bar. The noise and fog hits me like a wave. Men, voices raised, all talking and shouting about the witches and how they died. How the hangman was useless, how they would have done it better, but at least the pretty one showed her ankles and more, as she swung and struggled, and that made up for some of the others spoiling the show by jumping. The air is fetid and rank, filled with fumes of ale, sweat and excitement, the mood buoyant and cheerful. For they have finally been released from the threat of witchcraft that has hung over them these past months, they are cleansed and purified. I pour jug after jug of ale, smile my landlady smile, watch as faces get shinier, cheeks more flushed, jackets come off, cards are played and songs sung. And it is just like it was before; before the rock from the sky, before the accusations, before the Witchfinder. I wonder briefly where Master Hopkins is now, what other town he has slid into with his forked tongue and many skins.

And then someone shouts *'It snows!'* and all rush to the windows and door to see the sight, exclaiming and patting each other on the back. For the long period of cold has finally broken and, as if in blessing, white flakes are falling thickly, cleansing the Town. It is a sign of God's forgiveness.

CAPTAIN JOHNSON COMES TO THE LION THE FOLLOWING MORNING, striding down the hill through flurries of snow, his man with him, to settle my account. They step inside, brushing the wet from their cloaks and I pass his man a mug of ale, then show the Captain into my parlour.

'So it is done?'

'It is done, Mistress, and I am glad of it for, I confess, it has worn away at my very soul. That such wickedness was in our very midst . . .' He shakes his head and glittering drops fly and hiss into the fire. 'What is your bill, Mistress Howldine. For the rooms for Master Hopkins and his woman, their meals. Food and ale for the prisoners?'

I offer him my ledger so that he can see I have kept a true record of every expense but he brushes it aside.

'Four pounds and seven shillings, Captain . . .' His face brightens. '. . . and a further fifteen pounds for the costs of providing for the trial itself.' He looks sharp at me, and I push my account book towards him again, but he does not glance at it. He merely reaches into his cloak, brings out a leather purse, and counts coins carefully onto the table-top, placing them in glittering piles. We agree the amount is correct, and the coins chink and chatter as he returns them to the purse, pushing it across the table to me. He looks tired, spirit-sore.

'A mug of wine, Captain?'

'No, thank you, Mistress. I have other visits to make, other payments...'

I nod, and a thought comes of the women, sat in that filthy gaol for all those weeks, the vast amounts of money that have been spent on their destruction. I hurriedly push it back down.

'I hope I have carried out my duties as you required?'

'You have done well, the Town is pleased, the Witchfinder also. He made especial mention of you when he left.' A shiver runs through me, but I am safe now, Hopkins is gone, it is over. Except that the witches will not leave me – they haunt my every move, every thought, and I wonder how I shall bear it. I scoop up the purse as Captain Johnson stands.

He looks down at his hat as he turns it in his hands, then fixes his gaze on me. I see sadness, exhaustion, fear in his eyes.

'Those witches. You saw them more than all of us. Do you think, after all...?' So he, too has doubts. The women haunt him as well.

'I do not think, Sir. It is not my place to think. The Town did what it thought fit and that is good enough for me.'

He smiles wanly.

'You are right, Mistress Howldine, and that is how it should be. It is just that this business troubles me more now it is done.'

I am not here to salve his conscience. He has a wife, a family, to do that. I drop a deep curtsey.

'Please thank the Town for their prompt settlement of my accounts.' I open the door and he takes his cue to leave. He turns in the doorway, doffs his hat at me and, collecting his man from the warmth of the kitchen hearth, strides out into the snow, the whiteness fading and softening their footprints.

· · ·

It is another busy day, all talk is of the witches, who still hang, swaying, on the gibbet. Their bodies are to be taken down tomorrow it seems, left for today as an example to us all of what happens to the ungodly and wicked. I throw myself into endless and familiar tasks, blocking the horror from my mind as best I can, until it is late into the night and the last customer has staggered home. The tables have been cleared, the jugs and mugs put away for another day. The pot-boy is asleep in his box-bed in the kitchen, snoring contentedly. The Town outside is silent as I wearily climb the stairs to my bedchamber. As I unlock the door the smell of vomit strikes me, and I think I must scrub the boards thoroughly tomorrow with lye, to get rid of it.

The strong-box is heavy with silver as I pull it from beneath my bed and unlock it, lifting the lid. I have never seen so many coins, never owned so much. The Captain's purse squats like a toad, unopened, on the top and I reach forward to empty it, to pour his coins in with the rest, but something stops me. Instead, I sit on the edge of the bed and run the coins through my fingers, over and over. Nineteen pounds and seven shillings. Eighty-three pieces of silver. They are light and glittering, not like the marked and dented ones I get from the customers. These look fresh-minted, the silver shining like moons. I trickle them through my hands, feeling my treachery in their smooth coldness. I am so tired I lay down on the bed beside the pool of coins, just for a moment, and close my eyes. And, into my head comes a vision of the women, of their fellowship and acceptance and courage. They will not leave me alone. They call me still.

I wake just before dawn, my neck stiff, silver coins scattered over the counterpane, splashed through my fingers. My eyes are gritty and my body cold as I push myself to my feet. I have slept the night away curled up on the coverlet, and my bones ache, but now my mind is clear, clearer than it has been for many a month. My thoughts are finally quiet as I pour the coins back in the strong-box and close it. I am about to find the key on the chatelaine around my waist when a familiar sensation strikes hard at me. The feeling that I am being moved by another hand. It is the same feeling that I had when Joan Wade caused me to lift my hem, to unpick the stitches and push the packet of herbs from my fingers to Rose's.

Helpless, as if in a dream, I move to the table and find a piece of paper and a pen. I tear the paper in half and bend towards the window, as Matthew Hopkins did in this very spot, seeking the pale dawn light that comes in through the latticed panes, and, dipping the quill into the ink pot, I write.

For Robert, my faithful pot-boy, I leave this payment in grateful recognition of his services so cheerfully provided.

Signed Mary Howldine.

I pull the second piece of paper towards me and my quill scratches again.

To be used for aid and comfort of the poor of this Parish.

Signed Mary Howldine

I carry the notes back to the bed and open the strong-box again. I take the Captain's leather purse, discarded on the bed, fill it tight with silver, and put the paper for the pot-boy on top. I place the other paper on the coins in the strong-box and close the lid but I do not lock it, instead I take off my chatelaine chain and leave it, and the keys, on the coverlet. I hope this, my atonement, will be found. I hope it will be enough. Then I stand and look around. I put on a clean apron and my best cloak, straighten my coif and walk slowly down the stairs, past the sleeping boy. Opening the front door I step into the square.

Snow glitters in the early light, crisp and unsullied. The gibbet looms above me, and I stand and gaze at the seven bodies, sparkling with snow, shapeless and ethereal, swinging in the air. It is if they had never been. Snowflakes swirl and drift as the wind increases. The sea begins to roar its anger and I move towards the sound until I reach the pebbled beach. The sun is just rising now, thin and pale in a shimmering sky. It is one of those pure mornings when the world blends. Snow has even whitened the pebbles and I bend to pick one up. It is grey-blue, smooth, heavy, icy cold. I roll it over in my hand and think of the two flat stones I took to Rose, what she – we – did that night. I bend and take up another, then another, and all of a sudden I am as if possessed. I heap pebbles into the pockets of my apron, then lift the hem of my overskirt and fill that too, tying the edges so they will not slip out, moving ever forward, picking up more and more, until the white frozen sea-spume froths at my feet, coating my fingers. I am heavy now, weighted down with stones, but my spirit is lighter than it has been for many months, as I stand, then step into the sea. I gasp as the icy water comes over my shoes, swirling around my ankles, the cold of it piercing and sharp. I keep moving forward, pushing into the waves as they try to thrust me back, but the witches are calling to me, they will not leave me and I know they never will, so all I can do is go to join them. History, and this Town, will be haunted by them, by what it has done.

As seawater soaks through my clothes, the heavy wet wool and the weight of the pebbles pull me down until I am no longer able to stand. And, as I fall, the last thing I see is Joan Wade, smiling and beckoning. Rose, Alice, Catherine, Isbel and Sarah dance in the waves behind her, hands enjoined, laughing, as I move towards them, my arms outstretched, reaching them just as the water closes over my head.

FROM THE CHAMBERLAINS' ACCOUNT BOOKS

(SUFFOLK ARCHIVES, IPSWICH REF: EE1/1/2/2)

Given to Mr Hopkins the 8TH September for a gratuity he being in town for finding out witches. £ 2. 0s. 0d

Given Goody Phillips then for her pains for searching out witches £1. 0s. 0d

Paid Mr Bacon his fee for being Recorder £5. 0s. 0d

Paid to sundry men for watching days and nights with such as were apprehended for witches. 13s. 10d

Paid William Baldwine the 24TH November for the allowance of bread and beer to the prisoners and for making clean the gaol and some other this as re bill appeereth. £1. 18s. 05d

More to him for diet and lodgings and the room for Widd. Gardner being prisoner there the sum of. 7s. 03d

Given more to Mr Hopkins the 20TH December for being in Towne for finding out witches. £2. 0s. 0d

GIVEN MORE TO WIDOW PHILLIPS THE SEARCH WOMAN THEN £1. 0S. 0D

PAID MR THOS. JOHNSON THAT HE PAID MR SKINNERS MAN FOR FETCHING WIDOW PHILLIPS THE SEARCH WOMAN 12S. 6D

GIVEN MR HOPKINS FOR A GRATUITY FOR GIVING EVIDENCE AGAINST WITCHES IN GAOL THE 7TH JANUARY. £2. 0S. 0D

GIVEN WIDOW PHILLIPS THE SEARCH WOMAN FOR GIVING EVIDENCE AGAINST WITCHES IN GAOL AND HORSE-HIRE AND CHARGE £1. 5S. 0D

PAID 6 MEN TO WARD AT THE SESSIONS AND EXECUTION FOR TWO AND A HALF DAYS A PIECE AT 12D PER DAY AND 6D TO DRINK ALL IS 15S. 6D

PAID JOHN PAINE FOR HANGING SEVEN WITCHES 11S. 0D

PAID WILLIAM DANELL FOR THE GALLOWS AND SETTING THEM UP £1. 0S. 0D

FOR A POST TO SET BY THE GRAVE OF THE DEAD BODIES THAT WERE HANGED AND FOR BURYING OF THEM 6S. 0D

PAID HENRY LAWRENCE THE ROPER FOR SEVEN HALTERS AND FOR MAKING THE KNOTS 8S. 0D

PAID FOR WATCHING WIDD.WADE 3S. 0D

TO ROBERT KIDWELL FOR HIS HORSE AND MAN TO MANNINGTREE TO FETCH WIDOW PHILLIPS 8S. 0D

MORE FOR HIS HORSE TO SHRUBLAND TO MR BACON 2S. 6D

PAID TO MRS HOWLDINE FOR DIET AND WINE WHEN MR HOPKINS WAS IN TOWNE AND FOR CHARGES FOR THE WITCHES BILL £4. 7S. 0D

Paid her more in part of money due for diet and wine and other charges at the Sessions the 7TH January £15. 0s. 0d

Received of Mr Newgate March 12th in part for the charges of trying a witch in Aldeburgh £4. 0s. 0d

Received of Mr Richard Browne by the hands of Mr Bailiff Johnson May 25TH for the charges of trying a witch in Aldeburgh £4. 0s. 0d

HISTORICAL NOTES

The only original records relating to the Aldeburgh Witch Trails are in the Chamberlain's Account Book for Aldeburgh 1624-1649 (*Suffolk Archives, Ipswich, EE1/1/2/2*). They show that Matthew Hopkins, self-styled Witchfinder General, visited Aldeburgh three times, in September, December and in January for the trial itself. All the dates are shown as 1645, as the New Year in those days started in March. The entries show all the payments made to those involved and that a special rate was levied on the inhabitants of Aldeburgh by Mr Newgate and Mr Richard Browne, authorised by Thomas Johnson, who was bailiff then, to cover the huge cost of the trial. In an area which was in severe decline at the time, this would not have proved popular. What struck me forcibly about these records was that, amongst the considerable costs for searching out the witches, the men around the events are named, together with the amounts they were paid, but the names of those accused were not listed, apart from two brief entries *'[Paid]...for diet and lodgings and the room for Widd. Gardner being prisoner there the sum of 7s 3d'* and *'Pd for watching Widow Wade 3s'* and this became my reason for writing this novel, for it seemed to me so wrong that seven women should have been murdered, shown such contempt, thought to be worth so little, that their names were not even worthy of recording. And so 'The Unnamed' was born.

Mary Howldine is recorded as being the landlady of the Lion Inn in Aldeburgh, and she stood as a witness in the strange case of the curate Maptid Violet (*see below*). The Chamberlain's Accounts show how much she was paid for providing *'diet and wine when Mr Hopkins was in Towne'* and *'for charges for witches ye bill'*. (*Suffolk Archives, Ipswich, EE/1/1/2/2, p 249*). In two separate payments she was given a total amount of £19.7s.0d. This is the equivalent of £2,275 today and in the 1600s would have bought you three horses, three cows, 24 stones of wool, 5 quarters of wheat or 276 days of work from a skilled tradesman (*Source: nationalarchives.gov.uk/currency-converter*). Mary is referred to as the innkeeper of the Lion in the Chamberlain's Accounts and I wonder if it may have stood on the site of the White Lion, which still exists today, as records show that there has been an inn on that site since the fifteenth century.

On 4 August 1642 **Captain Thomas Johnson,** accompanied by fellow Aldeburgh Bailiff William Thompson, saw a stone fall from the skies, *'accompanied by a wonderful noyse heard in the ayre as of a drum beating most fiercely'*. He was so affected by this unnatural event that he wrote a pamphlet about it entitled *'A signe from Heaven or a fearful and terrible noise heard in the air at Alborow in the County of Suffolk'* which was published in London few days later (*British Library*). He took it as sign from God that the land had become corrupt and full of sin. I suspect that modern-day science would say that this was a meteorite, but it must have had a huge effect on the people who saw it and heard about it.

Only months later, on 24 January 1643, William Dowsing, the Parliamentary Visitor for demolishing all superstitious pictures and ornaments for churches, visited Aldeburgh. Unlike other churches, where the townsfolk stood back to watch Dowsing's men wreak their devastation, Thomas Johnson and the Reverend John

Swaine carried out the destruction themselves, a further sign of how the Captain was determined to bring the Town back to right-eousness. ('*The Journal of William Dowsing: Iconoclasm in East Anglia During the English Civil War' William Dowsing, Ecclesiological Society, Boydell & Brewer Ltd, 2001*). Thomas Johnson died on 23 December 1658. His Will is still in existence (*The National Archives, PROB 11/289/201*) and his tomb can be found in front of the altar, hidden under layers of carpet and underlay, in St Peter & St Paul's Church, which still stands high on the hill above Aldeburgh.

Styling himself 'Witchfinder General', **Matthew Hopkins** toured around Essex, Suffolk and Norfolk between 1644 and 1646 bringing a reign of terror. His beginnings are obscure but in 1644 he met an older man called John Stearne, equally Puritanical. It was generally assumed that they had been given a dispensation from Parliament to search out witches but, although John Stearne had obtained a magistrate's warrant to seize the first witches at Manningtree, this would not have been valid outside that area, and there is no evidence that the pair had any higher authority to carry out their actions. But news spread about their deeds and demand became such that, once they had worked through Essex, they moved on to Suffolk in the summer of 1645. It was at this time that Hopkins was invited to Aldeburgh to seek out witches. Much has been written about him and his reign of terror, and it is easy to assume that he was driven by money, but I have come to the opinion that he did truly believe he had a mission from God, certainly in the early days, and that he later became corrupted when he found out exactly how much he could earn from the persecution, trial and execution of witches. Although portrayed in images of the time and later films and drama as an older man, Hopkins was in fact only around 27 years old when he died at his home in Manningtree in August 1647, almost certainly of tuberculosis.

Goody (Goodwife) Mary Phillips accompanied Matthew Hopkins on his travels and was employed by him to 'search' the accused. She had been with him from the beginning in Manningtree, where she was known as a midwife, and was clearly relied on and respected by him, but it is hard to understand her cruelty towards other women, even if they had been accused as witches. She was famous for having a 'pricker', a bodkin or sharp needle, used normally for making holes in cloth, which was used to prick the bodies of the accused. No area was out of bounds. If there was no pain, or no blood came, that mark was claimed to be a Devil's Mark and was considered proof of the guilt of the accused. The more I have read about her, the more I think that she was motivated purely by money – she earned vast amounts during the witch persecutions and made herself invaluable to the witchfinders, seemingly agreeable to travelling all over East Anglia, often in horrendous weather conditions, to carry out her duties. Her presence also meant that Hopkins was able to detach himself from the more unpleasant side of his persecutions (he does not seem to have stayed in any town to see the executions that were the result of his work.)

There is mention of a **Widow Wade** in the Chamberlain's Accounts as having been watched during the trial. (*SuffolkArchives, Ipswich, EE/1/1/2/2, p 250*). I have traced a marriage record for a Margaret Walter who married Henry Wade at Aldeburgh in 1579. Henry was buried on 24 October 1580, less than a year later. I have taken the liberty of assuming that this was Widow Wade but I have given her the name of Joan to avoid any confusion with the character of Mary – I hope she will forgive me!

Widow Gardner is also mentioned in the Chamberlain's Accounts, in an entry dated 24 November 1645. Tantalisingly, the name of the payee is unreadable but I have assumed it to be the gaoler. I found a record of a marriage between Richard Gardner and Alice Mose on 17 July 1593 at Aldeburgh, and then a record of the burial there of

Richard on 26 October 1600. I have taken this to be the Widow Gardner referred to and called her Alice.

In the Dunwich Borough Records for 1645/6 there is a mention of monies paid for *'carrying ye Widow Clarke'* (*Suffolk Records Office EE6/3/3*) and, because of the dates, I have assumed that she was caught up in the witchcraft persecutions, so used this entry as the basis for the character of **Dorothy Clarke**.

The characters of **Catherine and Isbel Butts** and **Rose** the midwife are fictional, but the acts of witchcraft they were accused of have been recorded elsewhere, in other witch trials.

Richard Topcliffe was vicar of Aldeburgh from 1619 but was sequestered on 24 June 1644, when conflicts between him and the very puritanical Town came to a head. Amongst other things, he was accused of not preaching regularly and pulling down a gallery in the church so that fewer people could be accommodated. He also continued to bow at the name of Jesus, and turned the communion table back into an altar, which he compelled his parishioners to pray at. To an increasingly fanatical town, all these things smacked of the old Catholic habits, which had been banned, and so the Town moved to rid themselves of him.

At the same time, **Maptid Violet**, Topcliffe's curate, was charged with unseemly conduct. He was brought before the wonderfully named 'Suffolk Committee for Scandalous Ministers' accused of drunken behaviour in Aldeburgh and other local towns, accosting women and a maid-servant, using them 'most uncivilly'. Amongst the people that gave evidence and swore statements against him were George Nun and Mary Howldine, who both heard him speak out in the Lion Inn. The words I used in the story are theirs. There were many ministers ousted by this Committee, but Violet's is a rare case in that he provided a defence for his actions. (*The Suffolk*

Committees For Scandalous Ministers 1644-1646. Holmes, Clive, ed., Suffolk Records Society, 1970)

Mary Lakeland, known also as Mother was accused of witchcraft in Ipswich in 1645. Extraordinarily pious and godly, and known for preaching to congregations, which women were not allowed to do, it is thought that her strong religious beliefs might have been viewed with suspicion to the point where she was linked to one of Ipswich's radical sects. She was accused of causing several deaths, most significantly that of her husband, a barber, which was deemed an act of treason and punishable by burning. Mary Lakeland was burned in a barrel of pitch in Ipswich on 9 September 1645. Matthew Hopkins, who was responsible for her trial and execution, was in Aldeburgh, and so avoided watching this horrendous event.

Aldeburgh **Town Hall,** known since Victorian times as the Moot Hall, still stands today, and is considered one of the best Tudor public buildings still in existence. Built in around 1550, when Aldeburgh was a prosperous ship-building and trading town, the original layout of the ground floor consisted of dividing walls, forming six shops, which had hatches opening on to the street, and at one end, the Town Gaol. The offices and courtroom were above. The Moot Hall is now home to Aldeburgh Museum and is well worth a visit, although the inside of the gaol cannot be seen, as it now houses the Town Clerk's offices.

ACKNOWLEDGEMENTS

Once again, this book would not exist without the support and help of my husband, Brian who has patiently listened to my (often long) ramblings about all things witches, and who was the very first person to read The Unnamed. Thank you.

I first came across mention of the Aldeburgh Trials in Professor Malcolm Gaskill's excellent book 'Witchfinders: a Seventeenth-Century English Tragedy (John Murray, 2005) and if you are looking for a well-researched and readable summary of that period, I can highly recommend it.

I am hugely grateful, once again, to Ivan Bunn, for talking me through the processes connected with the seizure and trial of witches, for helping me to understand the contemporary docu-ments, for kindly sharing his vast knowledge, and for being so interested in my findings. Thanks also go to Charlotte and Lynne at Southwold Library – what would I do without you! To Diana Hughes and the staff at Aldeburgh Museum. To Simon Neal, researcher, for translating and transcribing original documents for me. To those who read the early version and passed on their feed-back. To Melissa West, for taking the time to read and re-read The Unnamed, and for her continued interest and encouragement. To Jerico Writers for their wonderful online courses and helpful staff, and to Louise Walters for her editorial report and support.

A very big thank you also to Sandy Horsley for designing yet another fabulous cover and bringing the story to life, and to Small Island Digital for the lovely website.

Lastly, a huge thank you to all those people who bought and read my first novel, 'This Fearful Thing', talked about it, and were kind enough to leave reviews on Amazon and Goodreads, and especially to those who took the time to email and message me about it. I cannot tell you how much this encouragement meant to a novice writer who wasn't really sure what she was doing!

I started writing 'The Unnamed' through a sense of injustice and anger. Anger at how these women were just a footnote to a process run by men, and the injustice of how, when details of the rope-maker, the carpenter, the hangman and the judge and jury are all recorded, only two of the seven women executed were felt worthy of having their names noted. They were ordinary women who had lives, had histories and feelings, who laughed and cried, felt happiness and pain.

They were like us – this book is for them.

ABOUT THE AUTHOR

L M West lives in Suffolk with her husband. Her first novel, 'This Fearful Thing', about the Southwold witchcraft trial, was published in May 2021. 'The Unnamed' is her second novel and a third, 'We Three', about witchcraft accusations in Dunwich, is underway.

For more information head over to www.lmwestwriter.co.uk where you can sign up for an exclusive free article about Matthew Hopkins.

An act of revenge. An accusation of witchcraft. A reckoning.
Southwold, Suffolk, 1645. Ann has fled from her past but when her childhood tormentor finds her in a busy street, she realises the past she thought long-buried has come back to haunt her. When rumours of witchcraft begin she knows that he will stop at nothing to destroy her...
Inspired by true events, 'This Fearful Thing' was published in May 2021

AND LASTLY . . .

Look out for the third book by L M West about the East Anglian witch trials, coming soon . . .

'She met the Devil midsummer last, like a black-haired boy 10 years old, by a whitethorns as she went to Westleton . . .'

At the same time that accusations are flying in Southwold and Aldeburgh, in the struggling port of Dunwich, three women, lifelong friends, are all accused of witchcraft by the same man. As Dunwich crumbles into the sea, so their friendship is weakened and destroyed, until events bring them together one last time.

A stranger-than-fiction story about wild accusations, again based on real events, 'We Three' is underway, and will hopefully be published in late 2022.
For updates pop over to https://www.lmwestwriter.co.uk

Printed in Great Britain
by Amazon